R/2015 Yahi

Chicken Caccia-Killer

Chicken Caccia-Killer

Liz Lipperman

W⬤RLDWIDE₀

TORONTO • NEW YORK • LONDON
AMSTERDAM • PARIS • SYDNEY • HAMBURG
STOCKHOLM • ATHENS • TOKYO • MILAN
MADRID • WARSAW • BUDAPEST • AUCKLAND

To all my Italian friends and relatives out there, for
keeping me chunky with your great Italian cooking.

Recycling programs
for this product may
not exist in your area.

Chicken Caccia-Killer

A Worldwide Mystery/November 2015

First published by The Story Vault.

ISBN-13: 978-0-373-26969-3

Copyright © 2013 by Elizabeth Roth Lipperman

Printed in U.S.A.

Acknowledgments

To my amazing agent and friend for life, Christine Witthohn. There is no way I could ever do this without you, nor would I want to. And to her husband, Jeff, who gives up precious time with her so that she can be my cheerleader, counselor and task master, as well as my first line of defense against all the bullies in the industry.

To Joni Sauer-Folger, my critique partner. Our friendship goes beyond line editing, and for that I will be forever grateful. Wish you lived closer.

To my awesome beta readers, Chris Keniston and Sylvia Rochester. You make me a better writer. And to Melanie Atkins, Phyllis Middleton, and my nephew Dick Flanagan, who walked me through the correct police procedures and lingo.

To the sisters and brothers who made sure that I grew up surrounded with both love and laughter.

To the bunko babes who supply me with all the funny lines in my books, and to all my writer friends whose support and friendship I cherish.

To Rhodes Bake-N-Serve for allowing me to print one of their wonderful recipes. To Jennifer Batchelder for the awesome Chocolate Bread Pudding Recipe, and to my sister Lill Magistro (and Rose and Cathy Magistro) for the mouthwatering spaghetti sauce and pizza bread recipes.

To Martha Hovers, who runs ARF House, a no-kill rescue shelter in Sherman, Texas, and to her wonderful supporters, especially Sally, who bought all my books at an auction benefitting this wonderful program.

And lastly to my husband, Dan, and my beautiful children, Nicole, Dennis, Brody and Abby, and my awesome grandkids, Grayson, Caden, Ellie and Alice. You all make me smile every day.

ONE

"So this is the girl who stole my job?"

That was the first thing Jordan McAllister heard as Jackie Frazier led her into the editor's office, and her jaw dropped at the venom behind the words. She didn't recognize the woman who had spoken, but before she could defend herself, Dwayne Egan beat her to the punch.

"Now wait just a minute, Loretta. Nobody stole anybody's job here. I distinctly remember you calling me the day you got out of rehab and telling me you'd quit. Did you forget that little detail?"

Jordan's boss leaned back in his chair and put his hands behind his head, making his huge ears look even bigger. She couldn't help staring, thinking back on the first time she'd walked into his office a little over a year ago. Expecting to see a tall, distinguished looking gentleman, she'd been surprised by the fiftyish man with bushy eyebrows and big ears. Stifling a grin, she remembered how at the time she'd sworn he could have been Mr. Potato Head's brother, minus the top hat.

"I did no such thing." The woman sprang from her chair and sprawled over the desk, pointing her finger at Egan's chest. "I called to tell you I was taking a little time off after rehab. That's all."

"Need I remind you it's been close to a year since you broke your hip, Loretta? That pushes the limit of 'a little time off,' I'd say. You must have known I couldn't hold your job that long." He motioned for Jordan to sit.

Taking the chair next to the irate woman, Jordan sucked in a gulp of air. *So this is Loretta Moseley.* She snuck a peek at the woman who wrote the Kitchen Kupboard for the *Ranchero Globe* before the job had been handed to her, first temporarily and then permanently after Loretta skipped town. Rumor had it she'd run off to Las Vegas with her smokin' hot physical therapist after she'd gotten the settlement money from a waterskiing accident. Seems the personal watercraft company decided that paying her off was easier than fighting, even though witnesses said the accident had more to do with Loretta's alcohol intake than a defect of the machine as she'd claimed.

"Need I remind *you* that my uncle Earl owns this newspaper?"

Egan leveled her with an icy stare. "I am well aware of that, Loretta, but I can't just yank the column from Jordan. She's worked hard to build a readership, and she's nearly doubled our sales."

Loretta turned to face Jordan. "I don't care what you say, it's my job, and no skinny redhead is going to take it away from me."

Skinny redhead? Excuse me?

Jordan tried to pull off an outraged look, but all she could think about was that it was the first time she'd ever heard her editor stand up for her. Since he never complimented her to her face, hearing him say that she'd worked hard was a surprise.

"At least this skinny redhead knows not to wear halter tops to work," Jordan fired back, mentally slapping her head for the lame, totally-uncalled-for response.

For a few seconds the two women glared at each other, each one daring the other to say something else that would reignite the fire between them. Jordan used that time to study her competition. Loretta Moseley stood about five two and had a body that should never have been squeezed into a halter top. The exposed layer of tanned belly fat had probably come from several months of partying in Vegas. Her short blond hair, cut in a seventies Dorothy Hamill style, accentuated hazel eyes that now flashed with anger.

"Okay, let's not get personal here," Egan said. He punched the intercom button. "Jackie, get Earl on the phone." Turning back to the two women who had finally quit giving each other the evil eye, he continued, "Let's see what he has to say about all this."

When his secretary buzzed back, he picked up the phone, leaving Jordan and Loretta sitting, quietly awaiting their fate while he talked to the owner of the newspaper—aka Loretta's uncle. A million thoughts ran through Jordan's mind as she tapped nervously on the arm of the chair, trying to pick out parts of the conversation without looking like she was actually eavesdropping. Most of those thoughts had the owner reinstating his niece as the culinary reporter and relegating Jordan back to writing only the personals again. That would not be a good thing, even if he let her keep the lousy hundred-bucks-a-month raise that had come with the promotion a year ago.

She'd really begun to enjoy the celebrity perks with having her own column, even though sometimes she felt like such a fraud masquerading as the culinary expert. When she'd first moved to the small town of Ranchero, Texas, located about seventy miles north of downtown Dallas, writing the personals was the only job she could get actually using her journalism skills. Truth be known, she had yet to make an edible grilled cheese sandwich on her own.

She could have stayed in Dallas and probably gotten a better job, but she wanted as far away from big "D" as she could get, bringing four suitcases, her goldfish, Maggie, and a broken heart with her. The fact that she'd graduated at the top of her class at the University of Texas and had covered every athletic event while she was there apparently hadn't influenced any of the editors of the many small newspapers she'd interviewed with. This job had been the only offer she'd received, and she'd jumped on it faster than a spider spying an unlucky fly caught in its web.

Although Egan dangled that sports writing carrot in front of her when he wanted her to do something he knew she'd balk at, the chances of that ever happening were slim to nil. Especially in this town where most of the people who worked at the *Globe*, including the acting director of sports, had grown up in Ranchero and worked there since high school. Loretta Moseley was one of those people.

Taking her mind off the angry woman sitting next to her, Jordan remembered the day she'd hobbled into Ranchero with her dreams shattered and her self-confidence at a record low. She'd felt like such a fool, having put her own career on hold while she'd followed her fiancé all over Texas chasing his perfect job.

Never once had she anticipated that when he finally got his dream job—which ironically, was also hers—as a sports correspondent for one of the biggest TV stations in Dallas, her life would come crashing down around her. It was bad enough that he'd cheated with the sexy weather girl, but the jerk hadn't even had the guts to tell her to her face and ended a four-year relationship with a 'Dear John' text.

How pathetic was that?

Moving as far away from her ex as she could, she'd been elated to land a job at the *Globe* even if it was only helping desperate people hook up. With her social life rivaling that of a nun's, she'd been tempted many times to slip her own sob story in there and see what happened.

Incredibly stupid, single white female with a broken heart looking...

Her life had changed dramatically when Loretta Moseley had broken both her hand and her hip and had to spend six weeks in rehab. Being related to the owner, she'd had a clause in her contract that required the newspaper to pay her full salary if she was ever disabled. When Egan offered Jordan the job with the promise of seeing her name on her own byline, it hadn't come with a pay increase, even though she was still required to write the personals. The measly jump in her salary came later when she landed the job permanently, and it was basically no more than a cost of living increase.

When Dwayne Egan rapped on the desk with a pencil, Jordan was jolted from her inner thoughts. "Yoo-hoo, McAllister, are you still with us?"

She looked up, embarrassed to have been caught daydreaming, especially when she noticed the smirk on Loretta's face.

"Okay, here's the situation. Earl agrees this is a dilemma." His eyes traveled from Jordan to Loretta. "But we think we have a solution."

Here we go, Jordan thought. *She gets the Kitchen Kupboard, I get the personals—or the boot."*

"For now both of you will write the column. Loretta, you'll take one day, and Jordan will take the other."

"I won't do that," Loretta interrupted, jumping out of her chair again. "And frankly, Egan, I find it hard to believe my uncle would agree to something like that."

The editor pushed the phone toward her. "You're welcome to call him yourself. Like me, Uncle Earl finds it difficult to discount how popular the column has become since Jordan's taken over."

Loretta huffed before sitting back down.

"Unless you've been living in a cave, you both know the Italian Festival is coming to Plainville next weekend. There'll be vendors from all over Dallas, and some from as far away as California and New York. The Italian-American Foundation has invested a lot of money advertising this event, and it behooves us to show them some love. For the next two weeks, we'll be covering the event from all angles."

He paused when Jackie Frazier walked into the room and handed him a stack of papers. After taking two envelopes from the top, he gave one to Loretta and one to Jordan.

"These are press passes for all the festivities, including the parties before, during, and after. We've promised the foundation that we would give them top notch coverage. That's where you two come in. I need both of you to attend everything—hell, pitch a tent and camp out there if you have to—then write about the food and all the activities. I've got Jim Westerville covering the bocce ball tournament and Sally Winters from Arts and Entertainment doing interviews."

He took a deep breath and blew it out slowly as if he knew the next thing out of his mouth would create a stir. "As I said before, you'll write the column on Tuesdays, Loretta, with Jordan taking Thursdays. When it's all over, Earl and I will evaluate how the public responds to each of you, and we'll make our decision about who keeps the column based on that."

Loretta slammed her hand down on the arm of the

chair. "I have never had to audition for any job in my life, Egan. I won't start now."

His expression remained unchanged. "Fine. Then that means Jordan will remain the culinary reporter permanently."

Loretta jumped up and leaned so far over the desk that Jordan was sure she was going to fall on top of the mountain of papers strewn all over it. "And my uncle agreed to this?"

"Actually, he was the one who suggested it."

"No way I'll let this girl take my job." She clucked her tongue. "I may not have a fancy college degree like she does, but I've lived in Ranchero all my life. We'll see who the good citizens of *my* town prefer." She stood and walked to the door before turning back once more to address Jordan. "Game on, Red."

In a huff, she walked out of the office, slamming the door behind her with enough force to rattle the autographed picture of Troy Aikman behind Egan's desk.

"Well, that went well," Egan said, a mischievous grin on his face. "You up for the challenge, McAllister?"

"What happens if I lose?"

His grin widened. "You really don't want to know."

"So I FINALLY get to meet the girl who talked my son into moving away from home?"

Jordan was caught off guard for a second time in as many days before her boyfriend's mother smiled. "Just kidding, Jordan. My daughter and I couldn't wait to get a look at you, especially since Alex has always kept us from his other girlfriends. Even tried to sabotage our meeting with you today." Natalie Moreland extended her hand. When Jordan reached for it, she grabbed her and hugged her instead. "You're as pretty as he said."

Jordan stole a quick glance toward Alex, who merely shrugged as if to say he had no control over his mother. Turning back to the petite woman who had just arrived from Houston, she said, "I've been looking forward to meeting you, as well, Mrs. Moreland."

Liar!

"Call me Natalie." She pointed to the younger woman standing beside her. "And this is Alex's sister, Kate."

Staring at the tall, well-built blonde in front of her, it was easy to see the family resemblance. Dressed in a navy blue suit with a powder blue silk blouse and heels that made her appear much taller than her five-eight or so stature, Kate Moreland could have been mistaken for a librarian—until you studied her face. With olive skin that accentuated the deep blue eyes, a career modeling anything she wanted was not too much of a stretch.

Kate noticed her staring and smiled. "Alex tells us you write for the local newspaper."

Jordan beamed. "I'm the culinary reporter at the *Ranchero Globe*," she answered, loving the way those words rolled off her tongue.

Purposely, she'd left out the part about how she still had to write the personals along with the column. Somehow, it sounded more impressive if they didn't know she was doing two jobs and only getting paid for one. And she definitely didn't want them to know what went down in her editor's office the day before.

Jordan lowered her eyes, not wanting Alex to see how worried she was just thinking about the possibility that she might be demoted. Here it was Saturday already, a day after the meeting with Egan and Loretta, and she still hadn't told either Alex or the gang at Empire Apartments.

At the thought of her friends, Jordan smiled to herself.

It had been one of the luckiest days of her life when she'd moved to Ranchero—population 22,000—and walked into the shabby apartment building owned by Victor Rodriguez and Michael Cafferty. She'd been greeted by the most loving group of friends she'd ever had.

Lucking into the temporary job when Loretta was in rehab was a gift from above, even though she knew absolutely nothing about cooking and hated most fancy foods. Since then she'd been biding her time until one of the sports writers either retired or moved on to the big arena in the sky, but that probably wouldn't happen anytime soon. Jim Westerville was still in his forties and had lived in Ranchero all his life. The only chance of him leaving was if he met a hot physical therapist and bolted for Sin City like Loretta had done.

Remembering Westerville as a happy-go-lucky guy who was always bringing his kids to work, she smiled. Not really the type to skip town with a floozy, but then again, she wouldn't have thought her ex would crumble under a mass of big blond hair and fake boobs, either.

And the other members of the sports team were just as entrenched in their jobs.

If she were being truthful, though, she'd have to admit that writing the Kitchen Kupboard twice a week wasn't a bad gig. Having people recognize her name and chat with her about the recipes she printed every week was exciting. But deep down she knew if her editor ever did give her the opportunity to move to the sports department, she'd give it all up in a heartbeat.

Sports had been her first love all her life. It was a given since she'd grown up in West Texas with four brothers who'd regularly counted on her to even out their flag football teams. When they'd discovered their baby sister could thread a touchdown pass between two defenders better than all of them, any chance her mother might have had at teaching her homemaking skills had gone out the window.

Had it not been for her weasel of a fiancé cheating on her after she'd followed him to Dallas like a loyal puppy dog, she wouldn't have felt the need to get as far away from him as she could and put her career dreams on hold. Nor would she have met the wonderful people at Empire Apartments who had taken her under their wing that very first day and made her a part of their close-knit family.

"Your lasagna recipe made it into her column, Mom," Alex blurted when there was a lull in the conversation.

Natalie Moreland perked up. "My great-grandmother's recipe always gets rave reviews. Did you try it before you put it in the paper?"

Jordan looked away, wondering if now was the time to tell Alex's mother that she was lucky she could boil water. She was positive Natalie Moreland, along with the rest of the good people of Ranchero, would wonder what the newspaper was thinking handing over the culinary column to someone like her, whose idea of gourmet food usually came with fries. If it wasn't for her neighbors giving her their personal recipes gussied up with fancy names, her tenure as a food connoisseur would have crashed and burned a long time ago.

"She did, Mom, and she loved it," Alex said, stepping in for her. He winked behind his mother's back, sending a silent message that her secret was safe with him.

She'd tasted the lasagna, all right, and it was as delicious as his mother had said, but he'd been the one to cook it. Jordan felt the heat crawl up her face, remembering how he'd seduced her that night with a tray of lasagna and a pitcher of homemade sangria. Thank heavens

Natalie Moreland had no idea her great-grandmother's recipe had been instrumental in what had turned out to be one of the most romantic nights of her life. If for no other reason, Jordan would have to add her own rave review for the dish.

"We'd better hurry if we want to grab some lunch. I have a meeting in North Dallas with the Italian festival planners at two," Kate said, impatiently glancing at her watch. "Oh, Lord, it's later than I thought. I'll have to take a pass and meet up with you all tonight at the party." She turned to Jordan. "I'll be working on the festival most of tomorrow, but why don't we do brunch before I head over to the fairgrounds? We can use the time to get to know each other." When Jordan nodded, Kate bent down to kiss her mother then stood on tiptoes to reach Alex.

As Kate was leaving, Jordan took a few minutes to study Natalie Moreland. It was obvious where both Kate and Alex had gotten their good looks. Shorter than her daughter, she had the same olive skin and deep blue eyes. Dressed in a pair of black slacks and a crisp, white, sleeveless shirt, she looked as if she could have been his older sister instead of the woman who had given birth to him. Dark blond hair with lighter highlights framed her perfectly shaped face in an up-to-date style. Jordan was pretty sure that, unlike Alex's hair, Natalie Moreland's had come from a bottle at a high price and wasn't the result of the sometimes brutal Texas sun.

Natalie entwined her arm with Jordan's. "What are we waiting on? I'm starving, and I can't wait to find out all about the girl my son has tried so hard to keep secret from me."

Alex rolled his eyes and held the door open as the two women passed. Once in the car, Jordan sat in the backseat so Alex's mother could get a better view of the small town her son now called home. Unfortunately, his job took him all over Texas, and he spent as much time away from Ranchero as he did in town.

During their last undercover gig in El Paso, Alex and his partner had put away a lot of big fish in the Texas/Mexico drug connection. After they'd tied up all the loose ends in the case, he'd jumped at the offer of a promotion as the FBI's Dallas assistant field commander. Even though Ranchero was an hour's drive from downtown Dallas, he'd chosen to live in the same house he'd occupied for several months while working undercover to break up an international diamond smuggling ring the year before.

Staring at the back of Alex's head as he entertained his mother with a tour of the city, Jordan was glad he'd decided to come back to Ranchero. Secretly, she hoped his decision to make that long commute to work had something to do with her.

With the Italian Festival in town, if she played her cards right, maybe she'd get a repeat of the lasagna dinner—and more.

TWO

JORDAN CLIMBED INTO Ray Varga's nine-passenger Suburban later that night, along with all her other friends from Empire Apartments, and everyone began talking at once.

"I can't freaking believe I'm finally going to see the inside of the fabulous Crown Royale Hotel. Heard the rooms go for a thousand bucks a night," Victor Rodriguez said from the back of the SUV.

Jordan turned to Michael Cafferty, Victor's partner, and pursed her lips to hide her glee. "You'd better hold him down, because when I tell him where the party is actually being held, he's gonna flip out."

Victor leaned forward until he was practically in Jordan's face. "Oh dear God, don't keep me in suspense. Are we going to be in the ballroom?"

Jordan shrugged. Victor was more like a brother to her than her landlord, and like her four older siblings back in West Texas, he was easy to tease.

He owned the local antiques shop in the town square and had a better eye for finding old stuff and turning it into a profit than anyone she'd ever known, but he was also the easiest of the Empire Apartment gang to impress. He and Michael had bought the rundown building on a lark and now socked every spare dollar they had into renovating it. That left little money for entertainment. Tonight was a big deal for all of them.

Jordan and Victor had hit it off right away and had quickly become good friends—and sometimes cohorts in crime. It seemed every time the two of them were off on their own, they always managed to get into trouble.

"Oh Lord, child. Put him out of his misery. I can't stand to see that look on his face." Rosie LaRue, the fiftyish, free spirit of the group, twisted around to face Jordan. "I'm dying to know, too. So give it up before we gang up on you."

"The Presidential Suite."

Ray whistled. "Whoa! I once worked security over there and couldn't believe the opulence. Don't know if it's true or not, but my boss said the suites upstairs started at ten grand a night." He leaned toward his favorite lady, Lola Van Horn. "You and I could do a lot of relaxing there, love, if you get my drift."

"Criminy, Ray! Who doesn't get your drift?" Rosie playfully punched Ray's arm.

Anyone with two eyes could see how much Lola and Ray cared for each other. What had started out as two neighbors sharing coffee every morning had progressed into the two sharing a whole lot more. It was cute watching the tough ex-cop turn to jelly in the hands of the seventyish woman who owned Lola's Spiritual Readings next door to Victor's antique shop and wore the latest caftans Walmart had to offer. It gave Jordan hope that love might be in the cards for all of them.

"Seriously, kiddo, we're really going to party with the rest of the Italian Festival people in the Presidential Suite at the Royale?" Rosie grabbed her purse and dug out the mirror. "I need more lipstick."

Jordan laughed. "Kate's firm represents the Italian-American Foundation."

"Who's Kate?" Lola asked.

"Alex's sister. Anyway, they're the ones putting on

the festival, and Kate's here to make sure everything this weekend goes without a hitch."

"His sister's a lawyer?"

"Yes. She lives in Houston, and apparently, she also was involved in last year's festival in California. She drove in yesterday to oversee the operation again this year. Alex's mother only came along for the ride—and to check me out, I'm sure."

"Oh my word! And you're meeting her tonight?" Lola shot Jordan a sympathetic look.

"Already did at lunch today. Thank God she's nothing like what I've been imagining since Alex first mentioned they would be coming. I was sure she would be another Marie Barone from *Everybody Loves Raymond*."

Rosie snapped the mirror shut, apparently satisfied with her makeup. "And is she?"

"No, thank God, although it's obvious Alex is still her baby boy. She put me on the spot a few times, but it wasn't anything I couldn't handle."

Jordan leaned against the cool leather seat and thought about the earlier meeting with Natalie Moreland. As expected she had been very protective of her only son and nailed Jordan with a few personal questions that bordered dangerously into none-of-your-business territory. Even Alex couldn't reel her in and finally had just thrown his hands in the air.

But Jordan hadn't minded. Something about Natalie Moreland reminded her of her own mother back in Amarillo. She'd answered the questions honestly, telling her the relationship with Alex was only in the beginning stages, explaining that they were taking their time getting to know each other. Slow and steady had seemed to satisfy her.

The only uncomfortable moment had come when they

were eating dessert and Natalie, as she'd instructed Jordan to call her, had quizzed her about how many children she planned to have. Alex had quickly jumped up and declared lunch officially over, admonishing his mother for getting too personal.

Leaving the restaurant, Natalie had whispered in Jordan's ear when Alex was out of hearing distance. "I have a feeling you two will make beautiful grandchildren for me."

Although they both knew it was way too early in the relationship to be thinking about things of that nature, Jordan had smiled back, wondering to herself what an Irish-Italian bambino would look like.

"There it is," Victor shouted from the back, his voice as excited as a kid getting his first look at a new bike under the Christmas tree. "Oh my God! It looks even more awesome up close." He leaned forward as Ray pulled the Suburban around the circular drive in front of the hotel.

"Kate said to be sure to use the valet. Otherwise we'll have to park too far away. They're expecting a huge crowd."

"How did you finagle an invite for all of us?" Michael asked, leaning across Victor to get a better look. "My boss said there were tons of important people coming to the party. He tried to get me in with press credentials, but they didn't go for that. Said it was a private party. He was really impressed when I told him I was going."

"Why would the radio station be interested in the party? I thought it was just for the planners and the bigwigs in the Italian American Foundation?" Ray asked.

Jordan answered for Michael. "According to Kate, it's just for the IAF people, but I can see why KTLK would be interested in covering it. It's the biggest thing to hit the Dallas/Fort Worth area since Arlington hosted the Super Bowl last year."

"I'll say," Victor added. "One of the guys who stops by the shop to chitchat every day said that people were coming from as far away as Palermo, Italy."

"That's true," Jordan confirmed. "And from all over the United States, as well. It's a pretty big deal."

"So how did you get an invite, Jordan, and not Michael with press credentials?" Ray repeated Michael's earlier question.

"The newspaper wants to make sure every aspect of the festival is covered. I'm actually on assignment tonight," she answered. "They want me attend every event that has anything to do with food and give a running review in my column…" She paused before finishing with, "My column for now, anyway."

Waiting for the valet, Michael turned to her. "What does for now mean?"

Jordan thought about changing the subject then decided her friends would find out sooner or later. "You remember Loretta Moseley who used to have my job at the newspaper?" When they nodded, she continued, "Well, she's back in town, and she's decided she wants her old job back."

"No way!" Victor exclaimed. "Isn't she the old bat who ran off with her lover?"

Jordan bit her lip to keep from grinning when Michael shot his partner a disapproving glance for calling Loretta an old bat. "That would be her."

"Who does she think she is? She can't just walk back onto the scene and ask for your job! More importantly, how can your editor, in his right mind, even consider it?" Lola huffed.

"Her uncle's the owner," Jordan explained with a shrug.

"I don't care who her uncle is," Lola said. "It's not right."

Jordan knew her friends would be outraged. "We're both covering the events at the festival and writing about them. She takes one day, and I take the other. Then Egan and the owner will pick the one who gets to keep the column." She tried not to sound too worried, but the truth was there was a good chance she'd have to give up the Kitchen Kupboard.

"You should've said that in the first place," Rosie said, with a wink and a swipe at a strand of her blond hair that had slipped out of her usual French braid. "The good people of Ranchero love you and your recipes."

"Your recipes," Jordan corrected. "Without you, my job as the culinary expert would be a joke."

Rosie patted her shoulder. "You could never be a joke, my dear. Maybe my recipes are a big hit, but it's your personality that comes through in the column. You're gonna kick that Loretta woman's ass."

A young man in uniform appeared, and Ray handed him the keys, then took the lead and walked through the elegant glass doors into the most beautiful lobby Jordan had ever seen.

"Would you look at this?" Rosie observed, doing a slow 360. "I can't wait to see what the Presidential Suite looks like if the lobby is this gorgeous."

An older man dressed in a dark gray suit that had definitely not come off the rack approached them. "May I help you?"

Jordan reached into her purse for her press pass and the gold emblazoned invitation Kate had given her. "I'm

Jordan McAllister from the *Globe*, and these people are guests of Kate Moreland. We're here for the IAF party."

After carefully inspecting the documents, the concierge instructed them to follow him to a private elevator around the back of the hotel desk. He scanned a card, and the elevator opened instantly.

"This will take you straight to the Presidential Suite."

Jordan felt a current of excitement course through her body when the door closed behind them. They were going to one of the biggest parties in Dallas. It would be a night to remember for all of them.

The sounds of a full-blown celebration could be heard even before the elevator door opened on the eleventh floor.

Stepping directly out into the largest hotel room she'd ever seen, Jordan stood in awe. The others were uncharacteristically silent, probably as star-struck as she was. A quick scan verified the room was twice the size of her entire apartment, and it looked like there were close to a hundred people milling around. A large, circular red leather couch wrapped around one entire side of the room, showcasing a magnificent stone fireplace with a theater-sized flat screen TV above the mantle.

Even with the recent temperatures topping the high nineties, there was a fire burning behind the glass enclosure, obviously more for ambience than heat. Jordan counted ten people sitting around the TV screen watching a video of a previous Italian festival. Hoots and hollers could be heard every few seconds as someone recognized a face on the screen.

In the center of the room, an impressive spiral staircase led to what Jordan assumed were the bedroom suites, with a balcony overlooking the lower floor. Off to the right was a bar nearly as big as the one Jordan and her friends frequented in Connor on Karaoke Night. Several people huddled around the dark oak structure either waiting for drinks or chatting with friends.

The rest of the party goers were moving from one group to another—*working the room*. Dean Martin's soothing voice crooned *Que Sera Sera* over the huge speakers in the corners of the large room.

Alex appeared out of nowhere. "You take my breath away," he whispered into her ear, causing the fine hairs on her neck to spring to attention. "New dress?" When she nodded, he put his hand on her shoulder and swiveled her around so that she was looking right at him. After his eyes moved up and down her body, they settled on her face. "Money well spent."

"She almost didn't buy it," Rosie said. "I had to twist her arm."

"I'll bet every guy in this place is thanking you right now, Rosie."

"Hush, Moreland! I'm already self-conscious enough without you adding to it." Jordan tried to look serious but couldn't pull it off.

She tugged at the hem of the red and white dress she'd bought on sale at Macy's that afternoon. Although it was a little shorter than she normally wore, Rosie had insisted it was perfect. She'd nearly flipped out when she'd seen the sales clerk adding in the matching stilettos that had cost almost as much as the dress.

Between Rosie and the young clerk who'd insisted the dress was nothing without the shoes, she hadn't stood a chance. Even though the spree would put a serious dent in her budget for the month, she'd left the store with both. Seeing the approval in Alex's eyes made it all worthwhile, though. Bologna sandwiches and chips would be her dinner staple for the next few weeks since eating out would have to be the first thing to go until she could get her finances back on track. That was if she didn't fall and kill herself trying to walk in the heels.

A small price to pay for the way Alex was smiling at her now.

After bending down and lightly kissing her, he greeted the others. "Come on. Let's get you all something to drink. You're gonna need it before you meet my mom."

They followed him to the other side of the room where a huge fountain was surrounded by a pyramid of cocktail glasses. Grabbing one, he filled it with the flowing liquid, and after attaching an orange slice for garnish, handed it to Jordan. "Taste this and then tell me you can stop at one." While he filled two more for Lola and Rosie, the guys helped themselves.

After only one sip, Jordan licked her lips. "What's this, Alex? It's fantastic."

"Italian Margarita. It's a staple at the festival, so you'll be drinking a lot of them next weekend. The amaretto makes it."

"It tastes familiar to me. Isn't this what George Christakis used to get me tipsy on the cruise the night I sat with him in the hot tub waiting for you to finish playing detective?"

"One and the same." Alex grinned. "And if I'm remembering correctly, because of the New York restaurateur plying you with these margaritas, you and I didn't get much sleep that night."

"Oh, no you don't!" Rosie exclaimed, stepping between Jordan and Alex. "No talking about that kind of stuff. Remember, I'm flying solo tonight. I'll need a few more of these before I can handle that kind of torture."

She refilled her glass and took a big swig. "Oh, this will definitely ease the pain."

"I'm betting when you get a good look at some of these Italian gentlemen here, that may all change," Victor said. "There are some hotties walking around."

Rosie's face lit up as Michael sent a dagger Victor's way. "I never could resist a cute *paesano*."

No truer words were ever spoken. Rosie was the femme fatale of the group and loved to flirt. It was an art form to her, and with four ex-husbands running around as proof, she'd gotten pretty good at it. She'd tried several times to teach Jordan how to do it, but each time Jordan had attempted to put it into practice, she hadn't been able to pull it off and had ended up feeling incredibly stupid.

Jordan remembered once when a really cute guy had tugged at the back of her shirt and looked at the tag. When he'd declared she'd been made in heaven just as he'd thought, all she could come back with after that corny pickup line was, "It was on sale at Target."

Sheesh! She was so lame when it came to interacting with men. Another side effect of hanging out with brothers whose idea of *protecting* her was scaring off any male who came sniffing her way. It wasn't until she'd gone off to college—and away from their watchful eyes—that she'd had her first serious relationship with a guy.

And look how that had ended—alone again with still no clue about how to purposely attract the opposite sex.

Rosie still cracked up every time they went back to that bar in Connor. Thank heavens, she hadn't run into the guy again. And lucky for her, she'd done better when she'd met Alex for the first time.

Actually, he'd picked *her* up, using a corny come-on line of his own at her favorite fast food Mexican joint.

Instead of being a bumbling idiot, she'd fired one back at him. But she'd been in her element. If there was one thing she could converse intelligently about, it was Mexican food. It wasn't until later that she'd learned Alex had been more interested in her involvement with a diamond smuggler than in her skinny redheaded self—to quote Loretta Moseley.

"Okay, everybody, fill up and follow me. My mom's been dying to meet you all," Alex said, flashing his pearly whites at her and making her heart skip a beat.

"What have you told her about us?" Victor asked. "Please tell me you only said good things."

"Even as a kid I couldn't lie to my mother." Alex grinned. "Okay, I didn't tell her *all* the bad stuff."

They followed him over to the bar where his mother was chatting with a nice-looking older man decked out in a dark gray jacket. Jordan stole a glance Rosie's way, knowing this guy was exactly the kind of man that would attract her fiftyish friend. She already imagined Rosie's status changing from 'single, party of one' to 'hooked-up, party of two.' Mentally, she high-fived herself for knowing her neighbor so well when Rosie got her first look at the older gentleman and immediately stuck out her chest.

"Excuse me for interrupting, Mother, but I wanted you to meet Jordan's friends." He turned to the man beside her. "You, too, Emilio."

Looking momentarily perturbed at being interrupted, the man quickly recovered, reaching for Rosie's outstretched hand and kissing it in an exaggerated show of chivalry. Jordan fought to hide a smile when Rosie nearly swooned on the spot.

"Natalie Moreland and Emilio Calabrese, I'd like you both to meet Jordan's neighbors."

One by one he introduced them, and as expected, Rosie turned on the charm, complimenting him on everything from his jacket to his dark black eyes. About five eleven, Emilio looked to be in his late fifties with a touch of gray at his temples. Even though he had yet to open his mouth and speak, Jordan got the distinct impression he was someone important.

Alex's mother wore a bright blue cocktail dress that fell below her knees and showed off curves even a much younger woman would envy.

"I've heard so much about you that I feel I already know all of you," Natalie said to the gang after hugging Jordan.

"Emilio is one of the sponsors of the festival," Alex explained. "His shipping company makes sure that everything, including all the alcohol and soft drinks for the weekend, arrives on time. And keeping all those Italians in *vino* for three days is no small feat."

Emilio repeated the hand kissing with both Jordan and Lola. Although he flirted openly with all of them, it was obvious he was more interested in Alex's mother. Jordan knew that wouldn't stop Rosie from putting her on-the-prowl persona into play.

A well-dressed man appeared out of nowhere and stopped in front of Emilio. "Do you have a minute? I need to talk to you about something."

"Not right now, Jeff. Whatever it is, it can wait until after the party." Then, as if he suddenly remembered his manners, Emilio faced the group. "This is Jeff Hamilton, my lawyer. Jeff, this is Kate's mother and brother and their friends."

The men shook the newcomer's hand while the women acknowledged him with a smile. Dressed in a dark gray suit that fit his svelte body perfectly, the man stood well over six feet tall with blondish-brown hair and green eyes. Jordan decided if she had to sum him up in one word, it would be classy.

"Okay, Make sure you find me when everyone leaves. We've got a problem." He started to leave then said. "If you see Kate, will you tell her I need to talk to her as well?"

"Will do," Emilio said as they all watched his lawyer walk away.

Jordan scanned the room. "Where is Kate, anyway?"

Alex and his mother exchanged glances before Alex shrugged. "She had a headache and decided to go back to my house to lie down." He linked arms with Jordan then addressed his mother again. "I'm taking Jordan and her friends for food, and then we're heading out to the balcony so I can show them how gorgeous the Dallas skyline is from here. Will you join us, Mother?"

Natalie waved her hand. "In a minute, son. Emilio was just telling me about his daughter's upcoming wedding."

Jordan didn't miss the disapproving look that crossed Alex's face. He had to have noticed the way Calabrese was standing close enough to his mother to brush against her occasionally. He'd mentioned earlier that his father was in Abu Dhabi on a business trip.

Was it possible Natalie Moreland was one of those people who believed in the old "when the cat is away" thing?

THREE

NATALIE AND EMILIO were quickly forgotten as Jordan got a look at the buffet table lined with elegant white linen and decorated with red, green, and white roses. It went hand in hand with the matching Italian flag sugar sheet that glistened from a huge cake in the center. Within minutes, they all had plates and were making their way around the table. Most of the food looked way too fancy for Jordan to ever consider, and for a second, she worried she'd have to resort to eating a bologna sandwich when she got home.

She'd only eaten a salad at lunch with Alex and his mother, not wanting the woman to think—as her son liked to say—that she could put it away like a lumberjack. Now she was starving and prepared to pig out on all the free food. But without recognizing the food on the platters, there was no way she'd take a chance and end up making the same mistake she'd made while judging the cooking contest on the cruise a few months back. She'd gotten into trouble after she'd scarfed down an entire plate of sweetbreads before discovering sweetbreads were actually the thymus glands of calves.

She'd nearly gagged and had made a complete fool of herself trying to spit it out. If it hadn't been for the kindness of a famous celebrity chef who had slipped her a mint under the table, her career as a culinary reporter might well be over.

Alex noticed her frown and slipped in beside her. "This is Italian food, Jordan. I promise you'll love it."

"Hello, Jordan," a voice from behind said, "It's nice to know you clean up pretty well."

Jordan turned just as Loretta Moseley approached with six-inch heels that had her wobbling like a drunken hooker. Dressed in an apple-green sundress that showed off an impressive cleavage, the ex-culinary reporter clung to the arm of a man who could only be described as a serious hottie.

Seeing her nemesis, Jordan touched her reddish-brown curls, wishing she'd gone for a more sophisticated look. Subconsciously, she smoothed down the front of her red and white dress, glad Rosie had talked her into buying it.

"Hello, Loretta. It's nice to see you again." She turned to the tall guy standing next to her, noticing the way his spiky blond hair accentuated dark green eyes that were blatantly moving up and down her body.

Jordan tapped her foot and waited until his gaze settled back on her face. "You must be the physical therapist I've heard so much about."

Loretta narrowed her eyes in an I-can't-believe-you-just-said-that glare. "Not that it's any of your business, but yes, Aaron is the one who helped me after the accident." She moved closer to her escort, obviously aware of the way he was smiling at Jordan.

Apparently, Alex had caught it, too, and slid in beside her, extending his hand toward the therapist. "Alex Moreland, Jordan's date."

The man finally took his eyes off Jordan and reached for Alex's hand. "Aaron Conley. I work at Ranchero Rehab Hospital off Texoma Parkway."

"I've been doing some checking on you," Loretta

said, glancing toward Jordan's empty plate. "My sources say you've been seen a lot at the fast food joints around town. That's kind of weird for a girl who writes about gourmet food, don't you think?"

Jordan swallowed back a groan, wondering if Loretta had somehow figured out she was a fraud. "No weirder than leaving town for nine months." She tilted her head toward Mr. America. "With your *friend* here, expecting to waltz in and get your old job back when you came home broke."

Loretta's gaze turned to steel. "So that's how we're going to play this?"

"You started it," Jordan said before lowering her voice. "I'm willing to be fair and do the best job I can. I guess we'll have to wait until after the festival to see who's the better columnist and let your uncle make his decision based on that."

Jordan heard Alex's sharp intake of breath behind her and cringed, realizing she hadn't yet told him about the conversation in her editor's office the day before.

"It's that old 'keep your friends close and your enemies closer' thing." Loretta grabbed Aaron's hand and pulled him from the table. "Good luck, Jordan. You're gonna need it because you're out of your league, out of your element, and soon you'll be out of a job," Then she walked away, dragging her therapist with her.

"She's a piece of work," Victor commented from the other end of the table where he was already digging into a plate of cannolis. "You got her pretty good, though, with that coming-home-broke zinger."

"What was that all about, Jordan?" Alex asked.

"Loretta came back from Las Vegas with her tail between her legs and demanded her old job back," Victor answered for her.

Alex moved closer and touched Jordan's hand. "I'm so sorry, honey. Does this mean you won't be writing the Kitchen Kupboard anymore?"

"I don't know," she answered, truthfully. "We both have to write about the festival, and then Egan will decide." She moved to the end of the table and the cannolis, resigning herself to the fact that if she didn't have her trusted Hostess Ho Ho's available to lift her spirits, cream filled Italian pastries would have to do. "Right now I don't want to think about that and ruin the party. Tomorrow's soon enough to worry about my job."

She wrinkled her nose before spotting a chafing dish in the middle of the table. Her smile returned after she made her way there and peeked under the lid. It was chicken parmesan, one of her favorites. She filled her plate, grabbed a hunk of bread, and followed Alex through the opened glass doors.

Seeing the balcony for the first time caused a collective 'ah' from the group. Dotted with six or eight tables sporting the same elegant white table linen and flag-colored roses as the main dining room, it was as big as her kitchen and living room combined. Only this patio came with a marble floor.

Finding a vacant table, they pulled more chairs around. Jordan sat next to Victor, noticing his plate was piled even higher than hers. She giggled to herself, knowing her friend probably hadn't eaten lunch, either. There were two things in life he loved besides Michael—eating and free food.

After cleaning her plate, she followed Alex to the depressed oak railing to get a better view. "Oh, my! Look how gorgeous this is." She pointed toward downtown Dallas. "I had no idea you could see the skyline this well from here."

"I hope you got enough to eat. You ate like a bird at lunch."

Jordan turned just as Natalie Moreland walked up with Emilio right behind her. Had Alex's mother seen her plate and was now being sarcastic? One look her way dispelled that notion. She was grinning at her like Jordan was something special, making her wonder if Alex kept his girlfriend's away from his mother for a reason. It would be embarrassing for him if Natalie Moreland treated every woman he brought home as her future daughter-in-law, and even more so if she asked them how many grandchildren they intended to give her.

"Mother, you'd better grab something to eat before they move the table out to start dancing. The band is already setting up." Alex sent her a disapproving glare. "I wish Dad had been able to come with you. You know how much he loves to dance."

Jordan bit her lip to stifle a grin. Alex wasn't fooling anyone with the dad remark. He was simply making sure Emilio knew his mother was married. Unfortunately, Emilio didn't look like the kind of guy who cared about small details like a wedding ring.

Or was it possible that Alex was reminding his mother?

"There you all are. I've been looking for you."

Jordan swiveled around just as Kate Moreland approached, her cheeks flushed, her charcoal silk blouse slightly disheveled.

"Oh, honey, how's your headache? I thought you were going to lie down for a while."

"I did, Mother, and I'm much better." She kissed Natalie then turned her attention to Emilio. "I need to talk to you later about the shipment from New Jersey. It still hasn't arrived, and I'm getting a little concerned."

"Don't you worry your pretty little head about it." Emilio patted her hand. "My guys are on top of the liquor situation. I guarantee it'll be here in plenty of time."

Apparently satisfied with the answer, Kate turned back to Jordan and motioned for the gang to come over. "These must be the friends I've heard so much about. I hope you all have a great time tonight and at the festi—" She glanced up when an older gentleman tapped her shoulder, and after a brief exchange with the man, she excused herself and stepped away from the group with him.

"She's not going to get much time to party tonight, I'm afraid," Alex explained. "Everyone seems to need her for one thing or another. She's—" He stopped when the sound of breaking glass was heard from inside.

Emilio stared into the living room. "Looks like a lovers' quarrel. You know how passionate we Italians are about love and war." Although his response was flippant, the serious look on his face was not.

Jordan followed his gaze and focused on one of the most gorgeous men she'd ever seen. Standing about six two and dressed in a black suit that had to be pure silk, the man was visibly upset. He was frantically trying to calm a woman who was screaming obscenities and waving her arms in the air with each new outburst.

Studying them from a distance, Jordan couldn't help thinking that if ever there was a mismatch it was the two of them. The woman stood around five three with black hair cut short and framing her round, olive face in a very unflattering style. Slightly overweight with a large nose, she wasn't what Jordan would expect to see on the arm of someone as debonair as the man she was arguing with. Jordan was about to say something to Alex when the good-looking man grabbed the woman's arm and marched toward them, stopping directly in front of Emilio and Natalie.

"Maybe you can talk some sense into my fiancée," he said, his voice dripping with anger. "She thinks I'm cheating on her."

"Your fiancée?" Kate asked, turning away from the man she'd been conversing with and stepping around her mother to face the new arrival. "Marco, what's going on?"

"Kate!" Surprise covered his face. "You said you weren't staying for the party. I thought you'd left."

"Is this the whore, Marco?" the short woman asked, tears now beginning to form in her eyes.

Kate's face flamed, and before Alex could stop her, she lunged at Marco and gave his face a stinging slap, leaving a bright red imprint of her hand. Without another word, she turned on her heels and stomped out.

"What are you talking about, Tina?" Emilio nailed Marco with an icy stare as he cradled his daughter in his arms.

Tina sniffed and pulled away, swiping at the tears running freely down her cheeks with the sleeve of her obviously expensive blouse. "I heard him talking to someone on the phone a little while ago, Daddy. He told her he couldn't quit thinking about her body against his, his mouth on hers."

Emilio turned to Marco, a stern look on his face. "Is this true?"

Marco shook his head. "She misunderstood me, Emilio. I swear. I love Tina and I haven't cheated on her."

Emilio studied Marco's face for a few minutes before he bent down and whispered something in his daughter's ear. Straightening up he gave her a nudge toward the living room. "Get yourself cleaned up, baby girl. The party's just getting started."

She stole a final look in Marco's direction, and then walked back into the hotel, still sniffling.

When she was gone, Emilio wrapped his arm around the man's shoulder and pulled him close.

"This is my future son-in-law, Marco Petrone."

Without warning, Natalie Moreland reached out and slapped the other side of Marco's face. "You're a lying bastard."

The silence following that statement was finally broken when a stunned Marco recovered enough to confront Natalie.

"And who exactly are you?"

Her eyes flashed anger. "The whore's mother."

FOUR

MARCO'S FACE REGISTERED the surprise before he glanced toward Emilio, whose eyes held the same questions the rest of the gang was thinking. He ignored Natalie and focused on his future father-in-law. "Tina's mistaken, Emilio. It all started when she overheard me on the phone earlier. Before I could explain, she threw a fit."

If looks could kill, Marco would have been six feet under as Natalie glared at him. Without a word, she side-stepped Emilio and stomped off.

Alex put a hand on Jordan's shoulder and bent down to whisper in her ear. "I need to find out what's going on. I'll be back in a few minutes." He hurried to catch up to his mother.

As soon as Alex was out of sight, Emilio spun around to face Marco, his eyes narrowed into angry slits. "I thought after you and I had our little talk last month that you'd made some changes in your life. I don't have to tell you how upset I'll be if I find out this is true, do I?"

Marco's eyes widened and he shook his head. "It's not true. If I'm guilty of anything, it's that I've neglected Tina lately. I've been so busy planning this festival, and it all came to a head the past few days. But I'll make sure she gets the attention she deserves. I promise."

"That's my boy!" Emilio exclaimed, slapping Marco on the back. He sounded more like a proud papa whose son had won a gold medal at the Olympics than a father who had just witnessed his daughter in tears. "Women are like African violets, Marco. They need a lot of care and attention, and when they don't get treated like the delicate flowers they are, they wither. Now go make things right with my daughter. I'll find Natalie and make sure she's okay, too." He grabbed Marco's arm and led him toward the entrance before he stopped. "Oh, and Kate tells me the liquor hasn't arrived yet. I hope you'll take care of that little problem immediately."

"There was a glitch at the warehouse. I'll make sure it's on the way." He allowed Emilio to nudge him inside, where the band had already begun to warm up.

Too stunned to speak, Jordan and the others stood at the railing watching the men walk away.

Finally Victor spoke up. "Holy cow!"

Jordan shook her head. "Yeah. Someone's lying. My money's on Marco."

"No kidding," Lola agreed. "I hope the two-timing jerk gets what's coming to him. Emilio doesn't look like the kind of guy I'd want to tick off."

"I hope Kate's okay. I don't see her anywhere in there." Michael cocked his head to rescan the living room. "Do you think what Tina said is true? That Kate really was fooling around with Marco?"

"Let's not jump to conclusions," Ray said. "We don't have all the facts."

"Spoken like a true ex-cop, Ray," Victor said. "But you've got to admit, it does look like Alex's sister had some kind of relationship with Marco. From her reaction, though, I don't think she had a clue that he was engaged."

"She didn't."

They all turned to see Alex walk up.

"Is Kate okay?" Jordan asked.

He shrugged. "She's holed up in the bathroom and

won't come out. Even my mother can't talk her into unlocking the door."

"Who is this Marco guy?" Rosie asked, moving over to stand beside Jordan.

"All I know is what Kate told us earlier. His family owns a huge vineyard in southern Italy. They export the wine along with a slew of other things from China and sell the goods all over the world. Apparently, he's got more money than he knows what do with and divides his time between New York and Matera."

"No wonder Emilio tried to smooth things over with him. Having his daughter marry into that kind of wealth has to be a strong motivator to overlook a few of his bad habits," Victor said. "Even if one of them is womanizing and making your daughter's life miserable."

"Victor! Why do you always want to believe the worst about people?" Michael scolded.

Victor rolled his eyes. "Please. Where were you a few minutes ago when that little scene played out? Marco is definitely a player."

"We knew there was someone special in Kate's life," Alex explained. "All she talked about today was how excited she was that we were finally going to meet him. I hope to God she wasn't talking about Marco."

Jordan reached for his hand. "I hope so, too, but I saw the hurt that flashed across her face, Alex. Hearing that Marco was engaged totally caught her by surprise."

"Where is that rat? Surely he's got enough decency to leave the party after all the trouble he's caused," Rosie said, clucking her tongue.

"That's not going to happen," Alex said, matter-of-factly. "This is his suite."

Ray looked around the room. "He *must* be rolling in some serious dough to afford this place. And without sounding cruel, I have to point out that Emilio's daughter looks way out of her league."

"Ordinarily, I would holler at you for saying such a thing, darling, but in this case, I have to agree." Lola patted his shoulder affectionately. "And I'm not only talking about the looks department. Emilio's daughter seems more like the type who'd rather be at home baking cookies for a house full of little Marcos than flying all over the world jet-setting with him."

"Alex?"

They all turned when Natalie approached, concern written all over her face.

"Kate finally came out of the bathroom, but she's still really upset. She's waiting on a cab to take her back to your place. I wanted to go with her, but she said she needed to be alone. Said she'd explain everything when we get back." Natalie sighed. "Do you think I should have insisted she let me go home with her?"

Alex shook his head. "Kate has always handled her disappointments internally. Remember the time she made it to the final cut at cheerleader tryouts and then lost out to another girl at the last minute? She didn't talk about it for a week—acted like it didn't bother her, even though I heard her crying in her room several nights in a row. Anyway, a week after she was cut, she got angry and put all her energy into making the girls' volleyball team."

Natalie bobbed her head, the beginning of a smile crossing her face. "I do remember. She could spike the ball better than most of the guys on the boys' team. Ended up making All State three years in a row."

"My point exactly. Getting pissed off was instrumental in molding her into one of the finest players ever at Sugarland High School," Alex said, pulling his mother closer to him. "Two state championships later, she used to say she owed the cheerleader snobs a debt of gratitude. Without that athletic scholarship, she might not've been able to go to law school." He kissed the top of Natalie's head. "Kate is a survivor, Mom. She'll get through this like she always does. We just need to give her time."

Natalie stepped back. "I know you're right, but I wish she'd let me help her through it. I feel so useless. Out of all my children, she's always been the most stubborn, and tonight won't be any different. I'll have to do exactly as she asked and give her some space. In the meantime, I have to pretend like I'm having a good time and hope she'll let me in when she's ready."

Michael stepped forward. "I'd be honored if you'd show me how they dance in Houston."

Smiling gratefully, she reached for his extended hand. "You're on, cowboy. Get ready to see my old lady moves."

Jordan choked up. Michael had a way about him that could make anyone feel better. He'd used it on her a few times in the past. Now watching him work his magic on Natalie, she wanted to show her appreciation and kiss him.

Victor grabbed Rosie and followed Michael and Natalie inside. The food table had been removed, and people were already two-stepping to a Willie Nelson classic.

"My lady?" Ray offered his arm to Lola, and the two of them meandered in that direction, too.

When they were alone Jordan turned to Alex. "Was that pep talk about Kate just for your mother's sake, or are you worried about her, too?"

Alex's brow furrowed. "Yes and yes. The talk was for her, but I am a little concerned. You should have seen her today talking about the new love in her life. Apparently, she met him last year at the Italian Festival in San Francisco, and unbeknownst to any of us, she's been seeing him for a year now. We assumed all those trips to New York were business-related, and probably, some were. But it's clear to anyone who watches her face light up when she talks about her special guy that there are deep feelings involved."

"Do you think that special guy is Marco?"

He pinched the bridge of his nose. "I sincerely hope not, but I'm not blind. Like you said, she was genuinely crushed when Emilio introduced Marco as his future son-in-law. Marco was lucky it was my mother who reacted first instead of me. I was ready to deck the guy."

"He would've been in big trouble if you had decided to avenge your sister's honor."

Alex laughed. "Dealing with Kate and my mother—and even me—is the least of Marco's worries. Trust me when I tell you it doesn't even compare to what will happen if Emilio turns against him."

"What do you mean? It looked like Emilio's willing to overlook a few things to have his daughter marry into all that money."

Alex laughed again. "I'm not talking about money, and FYI, Emilio probably has ten times more cash lying around than Marco ever will."

Jordan's eyebrow shot up. "Emilio's rich?"

Alex snorted. "He's definitely rich, but if I were Marco, I'd be worrying about more than that right now."

Jordan moved closer. "Yeah? Like what?"

Alex studied her face for a moment as if he were trying to decide whether to tell her something or not. Finally, he shrugged. "Ever hear of the Calabrese family from New Jersey?"

Jordan's eyes widened. "He's Mafia?"

"No one calls them that anymore, Jordan. Let's just say he's connected and leave it at that."

"Holy crap! Marco must be freaking out right about now and doing some fast talking to Tina."

"He didn't look too worried to me. It was like he knew Emilio wouldn't turn on him. Wonder what he has on the old man that would make him look away while his daughter's fiancé is obviously carrying on with another woman."

Just then the band ended the first song and went right into a slower one.

Alex tousled Jordan's hair. "Come on, curly, show me how good you can make an Italian guy look on the dance floor." He grabbed her arm and led her into the living room.

Jordan had missed being in Alex's arms and reveled in the sensation as he held her tight. With his body pressed into hers and swaying with the melody, all sorts of romantic fantasies danced in her head. He was wearing his favorite cologne—hers, too—and for a few minutes, she closed her eyes and let her body relax.

It didn't matter that Loretta Moseley was standing in the corner of the room shooting daggers her way, or that the Italian Festival might be the last event she covered as the culinary reporter for the *Globe*. She was with Alex, and the rest of the people in the room didn't matter in that moment.

Tomorrow, she'd deal with writing the best article she could about the festivities. And she'd take Kate up on that lunch offer and hopefully help her work out her feelings of being betrayed by her lover. If there was anyone with experience at being dumped, it was her. She'd been there, done that, and had the T-shirt to prove it, and she was anxious to use that wisdom to somehow help Kate.

Jordan looked over Alex's shoulder to see if she could spot Marco or Emilio's daughter in the room. When she didn't see them she assumed they'd worked things out and were probably off somewhere private making up. Laying her head on Alex's shoulder she wondered if maybe she should pick a fight with him for no other reason than the make-up sex.

"Oh my God!" a feminine voice shrieked.

Both Alex and Jordan stopped dancing and looked toward the patio where a middle-aged woman was bending over the wooden railing and screaming. They ran in that direction along with everyone else on the dance floor just as the woman backed away and began frantically shouting. The only words Jordan was able to pick up were "man" and "dead". Alex guided her through the crowd toward the oak rail.

Leaning over the barrier to get a better view, Jordan stared in disbelief when she realized she was looking at the body of a man lying face down on the ground eleven floors below. The river of blood making its way over the marble hotel entranceway gave Jordan a sick feeling of dread even before the hotel workers ran over to the body and turned the man over. Staring at the dark suit she'd seen up close just minutes earlier on the very same patio where she now stood, she didn't need to see the man's face to know it was Marco Petrone.

Before she could turn to Alex and tell him, there was another terrifying scream coming from inside the penthouse. Alex grabbed her arm and hurried back through the French doors into the living room.

"Sweet Jesus!" he said as his eyes followed the woman's pointed finger upward.

Staring over the balcony at the top of the spiral staircase, looking disoriented with her hair disheveled and her left eye bruised and swollen, stood his sister, Kate.

FIVE

ALEX RUSHED PAST Jordan up the staircase to his sister's side. Jordan followed, unable to keep up. Out of breath, she reached them just as he encircled Kate in his arms and pulled her tightly to his chest.

"Who did this to you?" His voice came out clear and calm, but Jordan knew better. When his sister didn't answer, he asked again. "Kate, who's responsible for this?"

Still no response. As a lone tear slid down her cheek, she shook her head, the only outward sign that she'd heard him. Her eyes remained fixated straight ahead on nothing in particular.

Alex held her at arm's length. "Kate?" Panic flashed over his face. His sister was in shock. He shook her then got right in her face. "Kate, look at me. Now!"

She blinked a few times before turning her eyes to meet his. Then she crumbled into his arms. It was like watching a paused TV image suddenly coming back to life. Hearing the gut-wrenching sobs now coming from her tore at Jordan's heart, and she swiped at her own tears that were threatening to spill over.

Natalie and the gang had watched the action playing out, and like the rest of the party-goers, had rushed upstairs to the bedroom to see what the commotion was about.

Natalie reached out for her daughter, but Alex shook his head, cradling his sister closer. Nobody spoke a word as he allowed her to cry for a few minutes. When her sobs subsided into an occasional hiccup, he handed her over to his mother who, despite the pain on her face, had somehow managed to keep her composure and her tears in check.

Even though more than half the people from the party were now crowding around, an eerie silence filled the room as everyone waited for Kate to explain what had happened. Out of the corner of her eye, Jordan looked over the crowd but didn't see Emilio or his daughter. More than likely they were both downstairs with Marco's body, probably taking the death pretty hard.

She glanced up at Alex, and there was no mistaking the look on his face. No longer trying to hide his rage at seeing Kate with her face badly bruised, his flexed fist and clenched teeth suggested he was ready to do serious bodily harm to whoever had dared touch his sister. Although Jordan barely knew Marco Petrone, she couldn't help thinking that if he was the one who had hurt Kate, he was better off dead.

Her hand shot up to cover her mouth at the realization of what she'd just been thinking. Her other hand rose to her heart. Oh God, what if Marco was to blame for Kate's black eye, and she'd fought back? Could it be that Alex's sister had something to do with his death? Could she have shoved him over the railing in a fit of anger or as a defensive move?

"Let her sit down on the bed for a few minutes," Emilio said, appearing out of nowhere and moving close to Natalie. "The police are on their way, and I'm sure they'll want to talk to her. Let's give her a few minutes to compose herself." His eyes were bloodshot and swollen as if he'd been crying. And why was he limping?

Natalie guided Kate toward the massive unmade bed in the middle of the room. The snow white comforter was half on the bed, half off, and five or six pillows were strewn all over the bed. One was even against the wall as though thrown across the room.

Alex stepped in front of his mother, blocking her path to the bed. "That's not a good idea, Mother."

"Why not?" Emilio questioned.

Alex looked first at Natalie and then turned his back on her as if he didn't want her to hear what he was about to say. "There's a good possibility Marco's bedroom is now a crime scene. We need to move out into the hallway."

When Natalie cried out, Kate lifted her head from her mother's shoulder long enough to nod. "I'll be okay out here," she said softly. "But I could use a drink."

Immediately, someone handed her a glass of champagne. Alex swiped it out of her hand on the way up to her mouth. "I'm afraid a soda will have to do, Kate." He turned to Victor and asked him to get her a soft drink before turning his attention back to his sister to explain. "You have a nasty cut above your right eye, and you might have a concussion." He paused, as if he were weighing his next words carefully. "And it's probably better if you have a clear head when the police question you about what happened here."

Again, Kate nodded. For what seemed like an hour, they waited on the second floor of Marco's suite, although it probably wasn't more than twenty minutes before the police arrived. Jordan found herself glancing back into the bedroom and trying to imagine what had gone on before Marco plunged to his death. No matter how hard she tried, every scenario had Kate smack dab in the middle of it.

Immediately upon entering the suite, the Plainville police took charge and began to round up the crowd on the first level and corral them to one side of the room. The band attempted to pack up their equipment but were ordered to leave it as it was and join the group in the corner.

A tall police officer giving orders glanced up at the balcony, then said something to another cop before making his way up the staircase. Jordan had a sinking feeling they were not going to like what came next.

Alex stepped forward to meet the officer after he topped the stairs. Rosie and the others who were still standing around outside the bedroom separated to allow the newcomer to pass.

"Are you in charge here?" Alex asked, shielding his sister and his mother behind him.

"Yes. Captain Walter Darnell."

"Alex Moreland, field commander of the Dallas FBI office." He held out his hand. Darnell reached out and shook it.

A puzzled look crossed the officer's face.

"I'm not on the job here," he explained, still completely blocking Darnell's way. "I was a guest at the party, and I'll be happy to answer all your questions." He took a step forward. "Is there some place we can go to talk privately?"

The captain studied Alex for a moment before shaking his head. "I'll definitely want to talk to you later, but for now, I need to have a word with the young woman behind you, Mr. Moreland. I've been told the victim probably fell from the balcony on this floor, and she might have some information that could help us in the investigation."

"I'd like to be there when you question her." Alex stood his ground and did not move out of the way. "Her name is Kate Moreland—my sister."

If Darnell was surprised by the comment, he never let on. Instead, he pulled Alex aside. "As long as you understand you have no jurisdiction in this investigation. This is my crime scene, but as a professional courtesy, I'll allow you to stay. Keep in mind, though, you're only an observer. If you can do that while my colleagues and I get to the bottom of this, we shouldn't have a problem."

"I'm staying, too," Natalie said from behind Alex.

Darnell peered around Alex's body. "And you are?"

"Kate's mother."

Darnell's eyes shot up to Alex's, probably looking for help. When none was offered, he said, "That's not going to happen, ma'am. Witnesses have said they saw you slap the dead man earlier. My men will need to talk to you by yourself."

"No way I'm leaving my daughter. I'm afraid your questions will have to wait."

Alex bent over and kissed his mother's forehead. "I'll be with her, Mom. The sooner we get this over with, the better." He turned to where the rest of the gang huddled close by. "Ray, can you stay with my mother while they question her?"

Ray took a step forward to stand beside Natalie.

Alex turned back to Darnell. "Ray Varga is a retired Ranchero police officer and a good friend of the family. I would like to have him with her at all times."

After thinking about it for a few seconds, Darnell waved his hand to another policeman. "I'll allow that as well, but the same goes for you, Mr. Varga. You are there only as an observer." Then he turned back to Alex. "Now let's you and me take your sister downstairs to somewhere private so my guys can cordon off this entire floor."

"I won't leave Kate," Natalie insisted. "She needs

me, Alex. You'll be so busy with all the police stuff, you won't be much help to her. Look at her. She's shaking so badly, I'm worried she'll go further into shock. Please don't make me go." She grabbed his arm. "I'm begging you, son."

Alex patted his mother's hand. "It's not my call, Mom. You'll be able to be with her soon, I promise. And Ray won't leave your side." He met Darnell's eyes before pleading, "Please, Captain. Kate is very fragile right now. If you won't allow my mother to stay with her, at least consider letting our friend in the room to be with her." He turned to Jordan and tried to smile.

Darnell stepped forward. "Because it's still just a preliminary investigation and we're only asking questions, I'll allow it, again as a professional courtesy. But be advised that the same rules apply. This is my investigation and I won't tolerate interference."

After hesitating for a moment, Natalie finally agreed to leave her daughter in Alex and Jordan's hands. Darnell barked an order for everyone to follow him down the stairs. After they reached the first floor of the suite, a group of men wearing CSI shirts rushed up the steps, carrying boxes of equipment.

Rosie, Victor, Lola, and Michael were directed to the corner of the room where the other party attendees waited to be questioned. A young officer approached and stood beside Darnell.

"This is Officer Wiedeman," the captain said, and then pointed to the other side of the room. "He's going to take Mrs. Moreland over there to interview her. It shouldn't last too long."

Ray introduced himself to Wiedeman, and then both he and Natalie followed him. Jordan glanced over and saw that they'd already set up a table next to the bar. It seemed a shame that they were so close to all that liquor and couldn't grab one measly drink to calm their nerves, but she knew that was out of the question.

When they were seated at the table, Natalie glanced over her shoulder, her eyes pleading one last time to be allowed to go with her daughter. Alex put his arm around his sister to reassure his mother that he would take care of her.

"I've had my men set up a place for us to talk on the patio. If you'll follow me, we'll get this over with as quickly as we can."

Jordan, Alex, and Kate followed Darnell past the crowd of people who were now all chatting at once. Jordan wondered what they were saying and hoped they hadn't seen Kate confront Marco earlier, although she knew that information would get out sooner or later.

Captain Darnell held out a chair for both Kate and Jordan before sitting down on the opposite side of the table. Alex took his place next to Kate, and patted her knee under the table.

"I'll get right to the point, Ms. Moreland. I've been told there was a problem between you and the deceased earlier tonight. Is that correct?"

Kate looked at Alex before answering, making Jordan wonder if she had always worked in corporate law or if she had any experience in criminal cases. "Yes. I had just learned that Marco—"

"Don't say anything else, Kate."

They all looked up to see Emilio's lawyer walk out onto the patio area. He pulled up a chair from another table and slid in between Kate and Jordan.

"Jeffrey Hamilton," he said extending his hand to Darnell. "I've been retained by Emilio Calabrese to advise Ms. Moreland. I'd appreciate it if you would direct any further questions to me, and I will confer with my client." He dropped his hand to his side when the policeman didn't reach for it. Turning to Kate, he said, "You can hire whomever you want tomorrow, but Emilio wanted to make sure you had representation tonight."

For the first time since all this happened, a smile tipped the corners of Kate's lips, and she let out a long, slow breath. "I appreciate the offer, Mr. Hamilton."

"Okay then," Darnell began again. "Back to the confrontation—"

"It hasn't been established that it was a confrontation," Hamilton interrupted. "My client will acknowledge that she spoke with the dead man earlier, but unless I missed something, she never once said what the conversation was about."

Darnell looked annoyed before he cleared his throat and began again. "Several people saw you speak to Petrone and then run from the room in tears. May I ask why you were so upset?" He sent a thinly-veiled look of disgust Hamilton's way.

The lawyer didn't flinch. "You can ask, and all she'll admit to is a misunderstanding."

If the cop was annoyed before, he was clearly ticked off now. "This interview will go a lot faster with just a little bit of cooperation. I'm simply trying to find out the facts here. No one is accusing your client of anything, counselor."

"Then we're in agreement," Hamilton said. "Both my client and Marco Petrone were involved in the planning of the Italian Festival this coming week. They've been working very closely to make sure everything goes as planned. Some minor problem surfaced tonight, and my client was upset when Marco reported it to her." He put his arm protectively on the back of Kate's chair. "Let me add that Ms. Moreland has been putting in eighteen hour days planning this event, and the lack of sleep has left her emotions fragile. She overreacted. End of story."

Jordan had never seen a real lawyer in action before, and she was totally impressed. So far, this man had not allowed Kate to say another word since her initial response, and even that wasn't anything that could be used against her. She'd heard both Ray and Alex say that interviewing a suspect immediately after the crime was committed before they could lawyer up usually produced incriminating results. She was grateful Emilio had the foresight to quickly send his high dollar lawyer to make sure that didn't happen.

"So, Ms. Moreland, is your statement that the reported confrontation with the deceased tonight was merely an overreaction?"

"We've already established that fact," Hamilton interjected. He glanced down at his watch impatiently. "It's been a long day, Captain. I'm sure my client would appreciate if we'd call it a night. I'll have her down at the station early tomorrow morning for further questioning. She's very emotional right now as Mr. Petrone was a friend. Can we allow her to grieve before you grill her?" He paused to glance toward Kate and give her a half smile before he leveled his gaze back on Darnell. "I've been told the deceased had a lot to drink tonight as well. It wouldn't be the first time a drunken man fell to his death."

Darnell narrowed his eyes. Clearly, he was not happy with the way his questions were intercepted by Hamilton. He pursed his lips and kept his focus on Kate. Jordan imagined him counting to ten before responding. "No, it would not be the first time, Mr. Hamilton, but in this case there were things that indicated Mr. Petrone may have had a little help getting over the railing," he said simply.

"Like what?"

"For starters, the railing is way too high to *accidently* fall over it. And then there are the problematic defensive signs—scratches across the railing as if he had tried in vain to keep from falling."

Hamilton smirked. "And you wouldn't have tried to catch yourself if you had slipped and fallen?"

The tips of Darnell's lips curled in a smile as if he had just seen the river card in a poker game and liked what he saw. "One of the valets heard the deceased scream and looked up in time to see him struggling with someone before he fell."

For the first time a concerned look crossed Hamilton's face. "Did this valet happen to see who that might have been?"

Darnell shook his head. "Unfortunately, he only saw a shadow."

"So, we're back to just thinking it was a possibility that someone other than the victim himself was responsible for his death."

"We will get to the bottom of this." He turned his attention to Kate. "One last question, Ms. Moreland. How did you get that black eye?"

"She walked into a door," Hamilton answered for her, standing up. "Are we done here?"

Darnell rubbed his forehead. "I guess we have to be. I expect to see you and your client at the station by—" He paused as a policeman who looked older than all the others approached and whispered something in his ear. When he finally addressed Hamilton again, he made no attempt to hide the grin on his face. "It seems we have a problem, and Ms. Moreland will have to hang around a little longer."

Hamilton was already halfway to the door. He turned back with a smirk. "And what might that be, Captain?"

Darnell motioned for the two men now standing in the doorway of the patio to come over. "My colleagues here will need to take swabs from under Ms. Moreland's fingernails."

"Not without a warrant," Hamilton reminded them rather smugly.

The shorter of the two men bent down beside Kate and opened the box he'd brought with him which held the equipment he would use in the investigation. He pulled out a pair of rubber gloves and slid them over his hands. Then he brought out an orange stick and a baggie and waited for the okay from Darnell.

"That's where you're wrong, counselor. It seems we have probable cause, but if you insist, we can all sit tight while one of my officers wakes up a judge and gets that warrant."

"What trumped-up evidence are you going to try to use now?" Hamilton's voice held a measure of contempt.

Darnell met his eyes and held them. "I've been informed the deceased had scratches all over his face. If I were a betting man, I'd guess we're going to find his DNA under your client's nails."

SIX

JEFFREY HAMILTON WALKED back to the table. As if to reassure Kate, he made eye contact with her when he sat down again. Without facing Darnell, he growled, "Get your warrant."

For the next forty-five minutes, they waited. Finally, a young officer walked out to the patio and handed the captain a document. He shoved it over to Kate's lawyer and nodded to the CSI tech.

Jordan kept her eyes on Kate while the man scraped under her fingernails. It was hard not to notice the panic spreading across her face as they bagged each specimen separately.

Oh God! Jordan thought. *She knows she's in trouble.*

She glanced at Alex to see if his reaction was the same as hers. Although he appeared to be cool and collected, Jordan knew the tiny scowl that wrinkled the corners of his eyes told a different story. It was beginning to look like his sister had somehow been involved in Marco's death, and he was powerless to stop the unfolding drama that he undoubtedly knew would follow.

Captain Darnell remained silent until the technicians finished up and walked back into the suite, but his eyes studied Kate the entire time. He was probably hoping her body language would give him some insight into her involvement in Marco's death.

He leaned forward in the chair. "We're finished for

now, Ms. Moreland. However, you'll need to come by the station first thing in the morning like we agreed."

"We'll be there," Hamilton said, matter of fact. "Until then, is there anything else?"

Using the table as support, the police captain got to his feet and addressed Kate. "I'd suggest you get some rest. I have a feeling tomorrow's going to be another long day for you." He pivoted and walked away, leaving her staring at his back, the shell-shocked look still on her face.

When he was out of hearing range, Alex turned to his sister. "Did you and Marco have some kind of physical altercation tonight, Kate? Will they find his DNA under your nails?"

Kate lowered her head and began to cry softly. "Yes to both questions."

"Oh, Christ!" Alex moved his chair closer to hers. "Kate, tell me you didn't have anything to do with what happened to him."

She shook her head.

"What were you doing in his bedroom? Mom said you went back to my place because you had a headache."

Before Kate could respond, Hamilton spoke up. "I'm a guest at this hotel, too. Why don't we all go down to my room and finish this conversation—away from all the chaos?"

"Good idea." Alex turned his back on Kate to address the lawyer. "On behalf of my entire family, I want to say how much we appreciate your showing up and taking charge, Mr. Hamilton."

"Call me Jeff."

"Alex." He held out his hand. "Let's see if they're finished with my mother. After I make sure she has transportation back to my place, Kate and I will come down to your room."

"I'll be waiting. Room 942."

Slowly, the lawyer made his way back into the living room as Jordan peered through the patio door. It looked like the cops were winding things down, and most of the people they'd corralled earlier for questioning were already gone. The few that remained were gathering their belongings.

Kate still hadn't lifted her head.

Alex's voice softened. "Do you want me to find another lawyer, or are you comfortable with Hamilton?"

She sucked in a large gulp of air and looked up. "If he's willing to represent me, I'd like to stay with him."

Alex nodded. "He was impressive. I'll give him that. We can ask him tonight about what it will take to retain him for the duration of this—"

"I know you think I had something to do with Marco's death, Alex, but I swear I didn't." Kate pleaded with her eyes for him to believe her.

"Is he responsible for your black eye?"

She dipped her head. "He'd had too much to drink, and we argued. He reacted to something I said and came at me all macho-like. When I threw my drink in his face, he punched me and threw me onto the bed, pinning me down." She steeled her shoulders before continuing, "For a few seconds I thought he was going to hit me again, but he didn't. He just suddenly rolled off me. I'd never seen him that angry before and certainly never violent. I was stunned. He must have realized he'd crossed the line because he rushed out onto the patio without saying another word."

"Did you follow him out there?

"I ran into the bathroom and locked the door. After

several minutes, I decided he'd had enough time to calm down, and it was probably safe to come out. When I didn't see him, I walked out onto the patio, but he wasn't there, either." She stopped to swallow before continuing, "That's when I heard all the commotion from the hotel entrance and looked over the railing. When I saw his body on the ground and all the blood…" She paused when her voice cracked. "I panicked."

"Was there anyone else in the room?"

She shook her head.

"What were you doing there in the first place?" Alex had switched from concerned brother into FBI agent mode, but he got choked up on the last question.

Kate took one look at his face and began to speak. "Marco called me when I was downstairs waiting for a cab. He begged me to listen to his side of the story. Like a fool, I wanted to believe there was no way our relationship had been built on a pack of lies—that he wasn't the two-timing scum I knew in my heart that he was. I prayed there was a logical explanation, so I agreed to go up to his bedroom to hear him out." She bit her tongue and looked up at the sky to keep the tears brimming in her eyes from rolling down her cheeks.

"When we got there, he tried to convince me he was in love with me, not Tina Calabrese. When he couldn't, he swore he was only going to marry her to get Emilio off his back. He laughed, saying why else would he agree to make love to a woman he couldn't even stand being in the same room with. He even tried to sweet talk me into climbing into bed with him—said there was no reason why we couldn't continue our relationship the way we have for the past year. That's when I lost it and tossed the drink in his face."

"And is that when he threw you on the bed?"

"Yes." Her voice was barely a whisper now as she reached up to touch her swollen right cheek. "Does it look bad?"

"Not as bad as the time you got slammed in the face with a volleyball and had two shiners." He brushed her cheek with the back of his hand. "Come on. You're going to have to explain this all over again to Jeff, so we might as well wait to hear the rest of the story."

Her head shot up. "There is no rest of the story. When I saw his body, I screamed and ran out of the bedroom. That's when you and everyone else came running up the stairs."

Just then Natalie pushed through the door with Ray right behind her and moved immediately to her daughter's side. Being in her mother's arms brought a new rush of tears. Natalie glanced up at Alex for some kind of signal that everything was okay. Unable to give her the reassurance she needed, he tried to smile.

"Are they through questioning her?" Ray asked.

"For tonight," Alex said. "They took samples from under her fingernails, and she has to go downtown with her lawyer tomorrow morning and give an official statement."

"Her lawyer?" Both Natalie and Ray asked in unison.

"Emilio sent his own personal lawyer to make sure Kate didn't say anything that might hurt her."

"Is that the guy we met earlier with the high-dollar suit?" Ray asked.

Alex shrugged. "You could be describing half the people at the party, but yes, he was the one Emilio introduced us to right before all the drama started."

"Thank God for Emilio," Natalie said. "He always did know what to do."

Jordan heard Alex grunt beside her. "We do owe him

a debt of gratitude. Jeff Hamilton made sure Kate didn't incriminate herself during the questioning. He did all the talking for her."

"So why did he allow them to get finger swabs without a warrant?" Ray asked.

"He didn't. Marco has scratches on his face, and they had probable cause, but Jeff insisted they get a warrant. That's what took so long."

Natalie was unable to stop herself in time and groaned. Without taking her arms from around her daughter, she asked, "And will this be a problem, Kate?"

"It could be," Alex answered for her. "But Kate's story should hold up tomorrow even with the swabs." He glanced at his watch. "We need to get down to Hamilton's room to prepare her for tomorrow's interrogation. Ray, can you make sure my mother gets home okay?"

"I won't stay in that house by myself," Natalie argued. "I want to go with you two."

"That's not a good idea, Mom. Some of the things Jeff will ask could be hard for you to hear. Plus, Kate might be reluctant to tell the whole truth with you in the room. You'll be okay by yourself for a few hours until—"

"I'll stay with you until Alex and Kate return," Jordan offered. "Tomorrow's Sunday, and I have nothing planned."

Natalie opened her mouth to argue then simply nodded. Alex stole a glance Jordan's way and smiled, sending a silent message that he appreciated the gesture and would show her how much later.

He focused his attention back on Natalie. "See, Mom, you have no excuse not to get a good night's sleep. We'll fill you in on everything in the morning over coffee." He tried to grin. "Maybe we'll splurge on Myrtle's Chocolate Chip Coffee Cake for breakfast."

Reluctantly, Natalie agreed and released her daughter. Jordan reached out and grabbed her arm and led the way back into the suite.

THE RIDE BACK to Ranchero was tense and seemed much longer than usual. There was little conversation in the car, and even that was centered on generic topics. Alex's mom leaned silently against the door and looked out the window. The past two hours spent at the hotel were never mentioned, and Jordan was glad of that, since it would do no good to rehash the events at the party.

Ray dropped them off at the Empire Apartments, and after throwing a few personal items into a tote bag, Jordan drove Natalie to Alex's house. She had no idea how long it would be before Alex and Kate made it back home, and she wanted to be prepared to spend the night if she had to.

She was anxious to do whatever she could for Alex and his family, not to mention that Myrtle's Chocolate Chip Coffee Cake was on the menu for breakfast.

Alex knew her so well.

By the time she and Natalie were settled in the living room and out of their party clothes, Jordan was already yawning as she prepared a palette on the couch. Even though it was the twenty-first century, with Natalie and Kate in the guest room it was probably not a good idea to sleep in Alex's room with his mother right next door.

"I'm not sure I can go to sleep until they get home," Natalie said, plopping down beside Jordan on the couch.

So much for getting some shuteye, Jordan thought. Truth be told, she was too keyed up to sleep anyway. They might as well wait up to find out what went down in Hamilton's room.

"Do you want me to fix you a drink, Natalie? Alex

has some wine in the refrigerator, and I'm sure there's a bottle of Scotch somewhere."

"No thanks, dear. I'm fine." She reached for her cell phone. "In all the excitement, I forgot that I hadn't called Kate's father to tell him about tonight."

"Why don't you do that now? For some reason I'm dying of thirst, and I'm craving ice water. Can I get you a glass? A wise person once told me that was the best thing to drink before you go to sleep after a night of alcoholic beverages. Something about the booze dehydrating you."

"Yes, I've heard that, too. It makes sense." Natalie sighed. "I suppose I should drink something. Those Italian margaritas went down way too easily tonight."

"I'll say." Jordan went out into the kitchen as Natalie spoke to her husband.

When Natalie hung up, she came back into the living room and handed her one of the glasses.

"He wanted to get on the next plane and come home," she explained after taking a drink of the cold water. "I talked him out of it—said we'd call every day with updates. God help me, I tried to minimize it all so he wouldn't be worried. This trip is so important to his company, and he's been talking about it for months."

"There's nothing he could do if he were here, anyway," Jordan said, wondering what else to talk about with Alex's mother. Since she'd only met her earlier that day—and what had happened at the party was definitely off limits—the silence was a bit awkward.

"So, let's talk about you and my son," Natalie started. She smiled when Jordan allowed a groan to slip out. "I know I came on strong today at lunch, but I worry so much about him. He's been surrounded by strong, independent women all his life, and that raises the bar when it comes to choosing someone to share his life." She paused to take another big gulp from her glass of water before turning to Jordan. "I have to admit, though, you seem perfect for him."

Jordan felt the heat crawl up her cheeks. It was uncomfortable discussing her relationship with Alex's mother even if the woman had just complemented her. She wasn't exactly sure where her relationship with Alex was headed yet, and hadn't even discussed it with her own mother. Just when she was trying to figure out a way out from underneath the romantic microscope, Natalie did it for her.

"You think Kate's in deep trouble?"

Jordan was surprised by the question and decided to answer as honestly as she could. "If you're asking me if I thought Kate had something to do with Marco's death, then the answer is no. However, if they find his DNA under her fingernails, that will make them crazy—give them a reason to pursue her as a suspect. I'm worried that it'll be a case of 'she said—she said' since no one else was in the room when it happened."

"I know. I wish I could tell the police that someone else entered Marco's bedroom, but I can't. And I watched like a hawk."

Jordan's head jerked up and she met Natalie's stare. "Why were you watching his bedroom?"

Alex's mother shrugged. "I saw Kate walk up the steps about ten minutes after she went downstairs to wait for a taxi. Since she'd already basically told me to butt out until she was ready to talk about her relationship with Marco, I did the only thing a mother could do—I kept my eyes on the door and waited, ready to pounce if I sensed trouble. Had I known the SOB was going to use her face as a punching bag, I would have killed him on the spot myself."

"And you're sure no one else entered the bedroom?" Jordan held her breath waiting for Natalie's answer. If just one other person had been in Marco's room and could confirm Kate's story, it might take the heat off her.

But Kate hadn't mentioned anyone else, either.

Natalie shook her head. "Unfortunately, I didn't even see Marco go up the stairs, so I figure he must have already been in the bedroom when Kate arrived. Like I said, I kept my eyes glued to that staircase except for the short time I walked over to the bar and shared a drink with Emilio."

"So it was only Kate and Marco?"

"Yes. I knew I should have marched right up and pulled my daughter away. Had I known Marco and she were up there in bed doing God knows what, I would have."

Jordan hoped she hadn't mentioned that in her interview with the police earlier and decided she didn't want to go anywhere near a conversation about Kate's sex life with Alex's mother. She quickly asked, "And your daughter never came out of the bedroom?"

"I don't think so," Natalie replied. "Everything happened so quickly, I don't remember seeing Kate again until she came out screaming, and everyone rushed up to the second floor. Then I saw Tina in the crowd before she took off and ran down the stairs. I assumed she'd heard that Marco was dead and was running out the door to go to him."

"Hmm. I'm not sure what it all means if anything, but it is something to think about. Did you tell the police any of this when they questioned you?"

She shook her head. "They didn't ask, and I never

mentioned it. Thankfully, no one knows I saw anything. And that's the way I'm going to keep it. The last thing Kate needs is for the cops to use her own mother as a material witness against her."

"It's probably a good thing you didn't mention it then," Jordan said. "I don't have any experience with legal stuff, but in the short time I watched Emilio's lawyer handle that police captain during Kate's questioning, I picked up a few pointers. The most important is not to volunteer information unless it's absolutely necessary."

"I'm glad Emilio had the presence of mind to send that man to represent Kate, even when it looked like she might be involved in the death of his future son-in-law. Although Alex was right there, she might have said something she shouldn't have."

"My first impression of Emilio is that he's a nice man, and I'm not surprised by his actions tonight," Jordan said. "He seems to have taken a liking to you, too." She hoped she wasn't crossing a line, but she remembered how Alex seemed put off by Emilio's attention to his mother.

Natalie stopped to run her tongue over her dry lips. "Emilio and I go back a long way."

Jordan sat up straighter, wondering if Alex knew this wasn't the first time his mother had met Emilio. She decided to probe, feeling a little guilty at first before thinking since Natalie had put her on the spot with a few personal questions at lunch, she shouldn't be too upset for getting one fired back at her.

"Did you meet Emilio at the Italian Festival last year?"

Natalie stared into space for a few seconds then turned toward Jordan. Sure the older woman was about to nail her with a mind-your-own-business remark, she was surprised when instead, Natalie smiled.

"I met Emilio right after I graduated from high school." She paused, maintaining eye contact with Jordan before she delivered the zinger. "At one point I was two weeks away from becoming his wife."

SEVEN

AFTER NATALIE'S STUNNING revelation, Jordan stared at her, sure her own mouth was hanging open. "You were engaged to Emilio Calabrese?" Remembering Alex's remark about Emilio being connected, she couldn't quite picture the petite woman sitting next to her on the couch as a Mafia princess.

"I was seventeen," Natalie explained. "I'd just graduated from high school and was visiting my cousins in New Jersey. My uncle was a longshoreman, and while I was there, we went to a company picnic sponsored by his employer, who just happened to be Emilio's father. That's when I met him." She sighed as she recalled those earlier days.

Jordan leaned closer when Natalie's voice dropped to a whisper.

"There I was, a naïve, young teenager from Texas, and he was this big popular, rich kid who drove a Corvette. It took him no time at all to seduce me with expensive gifts and fancy restaurants. Although he was four years older than me and already working his way up the ladder in his dad's company, there was a connection between us immediately. After the sheltered life I'd left back in Beaumont, Emilio and his bad-boy persona swept me off my feet." She stopped talking long enough to take a deep breath. "We spent nearly every day together my entire vacation, and by the time I left New Jersey to return home, we'd made plans for me to return in two weeks. We were going to go to Atlantic City and get married while we gambled the week away."

"Wow! That's quite a story," was all Jordan could think of to say. "What happened?" She hoped Natalie didn't think she was prying, but her curiosity was killing her.

"After I got away from all the glamour and excitement of the East Coast and settled back into reality at home, it dawned on me that I would be making a foolish mistake. The question I asked myself was whether or not I was willing to give up everything I'd worked for to marry a man I'd known less than ten days." She took a sip of water before continuing, "The answer was easy without all the distractions. I had a full academic scholarship waiting for me at SMU. I couldn't just throw that away."

Suddenly, Jordan's cell phone rang, and she jumped off the couch to retrieve it from her purse. "Hello."

"It's me," Alex said. "I wanted to call and let you know things are going well. I'm not sure when we'll be able to get out of here, but I wanted to make sure everything's okay back there."

"We're fine," Jordan said, wondering if Alex knew about his mother's teenage love story. Could that be why he was so obviously perturbed when Emilio went out of his way to stand close to her?

"My mom's not talking your ear off, is she? Please tell me she's not spilling any of my secrets."

"Wouldn't you like to know?" she deadpanned.

His mother was telling secrets, all right, but they had nothing to do with him. Asking about Alex's childhood hadn't even crossed Jordan's mind, but now that he'd mentioned it, it might be worth a few pointed questions, especially since Natalie was obviously in a talking mood. He loved to tease her about everything, and it would be nice to have some ammunition so she could give back as good as she got.

"Yes, I would. Jeff's back. Gotta go. Don't wait up for us. I'll see you in the morning."

"Okay. Tell Kate to hang in there." '

"Will do. Love you." And then he disconnected.

She stared at the phone, confused by his last words. Did he just say he loved her? She shook her head. No, it was just something you say to people automatically. It didn't really mean anything, did it?

"Is everything all right?" Natalie asked, apparently concerned when Jordan didn't immediately repeat the conversation with Alex to her.

"Oh, yes. Alex said they were getting a lot done and that we shouldn't wait up."

Natalie's face reflected her disappointment. "I guess I'll have to wait until morning to see Kate. To tell you the truth, I'm not sure how much longer I can stay awake, anyway." She reached for Jordan's hand and patted it. "Lord only knows why I'm telling you about what happened to me so many years ago when my own husband hasn't even heard this story."

Jordan yawned, glancing up at the clock above the entryway to the kitchen. It was two in the morning, and although she was exhausted, there was no way she was going to sleep without finding out how the story ended. "So, what did Emilio say when you told him you weren't coming back to New Jersey to marry him?"

"What do you think he said? Emilio, even then, was used to getting his own way. He called me every name in the book." She paused before adding, "Isn't it funny how men do that?"

"Do what?"

"React to every situation with anger? I know I broke his heart, but he would never admit it. I guess he needed to scream obscenities at me to be able to move on. I told him it didn't mean that we wouldn't see each other again—that we could stay in touch—but his bruised ego wouldn't allow it. He said if he ever saw me again, it would be too soon."

"And that was it?"

"Until tonight when I saw him at the party. It was like old times—without the romance, of course. Our past relationship was never discussed—almost like it didn't happen." She twisted to face Jordan. "Don't get me wrong. I care for Emilio, but only as a friend. There's an Englishman named Moreland sitting in Abu Dhabi right now who captured my heart a long time ago and won't let go."

Natalie leaned her head on the back of the couch and sighed. "Apparently, Emilio has gotten over his anger at me after all these years. And if this Hamilton guy is his lawyer, you can be sure he's one of the best. Emilio doesn't settle for anything less."

"Let's hope you're right," Jordan said, leaning her head back, too. "The sooner we get this ugly mess over and done with, the better."

As they waited in silence for Alex and Kate to return, Jordan found herself thinking back on the party before things went terribly wrong. Something Kate had said kept popping into her head, and she couldn't quit thinking about it. At the time it hadn't meant anything, but after getting a bit of insight into Emilio Calabrese's personality, Kate's words were beginning to make more sense.

When she'd been explaining to her brother what had happened at the party, she'd mentioned that Marco had denied ever loving Tina Calabrese. She'd said he told her the only reason he was marrying Tina was because her father was holding something over him. Jordan's mind raced with the possibilities of what that something could be.

Images of TV Mafia movies where the code of silence prevailed played in her head. Could Marco have done something he didn't want the world to know about? Was Emilio's silence about whatever Marco had done the driving force that had convinced the Italian playboy to marry a woman he didn't love? Or could it have been just money?

She quickly tossed that last idea out since both Marco and Emilio were wealthy. So what was it then?

She still hadn't come up with a logical explanation fifteen minutes later when Natalie said good night and went to bed. Finally, Jordan drifted off to sleep with that thought still on her mind.

JORDAN AWOKE TO the smell of freshly brewed coffee, and for a moment, she was confused about where she was. Slowly, she rose from the couch and was greeted with a kiss and a cup of coffee, along with a gigantic piece of something chocolate that looked fantastic.

Wide-eyed, she smiled at Alex, whose hair was still wet from the shower. Dressed in a pair of khaki slacks and a red golf shirt that showed off his chiseled upper arms, his eyes glinted mischievously when he saw her reaction. Scolding herself for the naughty thought that invaded her mind and sent a warm surge through her body, she reminded herself that his mother was in the next room.

She forced her eyes away from his face and reached

for the pastry. "This doesn't look like Myrtle's Chocolate Chip Coffee Cake."

"It isn't. By the time I got to the diner, she'd already sold out. You know how those good old boys like to congregate in there on Saturday mornings."

"What time is it anyway?"

"Seven thirty." Alex pinched off a little of the chocolate treat and put it into his mouth, running his tongue over his lips in a way that almost made Jordan forget there was chocolate in the house.

Almost!

"It's a new recipe she calls Chocolate Bread Pudding that she made for lunch today. I sweet-talked her into letting me have four pieces even though she wasn't selling it yet. She said since it's made with liquor, it would be sacrilegious to serve at seven in the morning."

He grinned when he saw Jordan's face fall. "I convinced her that it was five o'clock somewhere. I'm only sorry I won't be around to watch your face when you eat it. Just so you know, though, I will expect some kind of sexy reward for my efforts." He winked before adding, "Later, of course, and back at your place."

He bent down to kiss her just as Kate walked into the living room. Her eyes were bloodshot and a little puffy, and Jordan guessed she had cried herself to sleep.

"Ready, Alex?"

He turned and kissed his sister's temple before ruffling her hair. "Hey, wipe that sad look off your face. This will be over in no time, and I guarantee after Jeff works his magic at the station, they'll be glad to get you out of there." He tried to sound convincing but couldn't quite pull it off.

He followed his sister to the door, but before he walked out, he turned back to Jordan. "My mom's still asleep. Kate said she didn't sleep much last night, either. When she wakes up, her cake is on the counter. I know you have a lot of things to do today, and I think she'll be okay by herself."

"I'm good," Jordan answered. "I don't think she should be alone. If she's anything like me, her imagination will run wild if she's by herself." She peeked at the clock. "Any idea when you'll be back?"

He shook his head, his eyes telling her that he was more than a little concerned. "I have no idea how long this will take, but I'll try to call to give you some idea." He headed out the door before pausing, "I owe you big time for this."

Then he was gone, and she was left alone to think about what Kate would have to go through at the station. She wished they were going to the Ranchero Police Station instead of the Plainville one. Since Alex had worked with the Ranchero sheriff on an undercover assignment the previous year, they'd become pretty good friends. It might be advantageous to deal with a familiar face.

Jordan shook her head, finding it hard to believe so much had happened since she'd first met Alex. Had it only been eighteen months ago that she'd gone on her first assignment as a culinary reporter for the *Globe*?

She remembered that day like it was yesterday. She'd been sent by the newspaper to critique the food at a local steakhouse outside of town, and she'd ordered foie gras by accident. It had ended up in her purse when no one was looking after she'd found out it was fatty duck liver and knew there was no way she could eat it. When her dessert came, she'd still been starving, and the restaurant's chocolate decadence cake had been almost orgasmic.

She chuckled to herself as she remembered seeing

Alex sitting a few tables away and watching his face as she'd performed for him, licking her lips and making soft moaning sounds. He'd tried so hard not to smile but had eventually given in to her antics. It had been her first shot at flirting since her breakup with Brett, and apparently she hadn't been—and still wasn't—very good at it because he'd glanced away and hadn't looked in her direction again.

She'd found out later that he'd thought she was involved in an international diamond smuggling ring and had only forged a friendship with her to get information. But before he'd wrapped up the investigation and sent the bad guys to prison for a very long time, he'd managed to save her life and steal a piece of her heart.

They'd carried on a long-distance romance the entire nine months he was in El Paso on another undercover assignment, and they hadn't really had the opportunity to give the relationship a chance to work. It wasn't until he'd been promoted and transferred to Dallas as the field commander at the FBI headquarters downtown that they'd finally been able to spend time together. That was, until his mother and sister showed up for the Italian Festival.

Things weren't going so well for his family now, and Jordan was frustrated that there was nothing she could do to help. She smiled to herself as an idea popped into her head. She remembered Alex had once teased that the whole world needed to be on high alert when she got one of her hair-brained ideas.

But she couldn't just stand by and do nothing while he and his family were in crisis. She was in a unique position here with a press pass and an assignment to cover all the events of the festival. Today was the first day the vendors would be allowed to set up their booths in preparation for Friday, when the festival would officially open to the public.

Perhaps she could use the contacts to get the scoop on Marco. She might even find out what Emilio had held over his head to convince the playboy to marry his daughter.

A horrible thought burst Jordan's euphoric bubble. What if after seeing his daughter in tears at the party, Emilio had decided to confront Marco and *remind* him what he had to lose by being a jerk? And what if that meeting had heated up and ended up with Marco taking a dive over the railing of his balcony? Given that in the past twenty-four hours Jordan had heard stories about the short fuses both men possessed, was that so hard to believe?

She thought not.

She decided she needed a game plan, but not before she overdosed on chocolate and caffeine. Reaching for the bread pudding, she shoveled a huge bite into her mouth. It was even more fabulous than Alex had described, and she wondered if she could talk Myrtle into giving her the recipe for her column. Victor could give it some wonderful Spanish name like *Chocolate budin de pan*. The *Globe* readers would love it.

As she inhaled the delicious chocolate desert, she made plans to run out to the Plainville fairgrounds and do a little nosing around after Alex and Kate returned home. What would it hurt to check things out?

In the meantime, as she stared at Natalie's desert on the kitchen counter, she said a quick prayer for some serious willpower.

EIGHT

ALEX AND KATE showed up at the house a little after noon with meatball hoagies from Guido's, one of Jordan's all-time favorite restaurants. She caught Alex's eye and smiled, thinking the dark circles and concern she saw there belied his attempt to appear unfazed by what he'd just watched his sister go through.

"I told you I'd make it up to you," he said, trying to smile back.

"Alex?"

He turned to his mother whose forehead was creased with worry lines. "Come have something to eat, Mom. These hoagies are better than Uncle Undo's. Let's eat them while they're still a little warm. Then we'll tell you all about this morning." He directed her toward the kitchen table. "It's not bad news. I promise. It's just complicated right now," he added in an attempt to erase those lines.

"Unlike the TV shows, it may take weeks for the DNA samples to come back," Kate said. "Without that, the only thing Captain Darnell could do was ask me a few more questions."

Natalie's face lit up with renewed hope. "Maybe they won't find Marcus's DNA under your—"

"Yes, Mother, they will," Kate interrupted. "And when that happens, the police will pull off their kid gloves and come after me. But for now I don't want to think about it. I'm exhausted, and I'm starving." She sat down opposite Natalie at the table and unwrapped one of the sandwiches. "What do you have to drink, Alex?" she asked cutting off any further questions from her mother.

After they'd devoured the sandwiches, Jordan cleared the table, gently rebuffing Kate's attempt to help. "You've had a horrific night. Why don't you lie down and try to catch a nap?"

"That's a great idea," Natalie echoed, taking Kate's arm and guiding her out of the kitchen.

To everyone's surprise, Kate allowed her mother to lead her to the bedroom. As soon as Natalie closed the door behind Kate, she turned to Alex. "You should get some rest, too, son. I'm counting on you to get Kate through this, and I need you at the top of your game."

"You're probably right, but it's not *my* A game we need, it's Hamilton's." He chuckled. "A few times during the questions this morning I thought Captain Darnell might actually throttle him. As a cop I can tell you that lawyers are not our favorite people, especially ones who know their stuff. But as the brother of someone being interrogated, I felt damn lucky to have him in the room and on our side."

"Emilio wouldn't send a lackey," Natalie said, shooting a quick glance Jordan's way as a reminder that their conversation the night before was not to be shared.

Alex yawned before turning to Jordan. "What are your plans for today?"

Jordan knew better than to tell him she intended to snoop around over at the Plainville fairgrounds. He'd be all over that like a colony of ants on a discarded doughnut, insisting she keep her nose out of it. "I thought I'd run over and interview some of the vendors at the festival for my column," she said instead.

Okay, that part wasn't a lie.

"Good idea," Natalie chimed in, rescuing her from Alex's searing gaze—one she knew meant he was trying to decide if she was telling the truth.

She cursed the fact that he could read her so well.

"Would you mind if I tagged along? That way the house will be quiet for these two, and they can get a good rest," Natalie said.

Crap. It would be hard to do a little investigating with Alex's mother tagging along, but how could she say no without fessing up about her intentions? Besides, Alex was now grinning at his mother, probably thinking there was no way she could get in trouble with his mother around.

"I'd like that," Jordan said. "I don't plan on staying long, and I can have you back in a few hours, unless you want to run by the mall after that."

Natalie shook her head. "We'll see how I feel after traipsing around in the Texas sun all day, but there's really nothing I need at the mall. I'll probably be ready for a nap myself after we leave the fairgrounds."

"My mother is saying no to shopping?" Alex whistled, bending down to kiss Natalie on the forehead. "Somebody needs to check her temperature," he teased before kissing Jordan's cheek. "It's settled then. I'm heading to bed, and I'll see two of my favorite girls tonight." He winked at them both before making his way to the bedroom.

"Come on," Natalie said, pulling Jordan toward the door. "I can't stand sitting around watching my daughter go through this without doing something—anything. Talking to the vendors with you might be the perfect opportunity to find out what goes on behind the scenes. Trust me when I tell you that the worker bees know all the really good gossip. Maybe somebody out there has some dirt on Marco that will help my daughter, and you're just the pretty face that it will take to dig it out." She gave Jordan the once-over before saying, "Put some lipstick on and get ready to bat those beautiful eyelashes of yours. We need information."

Jordan stared at Alex's mother, positive the woman had just read her mind. Like an obedient child, she retrieved the new coral lip-gloss from her purse and smeared it on her lips. Looping her arm through Natalie's, she said, "Come on, Miss Marple, we have some sleuthing to do."

BY THE TIME Jordan pulled her Camry into the fairground's parking lot, she and Natalie had forged a fast friendship. On the twenty-minute ride over, Jordan had discovered so many new things about Alex she hadn't known, including his refusal to leave the family pet alone when the old yellow Lab was dying. According to Natalie, they'd had to pry his little body away from the animal long after the dog had taken its last breath.

Then there was the time during his sophomore year when Kate had begged him to play Mrs. Doubtfire in the school play. No other guy would do it, and according to Natalie, Alex had taken a lot of flak from his football buddies. But he adored his older sister, so he'd made the most of it. Wearing a fat suit and a wig, he'd turned in a memorable and hilarious performance. Was it any wonder that Kate adored him back?

Jordan had always known that Alex and his sister were tight, but it was fun finding out how he'd managed to grow up surrounded by all that estrogen and still turn out so macho.

"How should we work this? Do you want to take the

lead, or do you want me to?" Natalie asked, sliding out
of the passenger side of the Toyota.

Jordan thought about it for a moment before responding. "Let's just play it by ear. Some of these folks may
respond to you better because you're Italian, and others
may open up to me if they think there's a chance of getting some free publicity out of it." She giggled. "They
don't have to know I only write the culinary column."

She locked the car and the two of them headed toward
the fairgrounds, which had been turned into a mass of
tents, booths, and trailers. Scattered among the melee
was a motley crew of men and women with leathery
looking skin from too much sun, setting up the rides.

For a second Jordan was reminded of the Texas State
Fair, held at Fair Park in downtown Dallas each autumn.
A ginormous figure known as Big Tex was suspended
above the entrance and bellowed a Texas-sized welcome
to the fairgoers as they came through the gate. Unfortunately, the big guy had electrical problems and had
gone up in smoke the year before. A replacement now
stood in his place.

Here, instead of Big Tex, a huge balloon shaped like
an Italian flag flew high in the sky above the entrance.

The fairgrounds were set on ten acres of farmland on
the outskirts of Plainville and were the site of a monthly
huge flea market. In between, many big corporations
held their annual company picnics there and usually offered horseback riding and hayrides. Off to the right Jordan spotted a fenced-in area that she'd bet would house
those very same horses.

As they got closer to the actual area where the vendors were setting up, Jordan recognized a few faces
she'd seen at the party in Marco's suite the night before.

She was determined to do everything in her power

for information, and she nudged Natalie forward. "Okay, let's see if we're any good at this."

She followed a step behind as Natalie walked up to the first booth where a fortyish woman with jet black hair pulled back into a bun was busy setting up.

"Hi," Natalie began. "Can you spare us a few moments of your time? We have some questions we'd like to ask."

The woman stopped long enough to make eye contact with Natalie and to brush at a stray lock of hair that had escaped from the tight bun. "Sorry. It's already ninety-four degrees and supposed to hit triple digits today. I want to finish up before I melt."

Natalie stepped back and motioned with her hand for Jordan to give it a try. Like the other half of a wrestling tag team, Jordan inched forward.

The lady gave her a fleeting glance before turning around to hang a sign on the back wall of the booth. CARLITA'S ITALIAN CREAM CAKE BALLS. Jordan had no idea what an Italian Cream Cake Ball was, but just the thought of a sugar treat right now had her mouth-watering like Pavlov's dog.

Although she had no intentions of taking notes, she pulled out a pad and a pen from her purse for show. "I'm Jordan McAllister from the *Ranchero Globe*, and I'll be here all week interviewing vendors like you for my column." When the lady's head shot up, she felt Natalie squeeze her arm. But before she asked the important questions, her curiosity got the best of her. "What's an Italian Cream Cake Ball, anyway?"

"You're from the newspaper?"

Jordan flashed her press pass. "And I assume you're Carlita?"

The woman dried her hands on a rag she pulled from

under the counter, moving closer to them. "That would be me. Carlita Bruno. I'm from New Jersey, and my sister and I've been coming to the festival for a lot of years. I try to bring something new and different to sell every year." She pointed across the way where a much younger woman who resembled her was busy setting up a booth. "Ginny's Chicken Cacciatore usually sells out on the first day, even though she brings more every year. And her pepperoni bread doesn't even make it that long." She reached back under the counter and brought out a Tupperware bowl. "This is my latest concoction." After opening the bowl she took out two sticks with what looked like a huge chocolate bonbon on the end of each.

Both Jordan and Natalie took a step closer to get a better look.

"Go ahead and try it," Carlita prompted after handing each one a stick.

Needing no encouragement, Jordan bit into hers. She loved the Italian cream cake they served at Guido's, but she wasn't prepared for Carlita's pastry. It was a moist cake covered with dark chocolate that melted in her mouth. What was not to like?

She decided this little number could easily take the place of her beloved Ho Hos in an emotional crisis. After finishing the treat, she threw the stick into the trash can on the side of the booth.

"That was awesome. I don't know if I've mentioned it or not, but I print recipes, too. I'd love to include this one in the column. Of course, I'd give you full credit." So much for pretending she was more than a culinary reporter. But she could already imagine her readers going crazy over this dessert. Crossing her fingers behind her back, she hoped Carlita would agree.

The woman beamed. "Can you do a write-up on me

before the festival opens and then post the recipe after it closes?"

Jordan looked confused.

"I wouldn't want people to think they can go home and make these themselves. At least not until I've had a chance to sell out." She shrugged. "These booths aren't cheap, you know."

"Oh, of course. I get that. A girl's got to make a living, right? That's why I'm out here in this unrelenting Texas sun today." Jordan wiped her brow for emphasis before she leaned in and lowered her voice. She was going to have to warm this woman up if she hoped to get any useful information out of her—assuming Carlita knew anything at all that might help them. The fastest way to do that was to get her talking about herself. Who could resist that? "So, Carlita, tell us how you got started with the Italian Festival."

For the next ten minutes, they listened to the woman relate her entire life history as a river of sweat rolled down Jordan's back. Just when she thought the only thing she'd walk away with today was a great tasting treat and a recipe for her column, Carlita took a swig of water from a dirty-looking glass and lowered her voice.

"Guess you heard about the guy who was pushed off the balcony of his hotel room last night, right?"

Natalie pulled a tissue from her purse and swiped at the layer of sweat on her brow. She moved up as close to the counter as she could without falling over it. "Someone fell off a balcony last night?"

Carlita nailed Jordan with her eyes. "And you're going to write about me before the festival opens?"

Jordan would have agreed to just about anything now that the woman had brought up Marco's death the night before. Maybe this would be easier than she thought.

"Of course. I think the locals would love to hear how you grew up. But first, I'd like to hear more about the guy falling off the balcony." She stole a glance toward Natalie who was out of Carlita's view and was now rolling her eyes.

"I didn't actually see it, mind you," Carlita began. "But my sister is on the planning committee this year and was at a big party at some swanky hotel last night. She said one of the bigwigs from the festival took a nose-dive off the balcony and landed smack in the middle of the hotel entrance."

When she paused, Jordan plodded her. "Go on. Did your sister say who did it?"

"Some young home wrecker who was having an affair with him even though he was engaged to be married to…" She lowered her voice. "Emilio Calabrese's daughter."

Jordan saw Natalie's body stiffen but knew it was important to keep going. A respected journalism teacher at the University of Texas had always preached that when you had a person talking about controversial stuff, you should go in for the kill and ask the important questions to catch them off guard.

"Really. Why do you think that woman would want to harm the dead guy?"

"Why else? They had a lovers' quarrel in front of God and the entire room full of people, according to Ginny. She didn't get home until well after midnight because the cops kept them there asking questions. Everyone saw the two of them arguing and then later saw the woman screaming from the man's bedroom. It doesn't take a brain surgeon to figure out what happened in that room."

"Did you know the guy who was killed?" Natalie

asked, finally recovering enough from the home wrecker reference about her daughter to jump into the conversation.

"Who didn't? Marco Petrone was the biggest womanizer on the planet." She huffed. "Why, I've heard he had a harem of women in almost every country." She stopped to swipe her forehead with the same rag she'd dried her hands with earlier. "I'm not saying the man deserved to die, but it does seem like poetic justice that one of his Jezebels did him in."

This time Natalie gasped so loud that Carlita stopped talking and turned to her. "You all right? Here." She handed her the water from the countertop.

Natalie waved her off, scrunching her nose at the dirty glass. "I just choked on my own saliva," she explained, swallowing hard before continuing, "So are you saying there were a lot of women who might have wanted to see Marco dead?"

Jordan saw the hope light up in Natalie's eyes when Carlita nodded. "They didn't call him the Italian Stallion for nothing, if you get my drift. He went through women like a kid in a candy store, grabbing whatever he wanted and spitting them out after he'd had a taste."

Just then a commotion broke out behind them, and they all turned to see a middle-aged woman dressed in a short dress and heels arguing with a much younger man.

"Just between you and me, that woman right there had a pretty good reason to off Marco Petrone herself," Carlita said, clucking her tongue.

Jordan caught Natalie's eye and bit her lip to hide the smile before turning back to Carlita. If there were other women out there with a motive for killing Marco, chances were one or two of them had been at the party.

That would mean there might be reasonable doubt that Kate had been the one to push him over the ledge.

Natalie pointed to the couple who were still in a heated discussion not far from them. "Who is that?"

Carlita narrowed her eyes, tilting her head that way. "Georgette Calabrese. She's married to Emilio and is the mother of Petrone's fiancée." She lowered her voice and looked over her shoulder to make sure no one else was close enough to overhear. "Rumor has it she was one of Marco's throwaways."

NINE

NATALIE GRABBED JORDAN'S arm and nudged her toward Georgette Calabrese and the man she was arguing with. Jordan had just enough time to tell Carlita she'd be back later for the recipe.

"What about my story?" Carlita asked.

"As soon as I get the recipe, I'll write a review of you and your cake pops with the interview. Then I'll follow-up next week with the recipe, but I do need it now," she said just before Natalie propelled her away from the booth. There was no way Carlita was getting her name in the Kitchen Kupboard without giving up that recipe.

"I should've known Emilio would go for someone like this," Natalie said as they approached the two people who were obviously still in a heated discussion.

"You need to stand up for yourself, Frankie. Now's the perfect chance to show him you can step up and take charge if something happens to him. Convince him you're not a screw-up." The woman stopped talking when she noticed Natalie and Jordan closing in. The irritated look on her face left no doubt she wasn't happy about being interrupted.

"Can I help you?" she asked, not even attempting to hide the annoyance in her voice.

Jordan held out her hand. "I'm Jordan McAllister from the *Ranchero Globe*, and this is Natalie Moreland."

At the mention of Natalie's name, Georgette jerked her head around to make eye contact before focusing back on Jordan and shaking her hand. "I'm sorry you came all the way out here today, Ms. McAllister, but I have no desire to be interviewed. I have a lot of work to do before the festival opens, so if you'll excuse me." She dismissed the two women and turned back to the young man beside her.

"I'm not here just to interview *you*, Mrs. Calabrese," Jordan said, a little louder than before. "I was told I'd have access to the planners the week before the festival opens. I'm sorry to have bothered you. I'll let my editor know his information was incorrect." Jordan paused to see if Georgette was buying her story.

The old 'if looks could kill' adage popped into Jordan's head as the woman glared at her. "I misunderstood. I have a lot of people vying for my attention today, most of them reporters. I just spoke to someone else from your newspaper—a Loretta something or other."

Jordan mentally kicked herself for letting Loretta get one step ahead of her. "I'd like to report on what it takes to pull off a big event like this. I've been told you play a big part in it, and—"

"Who told you that, Ms. McAllister?" Georgette interrupted.

"Please call me Jordan. And I've already interviewed several other people who indicated that you're the one I needed to speak with about what goes on behind the scene leading up to opening day."

Just then a delivery man walked over and stood behind the younger man who had been arguing with Georgette, tapping a pen on a clipboard until she noticed him. When he announced he had a large shipment of game prizes and concession supplies waiting to be offloaded, she turned to the man beside her. "Frankie, go with him and make sure everything arrived in good condition."

Waving a hand in the air—one that sported a diamond the size of a cherry—Georgette barked out a few more commands to both the delivery man and the one she called Frankie. Jordan used that short time to check out the woman Emilio Calabrese had married after Natalie had rejected him.

Wearing a pale green sundress that showed off a tiny waist and a perfect tan, Georgette Calabrese had pulled her long blond hair off her face into a ponytail, making her appear to be in her late thirties. Jordan stole a glance Natalie's way and saw that she was also giving the tall, well-built woman who'd married her old lover the once-over.

When the two men walked away, Georgette finally turned to Jordan. "Sorry about that. You asked how this event goes off without hitches." She pointed to the delivery truck by the entrance. "It isn't easy. Everything has to be right on schedule, or it throws things off. We're still waiting on a liquor shipment that was supposed to get here a few days ago. That means a lot of people will have to hustle to make up for lost time when it does arrive. My job is to find out why that happened, and I'll start by having a long talk with the distributor to make sure it doesn't happen again. That's the kind of thing I need to stay on top of daily."

Natalie moved forward and asked the question before Jordan could. "And who is the distributor?"

Jordan remembered that Emilio had asked Marco about the liquor at the party and that Marco had assured him it would arrive on time. And Alex had mentioned that Marco was the owner of the company supplying all the liquor for the festival. Obviously, Marco couldn't take the heat for the late shipment, so who was Georgette going to "have a long talk" with?

"The Petrone Brothers."

"Marco had a brother?" Jordan asked.

At the mention of Marco's name, a flash of sadness registered in Georgette's eyes before she quickly glanced away. "Yes. Bernardo," she said finally. "Their company is based out of New York City."

Finding out that Marco had a brother gave Jordan another avenue to pursue. Maybe there was sibling rivalry between the brothers or a long-standing family feud. That would definitely throw a little reasonable doubt Kate's way if they could prove it.

"I'm sorry about what happened to Marco last night," Jordan began, thinking it was the perfect opening to see if Georgette could shed any light on his death. "I've heard you and he were close."

Anger lit up Georgette's eyes. "Of course I was close to Marco. He and my husband were business partners, and he was about to marry my stepdaughter."

"Tina is your stepdaughter?" Natalie asked.

Georgia bit her lip before replying. "Emilio's first wife died of breast cancer when the child was five. I've raised her since then and love her as if she were my own daughter. Everything I do has been for her."

Including test-driving her fiancé before the wedding?

Jordan stopped herself before blurting that out. What was the point in making this woman angry? They still needed information.

"Was Bernardo at the party last night?" Natalie asked.

Georgette narrowed her eyes. "Yes, he was, as were most of the people involved in the planning of the festival. Unfortunately, I had a business meeting in New York City that couldn't be postponed and missed it. I only arrived in Dallas this morning."

"And did Bernardo have a beef with his brother?" Natalie asked.

Georgette took a menacing step toward her. "They were brothers. Of course, they fought. Marco had a way about him that didn't sit well with a lot of people. Correct me if I'm wrong, but wasn't it your daughter who was having an illicit affair with Marco and pushed him off the balcony last night?"

Jordan reached out to keep Natalie from making contact with the younger woman.

"For your information, my daughter had no idea the man was engaged. So no, there was no illicit affair on her part. Although I can't say the same about you, since you were the one he sampled and tossed aside. I guess not *everything* you've done has been for Tina." Natalie's eyes turned defiant as she waited to see how Georgette would react to that remark.

"We're done here," Jordan said, grabbing Natalie's arm and turning her around. "I'll be in touch, Mrs. Calabrese," she said over her shoulder as she pushed Alex's mother in the opposite direction from the irate Georgette, who looked like she was close to committing murder herself.

ON THE WAY back to Alex's house, Natalie begged Jordan not to tell her son about the encounter with Georgette Calabrese. She was afraid if Alex decided to have a chat with her, Georgette might bring up the fact that Natalie was once engaged to Emilio—assuming she even knew about that. It didn't take much persuasion to get Jordan to agree. Telling Alex would also be confessing they'd been snooping around, and he'd pitch a fit. Both she and Natalie would have to listen to a long lecture about leaving police business to the police.

It was after four when Jordan dropped Natalie off and made it back to her apartment. There was no news about Marco's death, and Alex and Kate were meeting with Hamilton later that evening to discuss what to do next.

Alex had invited her to stay and have dinner with them, but she'd excused herself, saying she needed to get her notes straight so she could begin her article for Thursday's Kitchen Kupboard. She was anxious to see what Loretta Moseley had to say in Tuesday's column, secretly hoping the woman bombed. As much as she wished for a job in the sports department, the culinary reporter gig had proven to be a great second choice for her.

And she would do whatever it took to keep the job, although being related to the editor did give Loretta a huge advantage. Jordan would just have to work harder. She grinned, thinking she had a few tricks up her sleeve, too. She couldn't wait to see the readers' reaction to the Italian Cream Cake Pops recipe.

Crap! She'd left so quickly after Natalie and Georgette had verbally attacked each other that she'd forgotten to go back for Carlita's recipe. Even though she'd promised not to print it until the festival was over, she wanted it in her hands in case Carlita changed her mind about giving it up. Her plan was to write about all the food and tease the readers with the hint that Carlita's fantastic recipe would be coming out in her column the following week.

There was no way Egan could can her if she had the good people of Ranchero clamoring for her next column.

Halfway home, she decided now was as good a time as any to get the recipe, and she headed over to the fairgrounds. Maybe she'd even get another sample of the sugary treat as a bonus.

Just thinking about the pops made her stomach growl,

reminding her that she hadn't eaten since before noon when Alex surprised her with the meatball hoagie. Carlita had mentioned that her sister was famous for her chicken cacciatore and pizza bread. It might be possible to mooch a free sample of that, too. With a little luck, she'd get enough to count as dinner, and she wouldn't have to stop at Taco Castle on the way home. After splurging on the dress and heels for the party, she shouldn't spend the extra money.

It was just after six when Jordan pulled into the parking lot for the second time that day. She found a spot closer to the entrance and assumed most of the worker bees had already gone back to their hotel rooms. She hoped Carlita wasn't one of them. She got out of the car and walked toward the entrance, noticing that the Italian flag flying above the entrance was now flapping at a good clip. At least the wind had cooled things down since her earlier visit, and the breeze felt good.

As luck would have it, she spotted Carlita as soon as she walked through the gate. Waving, she approached the booth.

"There you are. I wondered why you'd run off so quickly," Carlita said, wiping her hands on the same dirty towel she'd used earlier. "I still have a lot to tell you about my life for the article."

Oh, great!

Jordan forced herself to smile. "Good. I came back for that as well as the recipe." She giggled. "I don't suppose you'd let me have another taste?"

Carlita's face lit up. "Of course. I want you to rave about them." She reached under the counter and brought out the Tupperware container. "Have two."

Jordan reached with both hands for the cake pops. It only took one bite for her to know that even if she didn't get the recipe right then, these little goodies were worth the trip back. After she devoured both of them, she declined Carlita's offer to wipe her hands on the towel and dragged her hands down the sides of her shorts.

"I wanted to tell you about how I came up with this recipe," Carlita began. "One day I was making my favorite Italian cream cake, and it didn't turn out so well." She frowned. "My oven was on the fritz, and the middle of the cake caved in. There was no way I could ice it that way, so I decided to crumble it up and make a dessert out of it. That's when I got the idea to turn it into cake balls. It was almost worth the money I had to put out for a new oven to get this recipe perfected." She patted the Tupperware, making Jordan wish for one more pop.

"That's a terrific story," Jordan said. "I'll make sure I use it."

Carlita reached under the counter and pulled out a notepad. She opened it up, tore out a page, and handed it to Jordan. "Here. I wrote it down as soon as you walked away. I thought for sure you'd come back for it."

Jordan snatched the paper from her hand as if it were made of gold. "My friend got an important phone call, and we had to leave right away," she lied. "That's why I decided to come back and talk with you tonight. The more I know about you, the better the article will be. I'd also like to include a small piece about your sister." She paused to scan the booths close by but didn't see another woman who looked like Carlita. "And you said she also has a booth?"

Carlita pointed to an empty stand across the fairway. "Hers is over there with the other food vendors. But she went back to the hotel already. Said she had a headache from the heat."

Jordan tried to hide her disappointment. She'd been

looking forward to tasting the famous pizza bread. "Too bad. I would have liked to have chatted with her, too. It will make for great reading if I can showcase both of you in my column."

"Ginny will be back tomorrow morning if you want to come by. But you'd better make it early. Like I said, she doesn't do well in the heat."

"I'll do that," Jordan replied, thinking she'd get Victor to run out there with her sometime before lunch the next day. The man loved free food more than she did.

Taking another glance around the food court, Jordan spotted the guy Georgette had been arguing with earlier standing by himself near the beverage station a few booths down from Ginny's Chicken Cacciatore booth. She turned back to Carlita and pointed in that direction. "I've got to run and talk to him. Tell your sister I'll be by in the morning to get her story."

"That's Frankie O'Brien," Carlita said, her gaze following Jordan's pointed finger. "He's Georgette Calabrese's son."

Jordan had already started toward Frankie but turned back immediately. "Georgette and Emilio have a son?"

"Frankie was Georgette's son from her first marriage, and from what I hear, he's a total loser. No wonder Calabrese doesn't want him running his business."

"What do you mean?"

Carlita leaned closer as if there was a chance that the man she was about to talk about could hear her. "I heard Frankie's tried every job in Emilio's shipping business. Apparently, he hasn't lasted with any one of them. Rumor has it that Emilio once joked he'd pay good money just to keep the boy out of the business."

Jordan's mind ran wild after that statement, and she remembered bits of the conversation between Georgette and her son when she and Natalie approached them earlier that day. Georgette had said something about now being the perfect opportunity for him to show Emilio that he could take charge. Could she have been implying that Marco's death might be to Frankie's advantage?

It might not be a smoking gun, but it could be interpreted as a possible motive for wanting Marco Petrone out of the way. Marco had been about to marry Tina Calabrese and become part of Emilio's family. If Carlita was right about Emilio not trusting his stepson with his business, Marco would be the perfect candidate to take over. And from the way Emilio had been willing to overlook the man's indiscretions the night of the party, it certainly didn't look to be much of a stretch.

That had to make Georgette and her son angry, knowing Emilio was planning to crown an outsider as the heir apparent to his empire and totally disrespect his own stepson.

But was it enough to commit murder?

Anxious to get over and talk to Frankie more than ever now, Jordan waved goodbye to Carlita and told her she'd see her in the morning. Nearly sprinting to get to Frankie just in case he decided to leave, she approached him, out of breath, and tapped his shoulder.

"I don't know if you remember me, but I'm the reporter who was here earlier."

Frankie turned around to face her, his face pinched with irritation. As soon as he saw her, he smiled, letting his eyes travel up and down her body, making her wish she hadn't worn cutoffs and a sleeveless top.

"I don't know what you said to my mother, but whatever it was left her in a foul mood the entire afternoon." He leaned in close enough that Jordan could tell he'd been drinking.

She allowed herself a few minutes to check him out before responding. Frankie O'Brien stood a little over six feet and was of average build. She wasn't an expert, but she'd bet the man had never seen the inside of the gym, nor had he participated in any sort of manual labor.

She decided to ignore the reference to Georgette and Natalie's altercation. "So, I've been told you're high up in the Calabrese shipping business. Is that right?"

The smile on his face couldn't have gotten any wider, and Jordan mentally high-fived herself for knowing how to butter him up.

"That would be correct. I'm in on all the important decisions the company makes." He leaned even closer, and Jordan took a step backward.

If what Carlita had said was true, this guy was lying through his teeth. And at the moment, Jordan was inclined to believe Carlita.

"Impressive," she said, not daring to say what she really wanted to. "So you're a big part of the festival?"

"That's right, sweetie, but I can still find time to party every now and then." He did another scan of her body, lingering on her chest before his eyes moved up to her face. "How about you joining me for dinner and drinks at the hotel right now? I'll show you how I let my hair down."

Sheesh! The man didn't even know her name, and he was already propositioning her. No wonder Emilio gravitated to Marco instead of him. But then again, Marco had a reputation as a womanizer, too.

"Sorry. I've already eaten, and I have an article to get ready for the newspaper." She hoped he didn't hear her stomach, which decided to growl at that precise moment.

Frankie touched her shoulder and let his fingers slide

down her arm. "Too bad. I have a pretty good feeling you and I would hit it off, sweetie."

Jordan gritted her teeth, thinking if he called her sweetie one more time, she'd barf. She had to get him talking about Marco instead of concentrating on putting the moves on her. She wanted to get out of there as fast as she could.

"So were you and Marco friends?" She watched his face, knowing his first reaction would tell the story.

And it did.

His brows narrowed into a V in the middle of his forehead. "Marco was engaged to my sister, but I wouldn't say we were friends."

"That's funny. Someone told me that Emilio was grooming Marco for a high-level position in the company. I would think that since you were going to be working closely with him, you'd be friends. After all, he was about to become your brother-in-law." She knew that was really reaching, but she hoped he'd take the bait.

"Friends don't sleep with your mother," he blurted before snapping his mouth shut and looking away.

But it was the perfect opening for Jordan—and she moved in quickly. "Did that make you mad enough to push Marco over the railing?"

This time Frankie didn't even try to hide his rage. "Listen, sweetie, I don't know where you're going with this, but let me set you straight. I was the one who introduced my sister to Marco. Why would I want to kill him?"

"So you were friends?"

"Business partners. We…" He stopped and smiled before pulling out a flask and taking a drink, then offering it to her. When she declined he said, "So what about tomorrow night? The hotel serves a mean ribeye." This time when he touched her shoulder, she moved away.

There was no way she was going anywhere with this guy—not even for a free dinner at the swanky hotel. And especially not for a steak. She hadn't eaten one of those since she was a teenager and her dad had forced her to try a rare one. The image of blood on the plate still gave her shivers. "Can't tomorrow, either." She took one last shot. "What did you mean when you said you and Marco were only business partners? Are you part of Marco's import/export business as well?"

Frankie stared at her for a moment then shook his head. "You misunderstood me. I never said we were business partners."

"Yes, you did."

His face was flushed with anger, his fists clenched at his side. Jordan had seen enough angry men in her life to know that the man standing in front of her was about to explode. She knew she should back off, but if Frankie O'Brien knew anything at all that might help Kate, she wasn't about to leave until she found out what it was.

"I misspoke. With Marco marrying into the family soon, it was family business," he said, simply. "Now, if you're not going to have dinner with me, I need to get back to what I was doing." He turned and walked away, leaving Jordan to ponder if finishing off that flask in his shirt pocket was part of that plan. Maybe she should stick around until he was good and liquored up and got chatty.

Deciding that was a bad idea, she returned to her car, wondering why Frankie had lied to her—first about being a bigwig in Calabrese's company and then about denying he and Marco were business partners after he had just admitted they were.

Business partners in what? She had no idea, but she

was darn well going to find out. She had a gut feeling it might be something helpful to Kate's defense.

A partnership gone bad was a perfect motive for murder.

TEN

ON MONDAY MORNING Jordan was surprised to see the older woman who used to occupy the cubicle next to hers settled into another space on the other side of the newsroom. Given the woman hadn't said two words to her the entire time she'd been a *Ranchero Globe* employee despite Jordan's frequent attempts to make nice, it wasn't hard to figure out she'd probably asked to be moved.

Oh well! With the exception of her friend Sandy who worked a couple of rows over, nobody else had gone out of their way to get warm and fuzzy with her, either. Sandy had suggested that since most of them had been at the *Globe* since high school, perhaps they saw her as an outsider and a threat to their jobs.

Sheesh! Like writing the personals was the job she'd deliberately try to steal from anyone!

But if she really thought about it, she could see how that misconception might have originated. She'd only been on the job for two months when Dwayne Egan had called her into his office and offered her the culinary column. Although he'd done it because of her journalism degree and success as a sports reporter at the University of Texas, it wasn't difficult to see why they might feel a little snubbed because he'd chosen an outsider over one of their own. She wished she could stand on her chair and holler that she had no interest in taking any other job—except maybe a position report-

ing in the sports department—but she knew that would
only further alienate her coworkers.

"Are you ready for the write-off this week, Red?"

Jordan snapped out of her daydreaming in time to
see Loretta Moseley drop a box on the empty desk beside her. She prayed Loretta had just stopped by to tor-
ment her and was not really planning to take over that
spot. Competing with the woman was one thing—having her just an arm's length away while doing it was an
entirely different story.

It didn't take long to realize that her nightmare was
coming true. As she watched in horror, Loretta began
unloading items from the box and placing them on the
empty shelf above the computer.

Crap!

"I'm as ready as I'll ever be," Jordan responded, turning away so Loretta wouldn't notice how worried she
really was.

When she'd agreed to compete with the woman who'd
originally written the column for so many years, she'd
asked Egan what would happen if Loretta won her job
back. She couldn't quit thinking about his response. He'd
implied that Jordan would be demoted back to writing
only the personals—or worse.

"Good. Even with your best stuff, you don't stand a
chance. I had dinner with Uncle Earl and Aunt Sarah
last night, and I can tell you there's no way that man will
pick you over me." She turned and gave Jordan a mock
salute. "Goodbye, Red. It was nice knowing you—not!

"I wouldn't get too comfy over there, Loretta," Jordan
fired back, surprised by the woman's cheeky attitude. "I
established a pretty good fan base while you were gone.
They might not take too kindly to me getting canned."

Loretta laughed. "You're forgetting that they were my fans long before you came on the scene."

Jordan could have reminded her that only half the people now following her column belonged in that category. Since she started printing Rosie's and Ray's great recipes, subscriptions to the newspaper had doubled. Technically, only half of the followers belonged to the arrogant reporter she'd now have to look at every day— or at least until one of them got the boot.

"No response to that, Red?"

Jordan smiled, thinking Loretta would probably win out in the end, but there was no way she'd go down without a fight. She mentally crossed her fingers that Carlita's Italian Cream Cake Pops were as big a hit as she hoped. It could turn out to be her secret weapon.

Thinking about the cake pops, Jordan remembered she was supposed to swing by and talk to Carlita's sister. Glancing at her watch, she silently cursed. It was already after ten and Carlita had said her sister would only be there until the Texas sun got too hot. The window to interview her about what she might have seen at the party the night Marco was killed was closing by the minute.

Grabbing her purse from the drawer, Jordan stood up.

"Where are you going?"

"Not that it's any of your business, but I'm going for an early lunch, and then I have an interview. If Egan calls, tell him I'll be back around three."

Loretta's eyes widened. "Who are you interviewing?"

Jordan smiled to herself. "Wouldn't you like to know?" She couldn't resist a quick peek over her shoulder.

Yes! she mouthed, seeing the concern in Loretta's eyes. It made her day knowing she'd wiped the cocky grin off her rival's face. She almost turned around to comment on that, then decided to play it cool and let it slide. Her time for gloating would come when Egan named her as the culinary reporter, although that would take a lot of great recipes to win out over the nepotism advantage—aka Uncle Earl.

It was only three blocks to Yesterday's Treasures, Victor's antiques store, and she headed that way first. She'd meant to ask if he'd go with her to question Carlita's sister when she'd returned from the fairgrounds the night before, but he and Michael hadn't been home. Then she'd gotten so engrossed in starting Thursday's column, she'd forgotten to go back over to his apartment later.

Sliding into the only available parking space in front of the antiques store, Jordan turned off the motor, climbed out of the car, and walked into the store. Victor was with a middle-aged couple who were examining a bedroom set in the far corner of the store. He looked up and waved when he saw her approaching, then turned his back to the couple and rolled his eyes.

Jordan bit her lip to stifle a grin. The one thing Victor hated was a customer who didn't know antiques and only saw them as overpriced old things. She'd bet money she was looking right now at two who fit that category.

"We love it, but you'll have to come down at least two hundred," the man said.

Victor pressed his lips together, and Jordan braced herself for his sarcastic comeback. Instead, he simply shook his head. "This is a fair price. I can show you a less expensive set if you want."

The woman whispered something into the man's ear before he said, "No, we really like this one. Is that your final offer?"

Victor nodded, sneaking a sideways glance Jordan's way.

Again the woman whispered to her husband and then

turned to Victor. "We'll leave our phone number with you. If this set doesn't sell and you're willing to come down on the price, give us a call." She pulled out a business card and handed it to him before they made their way to the door.

"Are you freaking kidding me?" Victor exclaimed when he glanced down at the card. "These people own Bubbles Champagne Bar in McKinley. Last I heard, that place was packing 'em in every night, and yet they're trying to squeeze me out of a lousy few hundred bucks." He tsked. "I paid good money for this set."

"Isn't this part of the new haul you got at the estate sale over in Greenville last weekend? The stuff you said made you feel like you should go to confession because you got it for such a steal?" She tried unsuccessfully to hide the amused look she knew had to be all over her face.

"A guy's got to make a living, Jordan. I have overhead." He giggled. "So what brings your smart-mouthed self down here at this time of day?"

"Had lunch yet?"

"No, and I only had an English muffin for breakfast. Want to run by the new all-you-can-eat place near the mall and pig out?"

"I'm thinking more along the lines of free chicken cacciatore and pizza bread."

Victor's eyes lit up. "Lead the way. Only I'm driving. You behind the wheel, my dear, scare the hell out of me."

"Should we see if Lola wants to come?"

Lola's Spiritual Readings was right next door to Victor's store, and even though taking too many people on a fishing expedition for information might not be ideal, it would be fun if all three of them went out there together.

"Lola's playing hooky today. She and Ray drove out to Lake Texoma to fish off Sandy's dock."

"That's nice. Sandy loves it when someone gets to use her place, especially now that she knows it isn't haunted." Jordan pushed aside memories of how solving her friend's ghost mystery a few months back had nearly gotten her killed.

"The car's parked out back. You can explain how we're going to get a free meal on the way to wherever." Victor grabbed his keys and followed her to the front, turning the OPEN sign around and locking the door. Then he snapped his fingers. "Chop, chop, Jordan. I'm starving."

FOR THE THIRD time in less than two days, Jordan found herself at the fairground entrance, this time with Victor at her side. On the drive over she explained about Carlita and her sister, and mentioned that their mission was to find out if Carlita's sister had seen anything that might help Kate's defense the night Marco died.

Halfway to the booth, Jordan heard someone call her name and looked up to see Carlita waving madly with a towel. Hoping it wasn't the same dirty rag as yesterday, Jordan smiled and waved back. Then she pulled Victor toward the booth across the way where a woman was having a difficult time trying to hang a sign on the front. One look at her left no doubt she was Carlita's sister.

"It looks like you could use some help," Victor said, reaching in and lifting the other end of the sign. "Where do you want it?"

The woman turned and stared, a light smile tipping the corners of her lips before she pointed to several nails protruding from the wooden plank. "There."

Jordan scrambled to help, but Victor had already lifted the sign up and had it in place before she could assist.

"My, my! You're a strong one," the woman said. "I like that in a man."

Victor moved away, and for the first time since she'd known him, Jordan saw him blush.

She turned to the woman and held out her hand. "Ginny, I'm Jordan McAllister from the *Globe*. I'm doing a story on you and your sister in Thursday's paper, and I wondered if you'd have time to answer a few questions for me."

"Lita told me all about you. Said you'd be coming by." Even though the woman was speaking to Jordan, her eyes had only left Victor's face long enough to do a body scan on him, causing the color in his cheeks to brighten. Jordan couldn't wait to tease him about that.

"Carlita tells me your specialty is chicken cacciatore and pizza bread. Is that right?" Jordan asked.

"Damn straight. Folks come from all over to sample it. I have to make bigger batches every year, and I still sell out. And my braided spaghetti bread is also a best seller."

"I'm sure it's delicious. I'll try to get by during the festivities to taste it," Victor said, now recovered from the earlier awkwardness of having this woman overtly ogling him. "Although I'm afraid that might be difficult since I'll be out of town all next week." He looked at Ginny to see if she'd take the bait.

She did.

"Are you hungry now?" Her smile was so wide Jordan thought her lips would split at the corners.

"Now that you mention it, I am a little hungry," Victor said. "I haven't eaten—"

"You have to try this," Ginny said, practically sprinting to the back of the booth where two large trays sat under a warmer. "You, too—what did you say your name was?"

"Jordan McAllister." There was no way she'd remember it even after the reminder. Her focus was on Victor, and Victor alone.

As if on cue, Ginny glanced up at him and batted her eyelashes. "And yours?"

Jordan fought to keep from laughing out loud. This woman was definitely coming on to Victor and making no bones about it. It was clear she was more interested in him than any publicity story Jordan had to offer.

"Victor Rodriguez. And I can't wait to taste your cacciatore and spaghetti bread."

"I didn't bring the pizza bread today, but you can taste the cacciatore and the braided spaghetti bread." Ginny grabbed two paper plates and filled them with the steaming Italian dish, setting them on the counter in front of Jordan and Victor. Reaching for two sets of plastic silverware, she said, "Eat this while it's hot. I'll tell you all about myself while you enjoy the food."

Neither Jordan nor Victor needed any further coaxing before they dug in. Carlita had been right. Ginny's cacciatore was the best Jordan had ever tasted, and she began plotting how she'd convince Ginny to give up the recipe for the Kitchen Kupboard. She stole a glance Victor's way, but he was shoveling the hot linguine into his mouth faster than she was. When he finally did look up, he winked, obviously pleased with himself for finagling the free food.

After another plateful and a slice of delicious, piping hot spaghetti bread, Jordan had heard Ginny's entire life history. Wiping her mouth with the napkin Ginny had placed in front of her, Jordan sized the Italian woman up. Standing about five-two with a body that could only be described as pudgy and dark hair pulled back into a tight bun, Ginny looked to be in her late thirties, making her a little younger than her sister, if Jordan's calculations were correct. Her round face was free of makeup and looked like it could use an industrial strength moisturizer.

When they were through eating, Jordan gave her a thumbs up. "Your chicken cacciatore is the best I've ever tasted. Thanks for letting us sample it."

"My pleasure. It was the least I could do for such a handsome, strong man like Victor, who helped me with the sign." Again, she batted her eyelashes, but this time Victor didn't blush.

Jordan decided to go for it. "I don't know whether Carlita told you or not, but my readers love recipes. Would you be willing—"

"Already ahead of you," Ginny said, pulling out two recipe cards. "I'd be honored to see these in print." She paused before adding, "But only after the festival is over. Deal?"

"Absolutely. My readers will go crazy over these."

Jordan grabbed the recipes and shoved them into her purse, deciding to dive right in and find the answers to the questions they came to ask. So far, the woman hadn't mentioned the party, and she was trying to figure out the best way to approach the subject.

Before she could do that, Ginny beat her to the punch. "Lita tells me you were at the party the other night at the Royale. That right?"

Jordan nodded. "I was covering it for the newspaper." She took a sip of the bottled water in front of her. "Were you there when all the commotion broke out?"

She was anxious to get to the heart of the matter and find out what this woman knew.

"Yes, but I don't remember seeing either of you," Ginny replied.

"We were both there." She hoped she could get Ginny talking. But even if she didn't, the mission was not a complete bust. She licked her lips thinking how good the food had been—and she had the recipes to print as a bonus. *Loretta Moseley, you'd better grab your butt and hold on with both hands after I post Carlita's and Ginny's recipes.*

"It was such a tragedy what happened to that man," Jordan continued.

"Certainly was. The guy deserved it, if you ask me."

Jordan's ears perked up. "Why do you say that?"

"Men can be such animals," Ginny began before turning to Victor. "I'm sure you're not, Victor. I only meant men in general. That Marco fella was up in his bedroom having some kind of orgy with two women…" She stopped abruptly as if she realized she'd said too much already.

"Two women? Are you sure about that?" Jordan and Victor both inched in a little closer.

"Positive," Ginny said, obviously deciding it was now or never to make a move on Victor. She leaned over the counter, and he backed away quickly.

Her eyes reflected her displeasure with his action, and she straightened up. "Well, if there are no further questions, I have more work to do." She walked back to the pan of cacciatore in the back, totally dismissing them.

"Say something nice to her," Jordan whispered to Victor. "We need to know who that other woman was."

Victor shook his head. "No way. She'd be all over me

like a cat in heat. She obviously doesn't have a working gaydar."

"Thank heavens, because you're our only chance to find out what she knows. If she thinks you're flirting with her, my guess is she'll tell you anything. Come on, Victor. Take one for the team."

"Have you gotten a good look at her? She has more hair on her arms than I do."

"I'm not asking you to take her out dancing. Just smile pretty once or twice for her and compliment her on something. Women love that." She pushed him closer to the counter. "I'll just start walking toward Carlita's booth across the way, and you work your magic."

He huffed. "You once told me I was as romantic as a horned toad. You're changing your tune now that you want something from me."

"If you won't do it for me, do it for Alex." She threw that in because she knew Victor adored Alex and would do anything for him.

"Okay, but don't go too far away. I'm afraid of what this woman wants to do to me."

Jordan kissed his forehead just as Ginny turned back from the warmer.

"Be sure and read Thursday's column, Ginny. I think you'll be pleased. Now, I have to go finalize things with Carlita." She turned and walked across the fairway, dying to sneak a peak to find out if Victor was talking to her.

By the time she reached Carlita's booth, her curiosity was killing her, but she forced herself to make small talk with Ginny's sister. A few minutes later, she heard a woman's angry voice shouting what she could only imagine were Italian obscenities. Both she and Carlita turned toward Ginny's booth in time to see Victor hightailing it away from the Queen of Cacciatore. Still screaming, Ginny was now shaking a big ladle in the air.

"Let's get out of here," Victor said, grabbing Jordan's arm when he got to Carlita's booth. When she didn't instantly react, he commanded, "Now."

She waved at Carlita as she allowed him to drag her out of the fairgrounds and toward his car. When they were safely inside and on the way back to Ranchero, she finally asked, "What was that all about?"

He bent over to catch his breath. "That crazy woman. She had a bloody meltdown. I'm lucky the pan of cacciatore was too heavy for her to throw at me."

"What in the world happened to make her so mad?"

"I swear I didn't do anything. We were just having a conversation, and I did what you said." He stopped and swiped at the beads of sweat on his brow. "Damn! She was mad."

Jordan was confused. "What did *I* tell you to do that made her blow a gasket?"

"You said to compliment her. Guess some women don't appreciate it as much as others."

Jordan narrowed her eyes in confusion. "You complimented her and she got mad at you?"

"Yes, and I have to tell you, Jordan, no more taking one for the team with that nut case."

"So what exactly did you say to her?"

"I complimented her about her face."

Jordan remembered thinking the woman had really dry skin and hoped Victor hadn't mentioned that. "Tell me exactly what you said to her—word for word."

"I told her I liked her mustache."

Jordan couldn't help herself and burst out laughing. Before long, Victor was laughing with her.

"I really liked it. You know how long I've been trying

to grow a good one like Tom Selleck's? Well, she had the beginnings of the perfect one."

That brought more laughter, doubling Jordan over. "You clod. That is the worst thing you could ever say to a woman. It's like telling a guy you like his man boobs."

"What's wrong with that?" he asked, causing another outburst of laughter.

When Jordan thought her sides would split, she finally pulled herself together. "I guess that means you didn't find out who the other woman was?"

He gave her a Groucho Marx eyebrow wiggle. "You underestimate me, my red-headed friend."

She turned completely to face him. "What did she say?"

"She said she had the perfect vantage point near the staircase and saw the woman who killed him go up the staircase first. Then ten minutes later, she saw another woman follow with a man she assumed was Marco."

"Oh my God! This could really help Kate. Did she say who the other woman was?"

He grinned. "Say you're sorry for calling me a clod."

She slapped his shoulder playfully. "You were a clod, and I'm not sorry, but if you don't tell me what she said I'm going to—"

"It was Tina Calabrese."

"What? She's sure?"

Victor grinned like the proverbial Cheshire cat. "And she said Emilio's daughter didn't go up those steps alone."

Jordan completely turned in her seat to face him. "Who was with her?"

"Say you're sorry," he demanded.

"Okay, okay, I'm sorry. Kate said Marco was already in the bedroom when she got there, so who was the guy?"

He pointed at her. "Gotcha. The mustache lady didn't recognize his face, but she'd said she's seen him around at the planning sessions, and she assumed it was Marco Petrone. And get this—she said whoever it was, the two couldn't get up to the bedroom fast enough. I was afraid to ask what she meant by that since she was already eye-balling me like I was dinner."

"She was sure it was Marco with Tina? 'Cause that's not what Kate said."

He shrugged. "She's never seen Marco, but she said it had to be him since it was his bedroom and he was the only guy up there."

Jordan sighed. This was indeed a new development that might help Kate. "That's weird, because Kate didn't mention seeing Tina in the bedroom with her and Marco. We have to assume that the cheating skumbag put Tina in the other bedroom and planned to talk Kate into a quickie first." She rubbed her forehead. "But Kate was adamant about Marco already being up in the bedroom when he called her. I tend to believe her. Why would he take both his fiancé *and* his girlfriend up to his bedroom after what had happened earlier?"

"He's a Casanova, remember?"

"That may be true, but I still think he was already up there when Kate arrived, which means the man Ginny saw with Tina couldn't have been Marco." She blew her hair out of her eyes. "So who was Emilio's daughter sneaking up to the bedroom with?"

ELEVEN

SHORTLY AFTER JORDAN arrived at work the next day, both she and Loretta were summoned to Egan's office. Neither said a word in the elevator, and it wasn't until Egan's secretary greeted them that Loretta finally broke the silence, hugging Jackie Frazier and asking about her kids.

Oh, great! Her competitor had an ally in the editor's office. That couldn't be good.

Egan was on the phone when they were escorted into his office and motioned for them to sit down without glancing up. When he slammed a file folder on his desk and raised his voice a few octaves, Jordan rolled her eyes, knowing he would be in a foul mood when he hung up. She had no idea why he'd called them here in the first place, but she figured it had something to do with the Kitchen Kupboard.

She worried that he and the owner had changed their minds about giving her a chance to show them she was the right one for the job. Loretta's little dinner with Uncle Earl and Aunt Sarah had probably been the nail on the coffin.

She felt momentary panic, waiting to hear if she was being sent back to writing the personals only.

"Heard that was quite a party the other night," her boss began.

Jordan nodded, and Loretta simply grunted.

Egan went on, "There's been a change in plans."

Here we go! Jordan braced herself for his next

sentence, convinced she was on her way out as a culinary reporter.

"We've decided to dedicate a full page every day to the Italian Festival from now until it ends." When neither woman reacted, he continued. "We're running a piece in the culinary column as well as the entertainment and sports column to showcase it. To make it even more interesting I've decided I want the two of you to write something for the column every day. That'll give the readers a chance to get a taste of both styles."

"That's asking us to do a lot of extra work," Loretta said, matter-of-factly. "I hope you know I expect to be compensated for it." She picked at a red tipped nail without looking at Egan.

Egan pursed his lips and narrowed his eyes. "You get a salary for being the culinary reporter, Loretta. Nowhere in your contract—which, by the way, was null and void when you failed to come back to your job after rehab—did it ever say how many articles you have to write every week. You should be glad for this opportunity. If it were up to me, you might not even be here. Once you gave up your position, that was it as far as I was concerned."

Loretta's shot out of the chair and leaned across Egan's desk. "Thank God it isn't up to you. I'll show you who's the better choice for the job, and then you'll eat those words." She turned to Jordan. "Game's still on, Red."

Jordan smiled, thinking she would be out of a job before she even finished that sentence if she talked to Egan like that. She wondered how much more of the woman's arrogance the editor would take before he reacted.

And had she just heard him right? Did he say he was rooting for her to win the job?

Well, maybe he hadn't said exactly that, but it sounded like he thought it was unfair that Loretta had just waltzed into his office out of the blue and demanded her old job back.

Suspecting Egan harbored at least a little animosity toward his former employee, Jordan vowed to take advantage of that and work her butt off to get good coverage of the festival. She decided to see if she could talk one of the Bruno sisters into letting her print a recipe in Saturday's column. That way she could run another one Sunday with a recap of the weekend long festival.

She got giddy just thinking about how the readers would love that.

"So, are you okay with that?" When they both nodded, Egan continued "I'll expect the reports on my desk before nine each morning." He waved toward the door. "Now go work on tomorrow's column. I have a couple of fires to put out here." He was already picking up the phone and dialing a number when they exited his office.

"Why didn't you speak up about the extra work, Red? We should at least get a little bonus for it," Loretta said when the elevator door closed behind them.

"I welcome the chance to prove I'm the one for the Kitchen Kupboard. Matter of fact, I already have a few ideas about what I'm going to write about."

Jordan stopped herself before she revealed her hand. She'd never been any good bluffing at poker when she played with her friends, but she was convinced if Loretta knew she had the recipes, she'd probably try to beat her to the punch and finagle them out of the Bruno sisters herself.

And there was no way the woman would honor Carlita's wishes to hold off on printing them until after the festival ended.

The elevator door opened, and Loretta pushed past, calling behind her, "You were probably a suck up in school, too."

"At least if I do get the job, it will be because I earned it and not because I whined to Uncle Earl over roast beef," Jordan muttered.

She walked by Loretta's desk and took a quick peek to see if maybe her first offering for the column was in sight. She'd love to know what her rival had up her sleeve.

No such luck.

Plopping down in her chair, she pulled out her notes from the interview with Carlita. She was planning to use them for her article the next day with teasers for the recipes to follow. Now all she had to do was persuade Carlita to let her print the recipes a few days early.

She'd go back to the fairgrounds before dinner—but this time she'd leave Victor at home.

GLANCING AT THE clock over the door, Jordan noticed several of her coworkers walking past her desk on the way to the exit. Already after five. She'd brainstormed a few stories for the column after she and Loretta had returned from Egan's office, and she'd lost track of time. She hadn't even taken a lunch break.

Sneaking a peek toward Loretta's desk, she wasn't surprised to find it empty. She'd probably slipped out early, still upset with Egan for not compensating her for the extra work. Loretta Moseley didn't seem like the give-the-job-100% kind of girl, but then again, she didn't need to be.

The woman had a benefactor.

The phone on Jordan's desk rang, startling her. She hesitated momentarily before answering, thinking if she had to listen to one more personal ad, she'd go crazy. For some unknown reason, today had been really busy for personals. More people had called in than ever before, making her wonder if there was a Lonely Hearts Club convention going on somewhere in Ranchero. The woman calling herself "Loves to party" had been her favorite one since the lady had confessed to being over sixty. How much over that she wouldn't say.

That had reminded her of her friend Lola, who had more energy and possibly a better sex life than most forty-year olds. She herself wasn't even thirty yet, but she'd bet "Loves" partied way more than she did.

She finally picked up the phone on the third ring. "Personals. McAllister speaking." She scolded herself for answering in the first place. Technically, it was a few minutes past closing time.

"Personals? That sounds sexy," Alex said, his voice bringing a smile to her face.

"Hey, you, I've almost forgotten what you look like."

"I know. I'm sorry, but between my job and meeting with Jeff and Kate about everything, I barely have time to sleep."

"I was teasing, silly. We'll have plenty of time after this whole mess gets straightened out. Besides, I've been pretty busy myself." She stopped before blurting out about all the detective work she'd been doing. She'd rather tell him the next time she saw him, thinking it might be easier to endure his 'quit snooping' lecture face to face.

"Actually, that's why I'm calling. My mom's taking Kate into Dallas to some kind of concert at Fair Park to cheer her up. I wondered if I could talk you into a nice quiet dinner tonight."

Her spirits were instantly elevated. "Mr. Moreland,

you have just made my day. What time should I expect you?" Spending a little time with Alex away from this mother and sister was worth putting off her return trip to the fairgrounds.

"I'll make a reservation for seven thirty at that new Italian restaurant on the outskirts of Plainville and pick you up around seven. Jeff said it was fantastic."

At the mention of Emilio's lawyer, Jordan was reminded that she hadn't heard the latest about Marco's murder. "How is Kate holding up?"

Alex sighed. "She's doing pretty well, given the circumstances. The DNA from under her fingernails still hasn't come back yet, but she has no doubt it's Marco's. She's kind of in limbo waiting, though, and to make matters worse, she's been relieved of her duties with the festival."

"Oh, no. That gives her more time to worry about all the police stuff."

"Exactly. Her boss drove up from Houston last night and officially took over for her. You can imagine how bummed she is about that. If it hadn't been for my dad, I don't think she would've come out of her room at all last night."

"Your dad?"

"He called from Abu Dhabi last night to see how things were going. Although she didn't sugarcoat it, my mother tried not to let him know who worried we are. Otherwise, he'd be on a plane out of there in record time. Since his big presentation to the Crown Prince is in three days, we convinced him to wait and see how this played out. He insisted on talking to Kate before he hung up, and like always, he had her laughing again."

"I'm so sorry, Alex. I feel so helpless. I want to do something, but I don't know what."

"There's not much anyone can do, Jordan. We just have to hope for the best."

Hearing the sadness in his voice, she decided to tell him about what she'd learned snooping around. "I've been interviewing several of the vendors at the fairgrounds, and I may have heard something that might help. It's probably nothing, but maybe Kate's lawyer can use it somehow."

"At this point, anything will help. Hamilton has nothing that might constitute reasonable doubt." He stopped to clear his throat, but not before Jordan heard the concern in his voice. "At any rate, I've missed you and seven o'clock can't come fast enough for me. You can tell me all about your new information at the restaurant. Wear something that makes me think twice about neglecting you again. And come hungry."

"Be careful what you wish for, Moreland. This may cost you a week's salary," she teased, hearing her stomach growl right then at the mention of food. "I missed lunch today."

He laughed out loud. "That's got to be a first. I'll lay odds you had a couple of Ho Hos, though."

"Maybe just a couple, but I'm still going to put a crimp in your budget tonight."

"I'm counting on it," he said. "I need a certain redheaded Irish girl to cheer me up, so be ready at seven."

She hung up, closed the manila folder with two of the recipes and her notes, and shoved them into the top drawer. She had two recipes ready to go and she was taking the other two home to work on making them print ready.

Halfway to the exit, she doubled back to retrieve them. No way she'd take a chance on Loretta sneaking back up to the newsroom and going through her notes.

As the woman had said, "game on," and she intended to show her just how well two could play.

After pulling the folder from the drawer, she placed it in the bottom one and locked it. Dropping the key into her purse, she headed for home. She was going to find something fantastic in her closet to ensure that Alex kept his eyes on her the entire night. Maybe if he was distracted enough he wouldn't notice how much snooping she'd actually done.

SEATED NEAR THE window overlooking a beautiful water fountain, Jordan stole a glance Alex's way. She really had missed him these past few days. His turquoise golf shirt made his smoky black eyes pop, and his khaki-colored slacks only accentuated his small waist and perfect butt. She had to admit, Alex Moreland was a "head turner," as her friend Ray always said when he saw a good looking woman. Jordan was proud to be seen with him, especially since every woman in the restaurant had watched him walk to their table.

When Alex caught her staring he smiled. "Hold that thought," he said before winking.

She smiled back but couldn't stop the warm rush spreading across her cheeks. Picking up the menu, she flipped straight to the desserts, hoping he wouldn't notice. "Oh look, they have tiramisu. I love that."

"Oh, no you don't. You have to eat something more substantial before you get dessert, young lady. You told me on the phone you haven't had anything to eat except a Ho Ho or two." He stared into her eyes. "I need to get your energy level up for later."

She tried not to blush again but couldn't help it. She was twenty-eight years old, for God's sake.

Of course, Alex picked up on it and teased her

unmercifully until the waiter finally appeared to take their order, basically saving her. Truth be known, though, she loved it when he teased her. It reminded her of growing up with her four older brothers and made her wish she lived a little closer to Amarillo.

But that would bring up a whole new set of problems for her. They still saw her as their baby sister, and like in high school, she was certain they would intimidate all her potential dates. If they had their way she'd be locked away in some secluded convent right now—with a chastity belt.

After she and Alex ordered, they made small talk until their salads arrived. When the waiter walked away, Alex picked up his fork, and said, "On the phone you said something about finding information that might help Kate."

Jordan wiped her mouth with the linen napkin. "I did." She took a second to search her brain for the right words so he wouldn't realize she'd been meddling. And she had to be careful not to mention that his mother had been right there with her while she was doing it. "Did you know that Emilio's wife had a fling with Marco Petrone?" When he didn't react, she hit him with the rest of what she'd heard. "And that apparently after Marco tired of her, he tossed her away?"

His eyes widened, and he put down the fork. "Who told you that?"

"The woman I interviewed for my column first told me about it, and then Georgette Calabrese's son himself confirmed it."

"Emilio has a son?"

"Stepson," Jordan clarified. "His name's Frankie O'Brien, and he's in his twenties. Anyway, he said that he and Marco weren't friends, but then he let it slip that they'd been business partners. When I called him on it, he denied saying that, but I know what I heard. When I mentioned he and Marco were about to be related, that's when he blurted out about his mother sleeping with his stepsister's fiancé."

The interest in Alex eyes spurred her on. "And we heard Georgette talking to him when we approached. She told him that with Marco out of the way, it was a good time for him to stand up and impress Emilio with his business skills." She paused. "Okay, I'm paraphrasing here, but it sounded like they saw Marco's death as a way for Frankie to step up and show Emilio that he's capable of running the show."

"We?"

Jordan mentally slapped her head for that slip up. After everything she'd just told him, what were the odds that he'd pick up on that one little word? She was never any good at thinking on her feet, and now was no different. "Your mother and me."

"My mother knows this and didn't tell me?"

Jordan crossed her fingers under the table and hoped he wouldn't hold it against her for lying. But she'd promised Natalie she wouldn't tell in case Georgette decided to blab about her teenage love affair with Emilio.

"Remember when your mother went with me to the fairgrounds so you and Kate could take a nap after you got back from the police station?" When he nodded, she continued, "Well, she was off talking to someone else when I overheard Georgette and Frankie talking, and I didn't want to mention it to her until I had a chance to talk to you."

Please God, overlook this one little lie.

She watched Alex's face, relieved to see he had bought into it.

"So Georgette and Marco were lovers at one time. Hamilton will have a field day with that. And her son trying to find a way to impress Emilio makes me think that maybe Emilio was showing favoritism toward Marco and perhaps even considering him as his heir apparent."

"Exactly," Jordan interjected. "According to the lady I interviewed, Emilio thought his stepson was a loser and wanted him as far away from the business as possible. But with Marco dead, there's no one else in the family to take over. To me, that's a pretty good reason for wanting Marco out of the way."

Alex's lips curled into a smile. "Don't get carried away, Jordan. I'll admit that it does cast a nice net for reasonable doubt, but it's a far cry from proving anything."

"I thought introducing reasonable doubt was all Hamilton had to do. No jury in good conscience could convict Kate of the murder if they think there's a possibility someone else may have pushed Marco over the railing."

Alex reached across the table and squeezed her hand. "It is, love, and Jeff will be glad you got this information, but I'm wondering why he doesn't already know all this. As Emilio's lawyer, he'd have to be aware that his boss didn't intend to pass on his business to his stepson. As for Georgette having an extramarital affair, Hamilton may have known about that, too. Hell, Emilio himself might even know about it." He paused and rubbed his free hand across his forehead as if in deep thought. "Come to think of it, the night of the party, I remember Emilio cautioning Marco about his womanizing ways. Maybe that's what he was referring to."

"Or maybe he and Georgette had one of those open marriages where anything goes."

"Even if that were true, I can't see Emilio looking past his son-in-law sleeping with his wife." He released her hand and took a sip of his Scotch. "I wonder if Tina knows."

"Oh my God! I forgot to tell you about Tina."

"What about her?" Alex eyeballed her suspiciously. "I have a sneaky feeling you didn't get all this information from innocently doing interviews."

Crap! She had to come up with a good story—and fast.

"I went back over there to try to talk the woman I had interviewed earlier into giving up her recipes for my column." Jordan leaned across the table and licked her lips. "Yum! You should taste Carlita's Italian Cream Cake Balls, Alex. They almost melt in your mouth."

"I should've known there was sugar involved."

Jordan ignored that remark and pressed on. "I took Victor with me to interview Carlita's sister who makes the best chicken cacciatore I've ever tasted. Anyway, she took a liking to Victor and told him she'd seen another woman follow Kate up to Marco's bedroom suite that night."

"This was one of the vendors at the party?"

"Yes and no. She is a vendor for the festival, but that night she was a guest. Apparently, she's part of the planning committee. Anyway, she saw another women go up the staircase with Marco right before he fell to his death."

"Did the vendor tell you who this other woman was?" Alex voice couldn't hide his increasing hope.

"She did. It was Tina Calabrese. And since Kate insists that Marco was already up there when she arrived, it must have been another man with her."

He raised his glass to hers and clinked. "Now you're

talking reasonable doubt." He motioned for the waiter, and when he arrived at the table, he said, "Can you bring this woman the biggest piece of tiramisu you can find in the kitchen?"

The waiter looked confused. "You mean after the meal, right?"

Alex shook his head. "No. Bring it now, please, and add a smaller piece for me. We're celebrating."

If it wouldn't have made a big scene, Jordan would have jumped up and kissed him right there. Instead, she settled for an air kiss and mouthed *I owe you*.

"Oh, yes you do, and I intend to collect," he replied before reaching for his phone which had begun to vibrate in his pocket. "Moreland," he said into the speaker, his eyes still staring at her and sending shivers up her spine for what they promised was to come later that night.

Jordan watched his face grow serious.

"Mother, calm down, and tell me exactly what he said."

Jordan waited patiently, her overactive imagination going wild with the possibilities of what had Natalie so upset.

Finally, Alex clicked off the phone and looked up at her.

"Jeff called Kate at the concert in Dallas. The Plainville police are waiting to talk to her tonight. My sister is no longer a person of interest. She's a full blown suspect. And if we don't get some hard evidence to clear her name soon, she could very soon be an accused murderer on her way to jail."

TWELVE

WITH THE DESSERTS in takeout containers, they left the restaurant before Alex had time to explain any further details. Once in the car, Jordan stole a glance his way. The concern that she'd seen earlier on his face had now turned into fear, and she felt helpless.

When they were on the Interstate on their way home, she couldn't stand it any longer. "Alex? What does all this mean?"

He swallowed hard, his hands white-knuckling the steering wheel. "I'm not sure. We expected the DNA scrapings to prove Kate had scratched Marco before his death. That's enough to bring her back for further questioning, but it's not sufficient to actually charge her with his murder. She admitted scratching him in self-defense when he threw her on the bed. Couple that with the injury to her face, and it should have been enough to keep the cops at bay." He shook his head. "They've got to have something else."

"What?"

A tense silence filled the car. "I don't know. I'm racking my brain for what it could be, but I keep coming up empty. Except for the DNA, there's really nothing else that suggests Kate was anywhere near Marco when he fell over the railing."

Just then his phone rang, and he dug it out of his shirt pocket. "Moreland." For a few minutes he listened intently before he finally said, "That's not what the guy said that night."

Jordan tried but couldn't figure out what that could mean. After another few minutes, Alex hung up and turned slightly to meet her gaze for a moment before focusing back on the highway.

"That was Jeff Hamilton. He got a call from Captain Darnell about an hour ago. Do you remember Darnell telling us that when they'd initially questioned the hotel valet he said he'd been standing in the middle of the driveway and looked up when he heard screams?" When she nodded, he continued "At first, he told the police he was too far away to see much of anything."

"I remember," she replied. "He said he only saw a shadow."

"Well, apparently, he's changed his story. He's now saying that since he's had time to think about it, he distinctly remembers looking up at the balcony and seeing a woman, although he's unable to positively ID anyone."

"Isn't it a little strange that he's so sure of that now?"

"You would think so, but it's not all that unusual for a witness to remember something days later. Usually, it's some minor detail, though, and not something this big. I have no clue how he suddenly got enough clarity to not only identify another person on the balcony with Marco but also to be so sure it was a woman from twelve floors below," Alex commented.

"Could it be that the police pressured him? You hear about that sort of thing happening all the time. I once met a woman who told me that after three days of relentless interrogation, bright lights, and no sleep, her son confessed to killing his cousin. When the truth finally came out, they discovered he was just as much of a victim as the dead girl." She remembered the agony on the woman's face when she'd related the story.

"When his mother asked why he'd confessed, he said the policeman promised him everything would be okay if he told the truth—the truth being the way the cops told him it had happened. Even though he had nothing to do with the crime, the police officers kept telling him he did. The kid was so confused he would have said anything to go home."

"Unfortunately, that happens more often than I'd like to think. I'll be able to get a better sense of it all after I talk to Kate's lawyer and Darnell. But even if it were true, the cops wouldn't admit to it."

"If the valet can't positively say it was Kate he saw on the balcony, why would the police think they had the smoking gun now?"

"With the DNA evidence still pending, the witness accounts of Kate fighting with Marco, and now the valet's story coming to light, they must think there's enough circumstantial evidence to formally charge her with the murder." He sighed. "She must be freaking out."

"I'm sure she is. None of us really believed it would get this far. We know she didn't kill Marco and assumed it wouldn't be too hard to prove."

When he passed the exit to Plainville, Jordan leaned toward him. "You don't have to take me home, Alex. You should be there when Kate and your mom arrive at the police station. It's a given your sister will need you by her side. I'll wait with you and then drive your mother home in their car."

He reached out and squeezed her hand. "I don't know what I did to deserve you, Jordan." He exited the Interstate and drove to the turnaround.

She smiled. "Do you want me to take your mother

to your house and stay with her until you get back from the police station? She must be frantic."

"I think she'd like that. She's taken a shine to you these past few days."

Jordan heard the catch in his voice and knew his heart was breaking for his sister. She concentrated on staying strong for his sake. "Then it's settled. I've got your mother covered. You take care of Kate."

They drove the rest of the way in silence until they pulled into the Plainville police station.

"We can sit out here until Kate arrives. By my calculation it will take her another ten or fifteen minutes to drive from downtown Dallas." He reached for the bag the waiter had given him. "You must be starving."

Up until now she'd completely forgotten that they hadn't eaten, but now that he'd mentioned it, sudden hunger pangs made their presence known. "I am a little hungry, but I don't think I can eat right now."

"We might need to stop at the emergency room and have a doctor check you out," he said, trying to lighten the mood. "Missing lunch and turning down dessert all in the same day has to mean…" He stopped talking when Kate and his mother pulled up beside him.

Alex got out of the car and walked around to the passenger side to open the door for Jordan. Then he did the same for his mother and sister. One look at Kate was all it took to know that she was more than a little rattled. As a lawyer herself, she had to know that things were about to go from bad to worse now that her status had changed from being a witness in a murder case to actually being a suspect.

Alex took a couple of steps toward her and pulled her to his chest. "Whatever we have to do to clear your name, we'll do. I promise you."

Watching Alex cradle her in his arms and hearing him promise that everything would be okay should have been reassuring to Jordan. And it would have been except that she heard the sadness in his voice and knew he was genuinely scared for his sister. She hoped Kate hadn't picked up on it as well.

"Alex?" Natalie moved up alongside Kate and cast a questioning look her son's way.

He opened his arms to allow her to be part of his co-cooning embrace. "Hamilton will be able to punch holes so deep into the valet's statement it will be useless. Without that testimony, the police have very little right now."

His eyes connected momentarily with Jordan's, and once again she saw the fear. She forced herself to give him a reassuring smile, but both of them knew it was going to be a long night.

They all turned as a dark sedan pulled up alongside Kate's car and screeched to a halt. The door bolted open and Jeff Hamilton emerged, looking like he'd just stepped out of the shower. His sandy-brown hair, normally coiffed in a modern style, was still wet and slicked back off his forehead.

"Don't worry, Kate," he said when he approached. "They're grasping at straws here. I'll have you back in your own bed by morning."

Kate wiggled out of Alex's arms and attempted to smile at her lawyer. "I hope you're right."

"Are you ready?" Jeff grabbed her elbow and led the way after she nodded.

The others followed behind. Jordan made sure she stayed close to Natalie in case what awaited them inside the station proved to be too much for her to bear. It would be very difficult for a mother to watch her daughter booked for a murder she didn't commit.

As soon as they entered the police station, Alex, Jeff, and Kate approached the desk and announced their arrival to the sergeant on duty. Almost immediately, the police captain who had interrogated Kate the night of Marco's death, sauntered down the hallway.

"I see you made it back from the concert," Captain Darnell said to Kate when he stopped at the desk. "I'm glad we were able to do this without a scene."

"You'd better have a damn good reason for dragging my client down here at this time of night, Darnell." Hamilton moved in front of Kate. "Something a little more incriminating than a young valet who just happens to remember that he saw a woman on the ledge with Petrone. A tad coincidental that just when you realized you have no case against my client, the kid suddenly has a total recall moment, don't you think?"

Darnell stared hard at Hamilton making it obvious there was no love lost between the two. "It was enough to get a warrant against your—"

"For now," Jeff interrupted. "I'll have her out of here before the judge has time to finish his first cup of coffee in the morning."

"That may be true, Mr. Hamilton, but right now, I'll need to proceed." He turned to Kate. "Ms. Moreland, you're being charged with the murder of Marco Petrone. My officers will take you to the back, read you your Miranda rights, and then book you."

A flash of panic crossed Kate's face, and Alex reached out to touch her shoulder. She hugged him, then turned to her mother, who was fighting back tears. "Mom, I'll see you in the morning. Please don't worry."

Neither woman wanted to let go, and it was only after Darnell cleared his throat that Kate finally pulled out of her mother's embrace. Then, like an obedient lamb being led to slaughter, she followed the officers down the hallway.

"I still can't believe you arrested her on the word of a young man who admitted on the night of the murder that the balcony was too high for him to see anything. Now all of a sudden he says he saw clearly enough to make out the image of a woman, and you buy into it like you had just found the murder weapon."

"Witnesses have been known to remember things the first few days after the crime," Darnell said with a smirk on his face.

"Just because he said he saw a woman doesn't mean it was my sister, Captain. There were plenty of other women at the party that night, and from what I understand, several may have had a good reason for wanting to harm Marco Petrone." Alex nailed the police captain with a smirk of his own.

"Again, this may be true, Mr. Moreland, but none of these other women were upstairs when the man was shoved over the balcony."

"And that's another thing, Darnell," Jeff interrupted. "The toxicology report I received just this morning from your office showed that Marco Petrone's blood was loaded with more than enough alcohol and cocaine to suggest there's a good probability the man accidently fell over the rail himself. With that amount of depressants in his body, any jury would agree that he would have had to have been more than a little unstable on his feet." He shrugged. "It isn't too much of a stretch to imagine him wandering out to the balcony after he hit my client and then leaning over a little too far, is it?"

"It wouldn't be if we didn't have an eyewitness who said he saw a woman out there with him, and according to everyone we questioned at the party, your client was the only woman upstairs at the time."

Alex glanced toward Jordan and she gave him the okay with a bob of her head. Turning back to Captain Darnell, he locked his hands across his chest. "There was at least *one* other woman up there with Petrone when he fell that night."

Both Darnell and Hamilton's head snapped around to face Alex.

"And how would you know that, Mr. Moreland?" the captain asked.

"Someone mentioned it to Ms. McAllister during an interview."

All eyes turned to Jordan.

"It's true. My source said she saw another woman go up the staircase right after Kate."

"And I don't suppose your source mentioned who this other woman was?" The tips of his lips curled in a smile, as if he was certain he had just caught her in a lie.

It felt like she was about to throw Emilio's daughter under the proverbial bus, but there was no other option. She looked up at Alex for reassurance. When he encouraged her with a half-smile, she said, "Tina Calabrese."

"What?" Jeff Hamilton turned to her "Why didn't you tell me this earlier?"

Jordan didn't like his tone. "Because I only found out myself yesterday. I was waiting to tell Alex tonight at dinner. I figured he'd know what to do with the information."

"So does your source have a name?" Darnell asked.

"I'd rather not say right now," Jordan said, hoping she didn't have to admit that Ginny Bruno had actually confessed to Victor and not to her.

Darnell took a step in her direction. "Look, Ms. McAllister, I know you write a culinary column over in Ranchero. It isn't like you have to protect your sources here. I just need the name of the woman who made that statement so I can investigate your claim."

Jordan looked at Hamilton, who was staring at her as if she had just confessed to the murder herself. "Her name is Ginny Bruno, and she's one of the festival planners. She was at the party and was sitting directly across from the staircase. She saw everyone who went up there that night. When I was interviewing her for my column yesterday, she blurted out that she'd seen Tina head that way right after Kate did with another man she thought was Petrone."

Darnell glanced down at his watch before turning to the desk sergeant. "Get Cummings and Jaworski to pick up this Ginny Bruno in the morning and bring her in for questioning." He twirled around to face Jordan. "Where did you say she lived?"

"I have no idea," Jordan replied, shaking her head. "If I had to guess, though, I'd say she and her sister were staying at a local hotel in Plainville."

"Have Cummings check that out. If necessary, call the head of the festival's planning committee to find out where we can reach her. I want this woman at the station first thing tomorrow." He paused as if contemplating his next move. "And send a couple of uniforms to pick up Tina Calabrese in the morning as well."

Alex turned to his mother who, up to this point, hadn't said a word. "Mom, Jordan is going to drive you home now. There's no sense in you hanging around here all night. I'll stay in case Kate needs anything."

"I won't go home," she protested. "Every time I look

at her empty bed, I'll think about her." She grabbed her son's arm. "Let me stay. Please, Alex?"

Alex shook his head. "I need you to do this for Kate, Mom."

Jordan stepped up and reached for Natalie's hand. "How about if you spend the night at my apartment? You can sleep in my bed, and I'll take the couch."

Natalie looked up at her son, probably hoping he would give in and let her stay. When he didn't, she slumped her shoulders in a gesture of defeat. "Okay, but I expect you to call me the minute you know something—anything at all, no matter what time of the night. Promise me."

"You have my word. Now go with Jordan so Jeff and I can work on getting Kate out of here."

Natalie handed Jordan the keys to Kate's car and followed her out of the building.

The fifteen minute ride to Jordan's apartment seemed like forever with little conversation between the two. Jordan wanted to believe everything was going to be okay for Kate, but she had a niggling feeling that it wasn't going to happen that way. So much could go wrong.

What if Ginny was still furious with Victor over his mustache remark and denied seeing Tina go upstairs that night? If, in fact, the valet really had seen a woman on the balcony, was it possible that Tina herself was actually the killer? She had certainly been mad enough at Marco earlier that evening, but was that anger enough for her to flip out and kill her fiancé? If that were true, what if Tina decided to save her own butt and verified the valet's statement? She might even say she actually saw Kate push Marco over the ledge. Then there was the mysterious man Ginny saw going up the stairs with her. A man who could or could not have been Marco Petrone.

Jordan's mind was still reeling with scenarios when they pulled into the parking lot at Empire Apartments. They got out of the car and walked through the back door and down the hallway to her apartment. For some reason it was eerily quiet, making Jordan wonder where all her neighbors were. A quick glance at her watch answered that question. It was already after midnight, and the next day was a workday for everyone.

She opened the door and allowed Natalie to enter first. She could only imagine what the older woman was thinking after getting her first look at the tiny apartment. Probably that it was a dump compared to the quaint little house Alex had rented. But if Natalie's thoughts ran along those lines, she kept them to herself.

"I appreciate everything you've done for me. Discovering that Tina had followed Kate up the steps should help, don't you think?" Her eyes pleaded with Jordan to agree.

"I hope so." Jordan saw a ray of hope cross the woman's face and decided to tell her the story of how Victor had gotten that information out of Ginny Bruno. At the very least, it would take her mind off her daughter's predicament, and it might even make her laugh a little.

"Victor was really the one who dug up that little tidbit, but not before he had to endure the woman's outrageous flirting. He—"

Startled by a knock at the door, she jumped. Any other time and she would have thought nothing of someone at the door at this hour, but under the current circumstances, her nerves were on high alert. It wasn't until she felt Natalie's fingers gripping her upper arm that the realization hit her. Someone was outside her door, and she and Alex's mother were alone and defenseless if that someone was looking to hurt them.

Grabbing a butcher knife from the kitchen counter, she shielded Natalie with her body as they inched their way to the door. She took several quick breaths for courage before standing on her tip toes and peering through the peephole.

Hoping to see one of her neighbors checking up on her, she was surprised to see who it actually was. But the surprise quickly turned to fear when she realized the man was not there for a social visit.

She took another quick peek and swallowed hard.

With a scowl on his face, Emilio Calabrese looked mad enough to kill.

THIRTEEN

SLOWLY, JORDAN OPENED the door.

An enraged Emilio Calabrese stormed into her apartment.

"What the hell did you think you were doing at the police station, Jordan?"

Jordan half expected smoke to shoot from his nose.

Natalie stepped from behind her and narrowed her eyes at her former lover. "She was doing what any other person would do if they were questioned by the police. She told them what she'd heard." She huffed. "And if I were you, I'd lose the attitude, or you can show yourself out right now."

His face registered the shock at seeing Natalie before he turned his gaze back on Jordan. "I apologize if I came on too strong, but you can imagine how I felt when I heard you had implicated my daughter in her fiancé's murder."

"I did no such thing," Jordan said, feeling a little braver with Natalie next to her. If Alex's mother wasn't afraid of Emilio Calabrese, why should she be? "I merely relayed a conversation I had with one of the vendors who said she'd seen Tina go up the staircase shortly after Kate."

"That's a bold-faced lie," Emilio shouted before lowering his voice a notch. "Tina was with me when all that commotion was going on."

Natalie moved toward him, and Jordan could have

sworn she saw Emilio take a step back. "That would have been hard to do, since you and I were standing at the bar and sharing a drink at the time. I was sitting on a barstool and you were beside me with your back to the staircase." She shook her finger at him. "Shame on you, Emilio. I want to help my daughter, too, but I won't resort to lying."

He stared at her for a moment before placing his hands on his hips defiantly. "Tina didn't kill Marco. I know it," he finally said softly.

"No woman likes to be made a fool of in front of all her friends," Jordan blurted before her brain had time to close her mouth. Once she started, she couldn't stop herself. "We all saw how upset your daughter was. If she walked in on Marco while Kate was still in his bathroom and imagined what had just happened in his bed, it could have sent her over the edge." She took a step backwards, sure Emilio would lash out.

Instead, he shook his head. "I know my Tina. She wouldn't even hurt a spider."

"And you think my Kate could kill someone?" Natalie fired back.

"Probably not," he agreed. "But trying to put the blame on my daughter isn't the way to go about proving she didn't." He stumbled and almost fell before he grabbed onto the side of the couch. "Mind if I sit down? I've had a long day."

Jordan motioned with her hand for him to sit. As soon as she was settled, she started in on him. "Let's get this straight, Mr. Calabrese. I only told the police the facts. At the very least, it casts reasonable doubt that Kate Moreland committed murder that night. Likewise, having Kate there does the exact same thing for your daughter. No one's out to get Tina. I can assure you. Best case scenario, they'll decide that Marco accidentally fell over the railing."

Emilio hung his head. "They've already officially labeled it a homicide," he said, calming down a little. "Jeff called tonight to tell me the police want Tina at the station first thing in the morning so they can question her. That's when he mentioned that they'd concluded that a spot of blood they'd scraped from the patio floor belonged to Marco. After the ME found a gash on the back of the man's skull during the autopsy, he ruled that at least one of Petrone's injuries occurred before the fall. Since he landed face down, that could only have happened before he went over the railing. More evidence indicates he didn't fall straight down like someone who had jumped. Thus, the homicide ruling."

Natalie threw her hands in the air. "Why didn't Jeff tell us that at the station?"

Emilio shrugged. "He may not have known about the autopsy at the time." He reached out for Natalie's hand. "This puts me in a precarious situation, Nat. It would have been unethical for Jeff to represent Tina in this matter after hearing privileged information from the accused. I had to bring in a local to make sure Tina's well represented."

Natalie opened her mouth to say something then closed it. After a moment, she reached out and grabbed his hand. "I'm sorry, Emilio. Really I am. I know you love your daughter as much as I love mine. Let's just hope the police decide there isn't enough evidence to try either one of them."

"She didn't do it," Emilio repeated. "It wouldn't have mattered if Marco had cheated on her. She didn't care. That's why she was so mad at me for making her..." He sucked in a gulp of air to cut off the rest of that sentence.

After glancing down at his watch he turned toward the door. "I'm sorry for barging in like this. I guess we'll just have to see what happens in the morning." He opened the door and walked out more slowly than he'd walked in. He seemed to be dragging his left leg, making Jordan wonder if he'd injured it somehow.

She raced over and locked the deadbolt as soon as the door closed behind him, then turned to Natalie. "Did you pick up on what he just said—and didn't say—a minute ago?"

"I did, and I'm still trying to figure it out. What could Emilio have meant when it slipped out that his daughter was mad at him?"

Jordan walked over to the couch and sat down. Leaning her head back she stared at the ceiling for a few minutes before responding. "I don't know, but my imagination is running wild. What if Emilio was making Tina marry Marco for some reason, and that's why she was so mad at him?"

"How could Emilio make her marry anyone? This is the twenty-first century, and we're not in an Old World country. Girls aren't forced into arranged marriages. They can marry whomever they choose."

"Unless the one who's holding the purse strings threatens to close the purse," Jordan said. She shut her eyes, trying to figure out what else it could be.

"But why would a girl like Tina balk at marrying someone who looks like Marco?" Natalie asked, plopping down beside Jordan on the couch. "From what I understand he had women all over the world trying to get him to settle down."

"I don't know why, but I promise I'm going to find out."

"How?"

"I'm going to ask her stepbrother."

Natalie straightened in her chair. "That's a brilliant idea, Jordan. I'll go with you."

Jordan shook her head. "This time I have to go alone, Natalie. If I'm going to squeeze any information out of Frankie O'Brien, I have to make him believe he's getting something in return. That won't happen with a chaperone present."

A twinkle brightened Natalie's eyes. "Wear that new lip gloss again."

JORDAN JUMPED UP from her makeshift bed on the couch when the phone rang. "Hello." She wiped the sleep from her eyes.

"Oh God! Your voice sounds so good to me," Alex said. "I would give anything to kiss the sleep off your face right now."

Natalie charged out of Jordan's bedroom. "Is Kate all right?"

"Tell her Kate's fine. Jeff did all they could last night before leaving. The police were gracious enough to let me crash on one of their office couches as a courtesy."

Tears threatened to spill over Natalie's face when Jordan relayed the message.

"Jeff's on his way back to the station now to find out about the woman who saw Tina Calabrese follow Kate up the steps that night. Hopefully, with that new information, the police won't have enough evidence to hold Kate. At the very worst, Jeff can persuade a judge to release her on her own recognizance." She heard the frustration in his voice, as well as the longing. "I can't tell you how much I need to see your smiling face."

"Me too," she said, sneaking a glance Natalie's way. She'd heard her tossing and turning most of the night just like she'd done on the couch, and the stress showed on the older woman's face.

"Tell my mother that I'll call her as soon as we find out anything. I know you have to go to work, but I can't leave Kate now."

"Your mom will be okay," Jordan said. "I'll have Rosie come over and sit with her until———"

"No! I want to be at Alex's apartment in case Kate gets to come home," Natalie interrupted holding up her hand." If you'll just let me follow you so I don't get lost, I'll be fine, and you can go to work."

"Your mother wants to wait at your house. Maybe she could take a nap while she's waiting," Jordan twisted to see Natalie's reaction to the suggestion.

"Doubtful," Natalie said, sitting down beside Jordan.

"Best case scenario, I'll bring Kate home and catch a few z's myself," Alex said. "I can't say for sure when I'll be able to get away tonight."

"You need to be with your family, Alex. I understand. Besides, I have something I need to do, anyway." She winked at Natalie before adding, "It's for my column tomorrow." If Alex knew she was going on a hunt for information from someone who might be the killer himself, he would freak out.

"I have to run. Jeff just walked in."

"Okay. Give Kate a hug for me."

"Will do."

She stared at the phone for a few minutes before shoving it into her T-shirt pocket and walking into the kitchen to fix Natalie a cup of coffee. "I'm sorry. The only things here that might double as breakfast are Chocolate Chip Cookie Dough Pop Tarts and Hostess Ho Hos." She felt the flush warm her cheeks, sure Natalie would wonder why she only had chocolate in the house. She made a mental grocery list that included English muffins and orange juice.

Instead Natalie clapped her hands. "I haven't had a Pop Tart in years." She sat down at the kitchen table and waited for the pastry to come out of the toaster. "And I can't even remember the last time I had a Ho Ho."

Jordan smiled and patted her back when she put the breakfast in front of her. "I've got to get ready for work. Help yourself to seconds if you want."

"I just might do that," Natalie said. "I always said that chocolate could make you forget all your troubles." She took a bite of the treat. "Well, maybe not all of them, but it certainly makes you feel better." She waved her hand toward the bedroom. "Go get dressed. And wear something sexy. You have a big job ahead of you tonight."

"AWESOME POST, LORETTA," the woman who sat two cubicles down said just as Jordan approached her own work station.

Loretta Moseley's smile couldn't get any wider as she thanked the woman, making sure Jordan heard. "I worked really hard on it."

"I can't wait to try it on my family. It sounds so delicious," the woman added before turning and heading back to her own desk.

That immediately caught Jordan's attention, and she tried to hide her surprise. Since arriving an hour late that morning she hadn't had time to look at the morning edition. But there was no way she'd give Loretta the satisfaction of knowing she was curious what her recipe was.

Thirty minutes later, Loretta got up to use the restroom, and Jordan pulled up the newspaper on her computer, going directly to the culinary page.

Her own article about the history of the Italian Festival was on the left side of the page. It was a good article with an in-depth look at the successes of past festivals. Jordan had been able to gather most of the information off the Internet and was proud of the way it had turned out.

She glanced to the right for Loretta's article and had to cover her mouth with her hand to stifle the scream that bubbled up in her throat. In bold letters besides Loretta's name, the words, Ginny's Chicken Cacciatore, glared at her, followed by the recipe for the wonderful dish.

No wonder people were congratulating Loretta. Swearing under her breath, Jordan wondered how Loretta had convinced Ginny into letting her print the recipe before the festival ever started. She'd upstaged Jordan and had taken round one of the competition. Next to the fantastic recipe, Jordan's article seemed dull and boring.

She opened the bottom drawer with the key from her purse and pulled out the files with her notes from the interview with the Italian sisters. Flipping through the pages, she looked for Ginny's recipe to compare it with the one Loretta had posted, secretly hoping the woman had left out a key ingredient or something. Grinning to herself, she imagined how angry the readers would be if they went to all the trouble of making the dish only to find out something was missing.

Her heart raced when she realized Ginny's recipe was nowhere to be found. An audible sigh escaped when she couldn't find Carlita's Cake Ball recipe in the folder, either. Going through her notes a third time, she felt panic rising. What could have possibly happened to the recipes? She had been vigilant about keeping the drawer locked, and the key had remained in her purse except when she needed it.

Just then Loretta walked back to her desk and noticed the look on Jordan's face. "What's the matter, Red? You look like you've lost your best friend."

Something about her tone and the look on her face had red flags waving in Jordan's brain. In that instant she knew beyond a doubt that Loretta had somehow managed to get into her drawer and steal the recipes.

"Give me the other one, and I won't go to Egan with this."

Loretta looked confused for a second, and then raised her eyebrows in question. "And tell him what? That you're mad because I printed the recipe before you did? He'll think it's just sour grapes."

"He knows you better than you think," Jordan fired back.

The other woman hissed. "That may be true, but even he can't prove I stole this recipe from your locked desk." She narrowed her eyes. "I told you that you weren't dealing with a rookie. I'll get my old job back no matter what I have to do." Although she turned toward her computer and pretended to be busy with something, the smile never left her face.

Fury almost choked her. Loretta was right. There was no way she could prove the woman had stolen her recipes. She might as well get used to writing only the personals again.

Putting the file back, something caught her eye in the back of the drawer. Reaching in, she pulled out a crumpled sheet of paper that had been jammed into the back. Smoothing out the wrinkles, she nearly jumped for joy. No wonder Loretta had seemed confused when she'd mentioned there was more than one recipe. Carlita's Cake Ball recipe must have fallen from the folder when Loretta grabbed it.

Jordan resisted flaunting it in front of her nemesis and simply tucked it into her purse. Maybe Loretta had won the first round of the culinary war, but she wouldn't win the next one. Jordan held the trump card. As good as Ginny's Chicken Cacciatore was, nothing compared to Carlita's Italian Crème Cake Balls.

Loretta was about to find out why you shouldn't piss off a redhead.

FOURTEEN

THE REST OF the workday dragged by without any further confrontations with Loretta, although it had been rather annoying listening to everyone stop by her desk to thank her for the great recipe. Jordan wanted to scream that the cheat had stolen it from her. Somehow, she managed to hold her tongue, but she couldn't quit thinking about how she would explain to Ginny and her sister why the recipe was in print before the festival had even opened.

At the thought of Ginny Bruno, she wondered how her morning at the police station had gone. That was another reason the Italian woman would be furious at her. Jordan did feel badly about involving her in the murder investigation. But what she'd told them about seeing a man go up the stairs with Tina the night Marco was killed was crucial if they were ever going to prove that Kate had nothing to do with his death.

As soon as Jordan was out of the building and into her car, she dialed Alex's cell phone. If anyone would know how Ginny's day at the Plainville Police Station went down, it would be him, since he had also spent the morning there with his sister.

He answered on the first ring. "Hello, beautiful. I was just thinking about you."

"Is Kate at home?"

"Yes, thank God. The police decided they didn't have enough evidence to hold her, and they released her with a warning not to leave the area."

Jordan's spirits were lifted. "That's wonderful news. Kate must be so relieved."

"For now, but if we don't get some hard evidence to clear her name soon, she could be on her way to jail again very soon." He paused briefly. "No more talk about that. Are you headed home?"

"No, I'm going out to the fairgrounds to see if I can get a couple of interviews before the festival opens this weekend and nobody has time to talk to me. I mentioned that this morning when you called, remember?"

She hated lying to him but it was necessary, and truth be told, it was really only a half lie, if there was such a thing. She *was* on her way to the fairgrounds right now, but she had no intentions of interviewing anyone. Her mission was to suck up to Frankie O'Brien to try to find out why his sister was mad at her father for insisting she go through with her marriage to Marco.

She remembered how Frankie's face had scrunched up in anger when he'd mentioned that Marco and his mother had gotten it on. She was counting on using that anger to manipulate him into spilling his guts about Tina and Emilio Calabrese.

"Wish I could go with you," Alex said, interrupting her thoughts. "But Jeff is coming over after dinner to brainstorm with us about what the next step should be. Trust me when I say there's nothing I'd rather do than take my best girl out to the fairgrounds for samples of food from my mother country. I'd especially enjoy plying her with a few decanters of chilled Italian wine so that she wouldn't be able to resist me."

Jordan laughed. "Hello? Do you know who you're talking to? You don't need a few decanters. All that would happen after maybe one and a half glasses of the good stuff."

He laughed with her. "Who said I was talking about you?" He didn't wait for her response before adding, "We both know I was, so there's no sense in trying to play it cool. Unfortunately, that fantasy will have to wait. I will take a rain check, though."

"You're lucky you added that part about it being me. I've already been reminded lately that I'm a skinny red-head, and you know what they say about redheads and their tempers."

"Yeah, well, a little Italian food will help with the skinny part but not the Irish temper."

"Maybe I can get Ginny Bruno to give me a little more of her chicken cacciatore and find some fine Italian wine to go with it. I promise I'll think about you the entire time I'm smacking my lips," she teased before she remembered why she'd called him in the first place. "Hey, speaking of Ginny, what happened when they interviewed her this morning at the police station?"

"Didn't I tell you? Ginny Bruno wasn't at the hotel when the police got there, so they haven't been able to talk to her. Jeff called a few minutes ago and said they still haven't been able to locate her."

"That's odd. She's rooming with her sister. Did anyone ask Carlita Bruno about Ginny?"

"As a matter of fact they did. She said Ginny got a phone call from someone from the Planning Committee early this morning. Something about the newspaper ads for the festival. Apparently, she's in charge of that." He tsked. "Anyway, she met whoever it was in the lobby and never came back to the room."

"Oh God, I hope she's all right."

"Why would you think she wasn't? The police believe she's just off somewhere taking care of business and hasn't bothered to call her sister yet."

Jordan swallowed hard. "I hope they're right." Even as she said it she couldn't stop worrying about the woman who'd been kind enough to feed her and Victor the day before. Even if she had gone a little ballistic with a serving ladle.

"Anyway, Kate is calling me now, so I have to run. I'll call you tonight after you get home. Maybe we can have a little phone sex."

"Don't let your mother hear you," Jordan teased. "She'll start naming our kids."

She slapped her hand over her mouth as soon as the words slipped out. What in God's name was the matter with her? Now, Alex would think she was pushing him in their relationship. "I didn't mean that the way it sounded," she said softly.

"Oh yes, you did, and you're right. My mother already adores you and would love to see a few more little Moreland babies running around." He paused before adding, "I can't say I find that notion unappealing myself."

Before she had time to digest that, he said, "Gotta see what Kate wants. We'll finish this conversation later."

She couldn't stop the grin from spreading across her face. Maybe when this was all over and Kate had taken her mother back to Houston, she and Alex could sit down and figure out if the relationship was headed toward bambinos or not. Even though they hadn't talked serious commitment yet, he had let a little "love you" slip out the other night on the phone, hadn't he?

She forced herself to shove all the romantic stuff to the back of her mind so she could concentrate on what was ahead of her at the fairgrounds. She was determined to get the lowdown on Tina Calabrese and her father, and instead of thinking about bearing Alex's children, she needed to figure out how she would seduce Frankie O'Brien.

As soon as she pulled into the parking lot, her heart picked up speed. It had already been established that she pretty much sucked at outright flirting, and the mission depended on her doing just that. She reached into her purse for the coral lip gloss and smeared it across her lips. Then with a newfound determination, she got out of her car. If she was going to fall flat on her face, at least her lips would be shiny.

The first thing she noticed after walking through the gate was that neither Ginny Bruno nor her sister Carlita was at their booth. Normally, that wouldn't have been unusual since Carlita had mentioned both she and her sister liked to work in the early morning hours to avoid the killer Texas sun. But there was something different about their booths, and Jordan had yet to figure it out.

She glanced at both booths on opposite sides of the fairway several times before it dawned on her what had caught her attention. The CHICKEN CACCITORE sign that Victor had helped Ginny Bruno post above her booth only days before was no longer hanging there.

She swiveled around to check Carlita's booth, only to find her sign advertising the Italian Cream Cake Balls missing as well. The whole thing was very odd, and she wondered if perhaps they'd skipped town to avoid Ginny getting involved in the murder investigation. But that made no sense. The police only wanted to talk to her, not put her in jail. Why would she feel the need to run?

She continued walking down the fairway, making a mental note to find out where the Italian sisters were staying so she could visit them at the hotel the next day. It was probably nothing, but she couldn't shake the bad feeling percolating since she'd first heard Ginny was missing. She hoped she was wrong—that it was only her overactive imagination stirring up trouble, as usual.

Searching for Frankie O'Brien, she walked up and down both sides of the fairway and was about to give up when she noticed a group of adolescent boys playing flag football in an open field behind the last booth. Smiling to herself, she remembered how she and her brothers had spent many hours doing that exact thing nearly every day after school back in Amarillo.

Since Alex would be tied up with his sister and Jeff Hamilton all evening, and with Frankie O'Brien MIA, she really had nothing better to do. No one even noticed when she wandered over to the sidelines where the boys were engrossed in their game. It didn't take long for her to get caught up in the match as well.

There were four boys total, all with olive skin and dark hair. The two on one side wore shirts while the other two were without. Within minutes, she figured out that the shirtless team was noticeably better. In the short time she'd been on the sideline, they'd scored three touchdowns while the less-talented "shirts" remained scoreless.

Unable to resist, she walked across the open field to where the boys in shirts were huddled up, preparing for the next play. When she reached them, both looked up, surprised to see a female on their field.

"You're holding the ball too long," she said to the shorter of the two who was the quarterback. Pointing to the taller one, she added, "You need to run along the sideline, then cross over to the middle as soon as you clear the defender." She turned her attention back to the quarterback. "And then you throw the ball down the middle even if your teammate isn't there yet."

Both boys stared at her like she had two heads.

"I'm just saying it's all in the timing. You have to trust that your receiver will be in the middle of the field to catch that pass."

"What would you know about it?" the taller one asked with a frown. "You're a girl."

She grinned. "That's what my brothers thought before I kicked their butts all over the field. And thanks for noticing that I'm a girl."

He was now eyeing her suspiciously. "You played flag football?" When she nodded, he said, "Wanna show us how to do it?"

This time she laughed out loud as she glanced down at her feet. "Not in these shoes, but I'll watch from the sidelines and give you pointers."

"I have an extra pair in my bag and a clean pair of socks," he responded as he pointed to his own feet. "It looks like they might fit you."

She contemplated the offer. One of the biggest things she missed about not living closer to her brothers was not being able to play football with them. What would it hurt to hang out with these adolescent boys and have some fun? Her reason for being at the fairgrounds in the first place was officially a bust anyway, with no Frankie O'Brien anywhere to be found.

She threw her arms in the air. "What the heck. Go get the shoes," she said before adding, "I'm Jordan, by the way."

"Gio," the young boy said over his shoulder as he ran to the sidelines and retrieved the extra pair of tennis shoes from his gym bag.

"And I'm Vince," the shorter one said.

"Glad to meet you both." She pulled off her flats and tried on Gio's shoes. "You were right. They're a perfect fit."

He grinned from ear to ear. "Told you." Then he turned to his friends on the other team and announced, "Jordan is our new quarterback."

"No fair," a pimply faced boy from the other team complained. "You have three and we only have two."

Gio turned to Vince. "Go on their team." After Vince had trotted over to the other side, Gio looked up at Jordan. "You want me to run down the sideline and cut toward the middle, right?"

"Yes, leave the defender in your dust and be ready to make that catch."

"You'd better be as good as you say you are," he said as they broke the huddle and lined up.

On the first play, Gio dropped the football, and on the second, Jordan mistimed it and the pigskin sailed over his head. But on third down and long, they connected on a perfectly executed play, and Gio scrambled for the touchdown.

For the next thirty minutes, Jordan forgot she was old—and a girl—and somehow managed to keep up with the twelve-year olds and all their adolescent energy. When she and Gio were up four touchdowns to one, she decided it was time to call it quits before she got a blister from wearing the shoes. Plus she hadn't eaten yet, and all that moving around had her stomach growling in protest—not to mention her muscles, which were beginning to scream at her as well.

"Wanna come back tomorrow and play again?" Gio asked as she handed him his shoes.

"As much as I'd love to say yes, I can't, Gio, but thanks for making me feel young again. This has been so…"

"Who's your new friend, Gio?"

Both the boy and Jordan turned to face the man who'd

appeared out of nowhere and was now standing in the center of the field with them.

"Oh hi, Dad. Did you see us play? We killed them."

"Indeed," the man said with just a hint of an accent. "And I was thoroughly impressed with both of you." He held out his hand. "Now, son, introduce me to the woman who threw those great touchdown passes."

"Her name is Jordan. That's all I know."

Jordan reached for his outstretched hand. "Jordan McAllister. I'm a reporter with the *Ranchero Globe*."

The newcomer's eyes showed his surprise, and he quickly smiled. "A girl reporter who throws better than most men. Now, I really am impressed." He shook her hand. "I'm Bernardo Petrone, but my friends call me Nardo."

Jordan nearly swallowed her tongue. "Marco's brother?" she asked when she'd recovered enough to speak.

His eyes squinted in question. "You knew him?"

She shook her head. "Not really. I only met him the night he…" She stopped short, watching for some sign of sadness in Bernardo's eyes. There was none. "The night of the party," she finally said. "From what I saw, he was a good man."

Subconsciously, she touched her nose to make sure it wasn't growing. She'd thought a lot of things about Marco Petrone when she'd first met him, and "a good man" was not on that list. But what else could she say to his grieving brother, although a quick glance up at Bernardo gave her the impression that he didn't appear to be taking his brother's death all that hard.

"I appreciate that," he said, turning to Gio. "Gather up your stuff and go with Vince to his father's booth for a few minutes. I'd like to talk to Ms. McAllister."

When the two boys were out of earshot, Bernardo leaned in. "After working so hard in this heat, I'll bet you could use a cold beer. Unfortunately, all I can offer is a glass of lemonade from one of the stands."

"Lemonade sounds perfect," she said, mentally sizing him up.

About four inches shorter than Marco, Bernardo Petrone had neither the looks nor the body that would even compare to his brother. Dressed in a pair of cargo shorts and a T-shirt that said PETRONE DISTRIBUTORS on the front, he seemed way too tame to have such a flamboyant sibling, making her wonder if they really were kin.

"Marco and I were half-brothers," he said as if he'd just read her mind. "My mother died in childbirth, and my father married Marco's mother a few years later."

"I'm sorry for the loss," she said when she could think of nothing else to say.

"Thanks. His body will be shipped back to New Jersey after the coroner releases it, and there'll be a memorial service then. In the meantime, I need to stay in Texas to see that the festival goes off without another hitch."

"Another hitch?"

Bernardo swiped at the perspiration spreading across his brow as he handed her a glass of lemonade from the vendor. "Somehow, the liquor shipment got screwed up and hasn't arrived yet. My people back in New Jersey tell me it was loaded on the trucks and on its way when Marco delayed it for some reason. Now they're not sure exactly where it is. The festival unofficially starts tomorrow night with the picnic for all the participants, and now we're scrambling to find out what happened and why Marco told them to hold off on the delivery in the first place."

"Why do *you* think he did that?" She took a sip of the cold drink, hoping he wouldn't think she was being too nosy.

"Who knows? It was his job to get it here on time, and since he isn't around to answer to Calabrese, I'm taking the heat for it not being here." He sighed and took a drink of his own lemonade.

Jordan detected a slightly bitter tone in Bernardo's voice when he spoke about his brother. She decided to go with her instincts and try to get some info out of him. Maybe there was a chance the long drive all the way out to the fairgrounds wouldn't be a total bust after all.

"Were you and your brother close?"

He tsked. "If you call him always putting me down in front of everyone close, then yes, we were. He always acted like I was hired help when I am—and always have been—an equal partner in the company."

She nearly spewed her lemonade. If Marco and his brother were at odds over control of the company, it was yet another reason for a jury to believe there was reasonable doubt that Kate was Marco's killer.

Determined to find out more, she leaned in. "With him gone now, will you and your father run the company yourselves?"

"My father is eighty-five years old and gave up the reins to the winery in Palermo five years ago after a mild stroke. He decided life was too short to spend working eighteen-hour days." He smirked. "That and the fact that he had a brand new thirty-year old wife who kept him happy in the bedroom."

Any normal self-respecting girl would have at least blushed a little after that remark, but Jordan was too busy trying to figure out how this all related to the murder.

"What about the distribution company? Did your father turn that over to you both as well."

"My father has nothing to do with that. Marco and I started that up before he ventured off into other things with…" He stopped short as if he realized he was telling her things he shouldn't have. "With another business-man," he said instead.

"Frankie O'Brien?" She held her breath, hoping he didn't tell her it was none of her damn business.

He eyed her suspiciously. "My brother did have some-thing going on with Frankie, but he pulled back when he got chummy with Calabrese."

"Do you think his future father-in-law forced him to?"

"Hell no," he shouted. "Emilio had no idea what Marco was doing on the side. All he cared about was marrying off his daughter to my brother so he could get a piece of the cash cow himself."

"I thought Emilio was a rich man in his own right."

"That's true, but after he found out about…" He stopped abruptly and took another drink of the lemon-ade. "I've talked about me too long. What about you? Since only the festival vendors and workers are allowed on the grounds until opening day, I assume you're here on official business. I hope everything we've talked about is off the record."

She shrugged. "Absolutely. You need to know that I write the culinary column. None of my readers would be interested in what you or your brother did or didn't do behind the scenes unless, of course, it involves a juicy recipe that I can print."

His eyes crinkled with amusement. "Good to know. I suppose you're a great cook?"

This time she threw back her head and laughed out

loud. "Depends on what you call cooking. I make a mean fried bologna sandwich."

He laughed with her. "I like you, Jordan McAllister. If I wasn't already in a relationship, I might even ask you out to dinner one night before I go back to New Jersey."

"Not sure your wife would approve," she fired back, thinking that Rosie would be proud of the way she was flirting, before she realized this wasn't what her friend would consider flirting in any stretch of the imagination. More like pumping him for information.

He lowered his eyes. "Gio's mother and I were high school sweethearts and never married. When she got pregnant, we decided a happily ever after was probably not in our cards, since she had already fallen in love with a rich, older man who wanted to show her the world. Gio was the best thing that ever came out of that relationship, and I got full custody when the old guy wanted no part of a newborn baby messing up his lifestyle."

"I must have misunderstood you. I thought you said you were in a relationship."

"I did," he responded. "And it looks like that's gonna work out just fine now that Marco…" He sucked in a gush of air before he lifted his paper cup and drained the rest of his lemonade. After he threw the cup into the trash can, he looked down the fairway where Gio and Vince were kicking a can around in the dirt. "As much as I would enjoy talking with you a while longer, I have to get Gio back to the hotel and into bed. We've got a big day tomorrow before the picnic. I hope I'll see you there."

With that, he turned and walked down the fairway, leaving her wondering what he'd meant by that last remark. She'd bet money he'd been about to say his relationship would work out now that his brother was out of the way.

Oh my God! What if Bernardo Petrone was the man Ginny had seen going up to Marco's suite with Tina Calabrese? Ginny had commented that they couldn't keep their hands off each other.

Little things were beginning to make sense now. Like Emilio letting it slip that his daughter had not been happy that he'd tried to make her go through with the marriage to Marco, even after the man had been caught cheating. Could it be that she and Bernardo were having a secret affair? That perhaps she was in love with him instead of his brother?

Jordan clapped her hands in delight. Wanting Marco out of the picture permanently made for one helluva motive for either Bernardo or Tina—or both.

FIFTEEN

AFTER STOPPING AT the Burger Hut for a quick dinner, Jordan finally made it home a little after nine. No sooner had she walked into her apartment and settled in on the couch than she heard a knock at the door.

"Hurry up," Victor said, knocking impatiently once again. "I have something to tell you."

When she opened the door, he breezed past her and walked straight into the kitchen where he opened the refrigerator and pulled out a beer. He held it out to her. "Want one?"

She shook her head. Beer always made her sleepy, and she had a few things to do before she could crawl into bed. Knowing the best time to talk to Carlita Bruno was in the early morning hours, she'd decided on the way home from the fairgrounds to swing by her hotel before work—assuming she was able to find out exactly where they were staying. She'd already prepared an excuse for being late if Egan gave her any grief about it. She'd simply say she was on assignment, which was partially true.

She walked past Victor into the living room and sat back down on the couch. "So what's so important that you rushed over here at this time of night to tell me?"

He took a quick swig of the cold beer and slumped down beside her. "Guess who came by the shop today and paid full price for that bedroom set I snagged at the estate sale last weekend?"

"No way! Mrs. Cheapskate talked hubby into giving

you the asking price?" She high-fived him. "I couldn't believe you let them walk away without caving and reducing the price the other day. I guess this shows you were right. I wish I'd known you were about to come into some money before I stopped and inhaled a burger, though. You, my boy, would have been paying for my dinner at some fancy restaurant."

He smirked. "Yeah, like you in a fancy restaurant on purpose is ever going to happen. With your taste for all the cheaper things in life, you must be the perfect date." He paused and took another drink. "Where were you, anyway? With Michael working, I had no one to tell about my unbelievable talent as an antiques dealer. Do you have any idea how much money I made off that old set?"

She laughed. "Keep talking, and I guarantee you're going to spring for dinner tomorrow night." She paused. "Darn it! I have to go to the pre-festival picnic. I'll never get that free meal out of you."

"Can I go with you?"

She shook her head. "I can't even take Alex. It's only for the planners, vendors, and the press."

"Okay, I'll buy you a big plate of Ginny's Chicken Cacciatore on Friday, then." He slapped his head. "But you'll have to go to her booth to get it. She'd probably put arsenic in it if I showed up there."

They both giggled before Jordan got serious. "She's missing, you know."

"Who's missing?"

"Ginny. I told the cops about her seeing Tina Calabrese and another man going up to the bedroom suite that night, but she disappeared before they could question her."

He looked confused. "Disappeared like in went to

visit a friend and spent the night or like something out of Creatures of the Dead? That's on tonight at midnight, by the way. Wanna stay up and watch it with me?"

"Can't. I have a big day tomorrow." She fought down the guilt that suddenly overwhelmed her. "As for Ginny, I don't know why she's missing, but if something happened to her because of me, I'll never forgive myself."

"You? Why would you think you had anything to do with her disappearance?"

She shrugged. "It just seems odd that it happened right after I sicced the cops on her."

Victor took another swig of the beer and again offered her the bottle. After she shook her head, he leaned back into the couch and propped his feet on the coffee table. "Did you ever think she might've found someone to party with and is just off doing what adults do when they're horny?"

That made Jordan laugh, and she leaned back and followed suit, positioning her feet next to his. "I'd forgotten how you have such a way with words. You're probably right, though. Regardless, I'm going by her hotel before work to talk to her sister. With any luck, Ginny will be there, too, and I can smooth things over."

"You're not going over there to apologize for what I said, are you? Because the lady very clearly came on to me, and I was flustered. And I meant what I said as a compliment. She should be the one apologizing for hitting on a gay guy."

"Don't be silly. I'm going because I think Loretta Moseley stole Ginny's cacciatore recipe out of my locked desk drawer and posted it in today's *Globe*. Since I promised both Ginny and Carlita that I wouldn't publish the recipes until after the festival ended, I feel like I need to explain to them why it showed up today. They're going to kill me."

"That sleazebag! Sounds like Loretta's taking the competition to a new level." He slapped his knee. "We need to move to Plan B, and since I know you're not as devious as me, I'll tell you what we're going to do."

She turned to face him. "Oh, no. I know that look. You're about to get me into trouble, aren't you?"

He shook his finger at her. "No, I'm not. I'm just gonna show you how to get revenge, my dear, and how to beat Loretta at her own game while doing it. She may have an advantage because Uncle Earl owns the newspaper, but you, Princess, have a lethal weapon—me. I'm about to save the day for you."

She laughed out loud. "You're not going to wear red tights or anything, right?" she teased. "Because I'm not sure I can handle that tonight."

"I don't need red tights. You and I are going to war with Loretta Moseley without even breaking a sweat. And if my plan works out the way I think it will, this battle will take place while we sleep."

He had her full attention now, and she leaned even closer to him. "Go on."

His eyes sparkled with mischief. "You have the recipe for that awesome braided spaghetti bread Ginny served that day, right?"

She gave it a lot of thought before agreeing.

"Here's what you need to do. I'll rewrite the recipe in my own handwriting so Loretta will think it's authentic, but I'll leave out one or two of the key ingredients. Then before you leave, make sure she sees you putting it in that same drawer she pilfered. I guarantee we'll see that recipe in Friday's column, and guess what, sweet-cakes? The readers are going to crucify her after they spend money to buy the ingredients, take the time to make it, and it sucks."

"I'm not sure I can lower myself to her level and do that," Jordan said, sadly. "I do have standards."

"What do you mean? The lady stole your recipe, and if this plan works, it means she's going to steal another one. Think about your readers in Ranchero. They deserve a culinary reporter with more ethics than that. Of course you can do it."

She pondered the idea for a moment before deciding that Victor had a point. If Loretta did as he was convinced she would, it would be her own fault for stealing a recipe once again.

"I'll do it," she said, finally.

She got up from the couch and walked to where her purse was laying on the kitchen counter. After pulling out Ginny's Spaghetti Bread Recipe, she handed it to him. "But I hope you're wrong, and she doesn't break into my desk again." Even as the words left her mouth, she knew the chance of that not happening was slim. It was obvious Loretta Moseley would stop at nothing to get her old job back.

Victor lifted himself off the couch and joined her in the kitchen. After throwing his empty beer bottle into the trash, he kissed her cheek. "I'll put the recipe in an envelope outside your door so you can take it with you to work tomorrow." He moseyed over to the door, and halfway there, he looked back. "Call me on your way home tomorrow. I want to know exactly how she acted and if you did it or not."

"Okay." Suddenly, she remembered that she hadn't told him about playing flag football with Bernardo Petrone's kid on the festival grounds. She was about to call him back, then remembered she had to make a few phone calls before it was too late. She'd see Victor tomorrow and could bring him up to speed on her snooping then.

After he was gone, Jordan called Alex to tell him she was going to tell Carlita about the recipes in the morning, and she asked if Kate could find out where the sisters were staying.

"Jeff talked to Captain Darnell after dinner tonight. They pulled the hotel security tapes and were able to see Ginny Bruno when she got off the first floor elevator and met someone in the lobby."

"Could they tell who it was?"

"They're not a hundred percent sure, but it looks like it could've been Georgette Calabrese"

"What? She's not even on the planning committee, is she?"

"Not according to Kate, but she is one of the major organizers of the festival. Darnell is having her brought in as we speak to question her about it. But here's the kicker. After Ginny walked away from Georgette or whoever, a man approached her at the elevator. They spoke briefly before they left by the side door, and the cameras lost sight of them."

"Holy crap! And the police have no clue who the man was?"

"They're not even sure it really was a man. Whoever it was had on a hoodie and must have known where the cameras were because he or she made sure not to look directly at them."

"I hope Ginny's alright," Jordan said.

"Me too. The police will see how Georgette fits into all this, but I doubt they'll find anything useful. The camera showed Georgette walking out the front door by the time Ginny reached the elevator." He paused. "We won't know anything more until the morning. In the meantime, I'll find out from Jeff the name of Ginny's hotel and get back to you."

Ten minutes later she had that information and was already planning what she'd say to Carlita. She said a quick prayer that Victor was right and that Ginny was just off somewhere with the mystery man having the time of her life. She hoped the woman had already called her sister to let her know where she was.

Jordan twisted around suddenly, feeling a sharp pain in her lower back. Grinning to herself, she decided that playing flag football with a bunch of twelve-year olds might not have been one of her better decisions. She turned off the lights and walked gingerly to the bedroom.

Since the drive to Plainville fairgrounds would take about a half hour, she set her alarm for an hour earlier. Then she climbed into bed, but as tired as she was, she couldn't get to sleep. Her mind raced with thoughts about her earlier meeting with Bernardo Petrone and what it all could mean.

Finally, after forty-five minutes of tossing and turning, she got out of bed and padded to the kitchen for a beer.

AS JORDAN PULLED into the Dream Weaver Inn at the outskirts of Plainville, she immediately noticed the difference between this hotel and the Crown Royale where Marco had fallen to his death. The Crown had a cobblestone port-au-cochere and several valet attendants waiting to park cars. The Dream Weaver had neither.

After parking her Camry out front, Jordan walked into the lobby, pleasantly surprised to find it wasn't the dump she was afraid it might be. Her eyes scanned the area and finally located the security cameras that had captured Ginny Bruno before she disappeared.

With the security footage in mind, she thought of the police questioning Georgette Calabrese about why she was in the lobby with Ginny. Curious how that interview had gone, she made a mental note to call Alex on her way to work to find out.

She walked up to the reservations desk. A middle-aged, bleached blond clerk looked up from the computer where she'd been playing Solitaire.

"Can I help you?"

"I'm looking for Carlita Bruno," Jordan said, trying hard not to prompt her to put the black jack on the red queen.

The woman clicked off the screen and pulled up the list of guests, turning the monitor slightly so Jordan couldn't see. When she looked up again, she said, "Sorry. Hotel policy prevents me from giving out her room number. I can call her, though, and let her know you're down here. What did you say your name was?"

"I didn't, but you can tell her that Jordan McAllister from the *Ranchero Globe* is here for a follow-up interview with her."

The clerk looked totally unimpressed before she picked up the phone and called Carlita's room. After announcing that Jordan was in the lobby, she talked for a few minutes before disconnecting.

"She's in 782." She pointed to her left. "Take that elevator over there." She didn't even wait for Jordan to thank her before she returned to her online card game.

On the elevator ride up, Jordan went over in her mind once again what she'd say to Carlita Bruno. The last thing she wanted to do was let her see how worried she was about Ginny. That would only make matters worse,

especially if Carlita was already freaking out and thinking the worst.

She stepped off the elevator and followed the arrows
to 782, swallowing the big lump that had formed in her
throat. This was not going to be easy. When she got to
the room, she knocked lightly on the door, and within
seconds, it opened.

Carlita Bruno's eyes widened when she saw her.
"Didn't expect to hear from you again."

Jordan tried to smile and almost made it. "May I
come in?"

Carlita stepped aside to allow her to enter. As soon as
she was completely inside, Jordan turned to the woman,
noticing the bags under her eyes from an apparent lack
of sleep.

"Have you heard from your sister?"

Carlita lowered her eyes and shook her head. "I'm
trying not to be worried, but I can't help it. I keep telling myself that it's just Ginny being Ginny. She's been
known to go off on her own for a few days to sort things
out whenever her life becomes messy, and I'm hoping
that's what she's doing now."

"And is her life messy now?"

"I didn't think so. We were both looking forward
to a profitable festival, and then we were going to take
our time driving back to New Jersey. Even talked about
spending a few days in Branson." She motioned for Jordan to sit down at the small desk. "Do you want something to drink? We have a cooler with sodas."

Jordan shook her head. "I'm fine. I stopped to find
out about Ginny, of course, but also to tell you that her
recipe for chicken cacciatore was printed in yesterday's
newspaper. Another woman at the paper stole the copy
from my locked desk drawer and published it without

my knowledge. Since I promised not to print her recipes until after the festival ended, I wanted her to know I didn't renege on our deal."

The news didn't seem to bother Carlita, and she shrugged. "In the big scheme of things, that seems unimportant right now. Unless I hear from Ginny soon, neither one of us will be participating in the festivities this year, anyway. I had them take down both of our signs until we know something one way or another."

A mental picture of all those Italian Cream Cake Balls going to waste popped into Jordan's mind before she mentally slapped the thought away. "Did Ginny find someone she was interested in?" she asked as delicately as she could.

Carlita picked nervously at the cuff of her blouse before a half smile covered her face. "Only your friend, but after he insulted her, she swore off men altogether."

"My friend didn't mean to hurt her feelings," Jordan said, quickly defending Victor. "He actually thought he was complimenting her."

Carlita tsked. "Isn't that just like a man? I once had a guy who was courting me say that for a fat girl, I didn't sweat much. Like I was supposed to be happy about that." She tsked again before grabbing a Diet Pepsi from the ice chest. After pouring it into one of the clean glasses from the dresser, she looked up at Jordan with a twinkle in her eye. "I've been on Ginny's case for years about her mustache, but she didn't see anything wrong with it since our mom had one, too. I tried to convince her that back in Mom's day, all the women had them, but the new generation of Italian females now go for bare upper lips."

She paused to take a sip. "Two hours after your friend told her he liked her mustache, she made an appointment at the beauty salon down the street and had it waxed off. Looks a hundred percent better now."

"Really? So Victor's ignorance didn't totally ruin her day?"

"On the contrary. When she returned from the salon and checked out the finished product in the mirror, she even commented that maybe now, he'd like what he saw."

It was Jordan's turn to laugh. "I'm here to tell you that'll never happen. My friend isn't interested in women."

Suddenly getting it, Carlita's eyes twinkled with merriment. "Obviously, neither one of us is very observant."

Jordan chuckled with her. "I still tease Victor about it. At any rate, he wanted me to tell her that he was sorry if he upset her."

Carlita's eyes again clouded over with worry. "I pray that she's okay."

"I'm sure she is, Carlita. Let's hope she's off somewhere working out the problems in her life." Even as she said it, Jordan couldn't help thinking it may already have been too late for hope or prayer.

"I appreciate you stopping by to tell me all this. I saw the article you wrote about me and Ginny, and I want to thank you for that, too." She stood up. "Can you stay and have breakfast with me?"

Jordan sighed. "I wish I could, but I'm already going to get a lecture from my boss for being late." She got up and walked to the door before digging into her purse for one of the business cards Egan had made when she'd taken over the job as the culinary reporter permanently. After she scribbled her cell phone number on the back, she handed it to Carlita. "Will you call me when you hear from Ginny?"

"I will. I appreciate you coming out here to check

on her. Can I at least send you to work with a few cake balls?"

"As much as I love your cake balls, the next time I eat them, it will be Friday night at the Italian Festival, along with Ginny's cacciatore."

"God bless you for saying that."

Jordan opened the door, waving one last time before she walked out. At the elevator, she slapped her head. What was the matter with her? She had just turned down a dessert that had to be ranked right up there in her top ten favorites of all time.

After stepping off the elevator on the first floor, she made it all the way to the exit, before suddenly turning back. Slipping past the desk clerk who was so engrossed in her computer game that she didn't even bother to glance up, she bypassed the elevator and walked to the stairwell door beside it. This was where the cameras had picked up Ginny Bruno leaving with an unknown person the last time she was seen.

She followed the steps down to the basement where she heard what sounded like dryers going full blast and spotted the laundry room in the back corner of the huge room. Walking in the opposite direction toward a door that looked like it opened to the outside, she let out a squeal when an older man in a janitor's uniform touched her arm.

"Sorry I scared you, miss. Are you lost? The guest rooms are all upstairs."

She put on her best girlie face and giggled. "Guess I am. Since I'm here, I'll just go out this way."

"That door takes you right out to the alley. The only things out there are garbage cans and a few stray cats."

"I'll be fine," she said, walking away before he could stop her. She turned around, deciding to play a hunch.

"Were you by chance on duty yesterday morning at the crack of dawn?"

"I live here, missy, and I work a split shift every day. Four hours in the morning and four in the evening. So, yes, I would've been here then."

Her hope mounted. "And did you see a woman in her thirties with olive skin and dark hair leaving out this door?"

He rubbed his chin as if he had to think about it for a moment. "Sure did. She was with a man in a hooded tee-shirt, I believe. There was something on the back, but I couldn't really see what it said."

Her hopes skyrocketed. "Did you see maybe a picture or something else on the shirt?"

He looked pensive before replying, "I kind of remember the letters ON."

"Did it appear she was being forced to leave?"

"Not really. Matter of fact I saw her smile up at him and say something as they went out the door, like she knew him."

SIXTEEN

THE DAY DRAGGED on until it was finally time to leave for the picnic. Jordan was going straight from the office to the fairgrounds and planned on staying only about an hour—long enough to get a few more recipes and maybe a good story or two before sneaking away. Even after drinking a beer the night before, sleep had evaded her, and she hadn't been able to stop yawning since lunchtime.

"Late night, Red?"

She swiveled her chair around to face Loretta Moseley after another long yawn. "Wouldn't you like to know?"

Staring at her nemesis, she remembered Victor's idea of leaving the spaghetti bread recipe that he'd rewritten in the locked drawer of her desk. He'd been so excited about beating Loretta at her own game, there was no doubt he'd lecture her for hours if she forgot to do it. Turning her back to the other woman, she made a big production out of digging the envelope from her purse.

After unfolding the paper, she pretended to read it over, trying hard not to glance Loretta's way to see if she was watching. As promised, Victor had left out the key ingredient—the spaghetti sauce. Without it, the entrée would just be dry noodles and cheese in the middle of a loaf of bread.

Jordan counted on Loretta having never actually tasted the finished product and not realizing something was missing. Sneaking a glance over her shoulder, she could see the woman pretending to be working away on her computer, yet watching her every move.

She leaned over, opened the drawer, and slid the envelope in. Then she locked it and threw the key into her purse, just like the last time. She glanced furtively over her shoulder to verify that Loretta was indeed still watching her. In that instant she knew Victor had been right and that her coworker would take the bait. After shutting down her computer, she turned out the light over her desk before gathering up her purse and walking toward the exit door.

Twisting around halfway there, she made eye contact with Loretta who was outright staring now. "Are you going to the picnic?"

Loretta shrugged. "Maybe later. Right now I have to finish up tomorrow's column."

Jordan waved goodbye and continued to make her way to the exit, biting her lower lip to keep from smiling. If tomorrow's column included the spaghetti bread recipe, Loretta was in for a rough weekend as her readers baked it using her directions.

By the time she slid behind the wheel of her car, she was already checking her watch to see how long she'd have to spend at the picnic before heading home and crawling into bed. With tomorrow being opening day of the festival, tonight was more or less a test run for the food vendors and arcade employees to work out any kinks before tomorrow night's opening. It was also the only time they'd be able to engage in a little festivities themselves.

Jordan and the Empire Apartments gang had already made plans to be there when the gates opened Friday at six. Alex had to be in Dallas all day on official FBI business, but he'd join them around seven. Kate and Natalie had elected not to attend on opening night and opted, instead, for a nice quiet evening with pizza and a salad.

She made a mental note to find some time to spend with Kate and her mother over the weekend to try and cheer them up. But that would have to wait until Saturday or Sunday since she planned on dragging Alex away from the gang on Friday after the festival for a little one-on-one time.

When she drove into the fairgrounds parking lot, there were already several rows of cars lined up. Pulling in beside an SUV, she thought about what she hoped to accomplish tonight. She wanted to try a few more of the food offerings and hopefully, talk the vendors into giving up the recipes. Although she might not be the *Ranchero Globe's* culinary reporter come Monday morning, she fully intended to give it her best shot and make it as difficult as she could for the woman who would do anything to steal her old job back.

For a fleeting moment, she felt a little sleazy for setting the trap, but she had to be prepared to fight for her job. If that meant playing by Loretta's rules, so be it.

She reminded herself that just like in war, you had to give as good as you got or go down in a hurry. She had no intentions of going away without a fight.

She walked across the parking lot to the entrance and handed her ID to the man at the gate. After checking it, he gave it back to her and waved her through. As soon as she got about a hundred yards into the fairgrounds area, she could already tell the picnic was going strong, probably the highlight of the weekend for the vendors. It was their only chance to let down their hair and party with their friends, since they'd work the booths the rest of the time.

And from the looks of it, Emilio had finally come through with the booze delivery. She hadn't even made it to the first booth before a man carrying a tray shoved a glass of red wine into her hands.

After thanking him, she took a sip and sauntered down the fairway, feeling a gush of sadness pulse through her as she passed the empty booths where she'd first met the Bruno sisters. Since she hadn't heard from Carlita she could only assume that Ginny had not returned to the hotel or called to say where she was. She looked upward and said a silent prayer to St. Jude, the patron saint of hopeless cases, for Ginny's safety.

Continuing down the fairway, she heard raised voices in a heated argument. She looked in that direction and saw Georgette Calabrese screaming at someone, her face scrunched in anger. The person on the other end of the petite woman's rage was behind the booth and out of Jordan's visual range. But whoever it was, he or she was getting a big dose of Georgette's temper, as she used her hands for emphasis and reverted to what Jordan could only imagine were Italian swear words.

She stopped at a booth about thirty yards from where the argument was taking place and leaned against the wooden counter so as not to appear too obvious with her eavesdropping. She was able to pick out the words "outsider" and "a nobody," but she was too far away to make out anything else Georgette was saying. She concentrated, wondering why the other person hadn't said a word through all that screaming.

Before she could hone in on what they were saying, a plump fortyish man beckoned to her from inside the booth with a sample of some kind of food in a small Styrofoam bowl.

She shook her head and held up her hand to decline

the sample and once again turned her attention to the heated action going on over by the next booth.

But the Italian vendor apparently had spied the press ID hanging from her neck and wasn't about to be rebuffed. He came out from around the booth and stood directly in front of her, waving a steaming bowl of pasta in front of her nose. "Try this, miss. It's the best baked ziti you'll ever taste."

Jordan glanced one last time to where Georgette had been standing only to see that Emilio's wife had disappeared. Frustrated that she might have missed an opportunity to help Kate, there was nothing else she could do right now. Turning back to the vendor, she returned his smile and reached for the pasta sample. Knowing he was anxiously waiting for her to try his offering, she took a small bite, just in case she hated it.

After a moment of silence, he shrugged. "Well?"

Jordan licked her lips and ate the rest in record time. After the last bite, she looked up. "I believe you speak the truth, Mr...." Her eyes darted to the sign across the top of his business. DEZI'S BAKED ZITI. "... Mr. Dezi?"

He laughed. "I told you so. Now drop the mister and call me Dez."

She reached across the counter and offered her hand. "Jordan McAllister. I write the culinary column for the local newspaper. What are the chances of you letting me print a copy of this recipe in tomorrow's edition?"

His smile stretched across his entire face. "I'd be honored. It's an old family recipe that my great grandmother brought over on the boat from Bologna." He grabbed her empty bowl and refilled it from the casserole dish on the warmer in the back of the booth. "My ziti is like those potato chips they advertise. You can't just have one serving." After he set it down in front of her, he leaned on the counter to watch her eat.

She didn't need coaxing and finished off the entire bowl in a few bites. Giving him a thumbs up, she said, "My compliments to your great-grandmother. And you, Dez, are about to make my readers very happy. I'm sure after I print the recipe, they'll be flocking to your booth this weekend to taste this awesome dish for themselves."

After shooting the breeze with the man for a few more minutes while he wrote out the recipe, Jordan thanked him and moved on. By the time she'd reached the other end where she and Bernardo Petrone's son had played flag football the day before, she'd sampled five other delicious Italian entrées and had scored recipes for all of them. Mentally, she high-fived herself for a job well done.

Glancing down at her watch, she decided she'd stayed long enough to be considered sociable. With the wine flowing like a downhill stream after a particularly wet rainy season, it looked like the party would go until well after midnight, and she needed to get home.

Setting her empty wine glass on a counter with a few others, she hastily declined the offer of a refill from a pretty Italian woman dressed in the traditional red, green, and white colors of the flag of Italy. Walking back to the entrance, she felt a tap on her shoulder from behind.

"Hey, beautiful, where've you been?"

She turned to face Frankie O'Brien who looked quite ridiculous in cutoffs and an NYU tank top. *Skinny arms like his should never be on display in a shirt like that,* she thought.

"It's good to see you, Frankie, but I was just leaving. Tomorrow's the big day for all of you, and I thought you'd want to party by yourselves. You all deserve to have fun without the press looking on."

He ran his fingers up her arm, sending involuntary chill bumps all the way to her elbow. "You can't go home yet. The real fun's just getting started."

"I see the liquor arrived," she said, backing up when he moved closer and she got a whiff of breath that reeked of alcohol. She moved a few more steps to her left to get away from his fingers still doing a slow dance up and down her arm.

"You got that straight. I was beginning to worry about it before—" He stopped talking as three men approached and stood directly in front of him.

"What's up, Frankie?" Speaking with a slight accent, the man sandwiched between two bigger ones had a smile on his face, even though his eyes remained hard when they zoned in on Frankie O'Brien.

If Jordan hadn't been looking right at Frankie, she would've missed the sudden shudder that coursed through his body before he smiled up at the new arrival. "We're partying, Romano. Let me get you a beer." He turned to walk away when the bigger man held up his hand and stopped him.

"That can wait. Right now I want to know why I had to make a trip all the way out here to find out why you're not holding up your end of the bargain."

Jordan knew the polite thing to do would be to walk away and let the two men have a private conversation, but she couldn't make herself do that. If there was even a smidgen of a chance that she'd learn something that might help Alex's sister, she had to be rude and stay put.

While the two men talked, she sized up the new arrival. Standing about six-two with black hair and eyes to match, the man loomed over Emilio Calabrese's much smaller stepson. Although he had on a T-shirt with sleeves, it was obvious he worked out because his muscles strained at the thin cotton covering his upper arms. Jordan couldn't help wondering how he'd look wearing the tank top that was so pathetic on Frankie O'Brien.

When she heard Frankie begging the other man for more time, she was jerked out of her imagery. She leaned in closer, hoping they wouldn't call her out for the overt snooping, but she needn't have worried about that. They were so engrossed in the conversation, they wouldn't have noticed a five hundred pound gorilla standing beside them.

"I think I made it perfectly clear what happens to people who don't come through on their promises," the big man was saying.

"It wasn't my fault the shipment was stolen, but I'm going to get it back." Frankie's face reflected his fear.

"I don't give a rat's ass whose fault it was. All I know is I've got a lot of money riding on that delivery. I'm tired of listening to my customers griping at me." He reached over and yanked Frankie's upper arm, almost lifting him off the ground.

The fear on Frankie's face escalated to terror. When Romano eased his grip and Frankie realized the guy wasn't going to smack him around, his shoulders relaxed, and he tried to smile. "I just need a few more days. Next week you'll have the shipment. I promise."

"Need I remind you of what happened to your partner the last time he didn't deliver?"

Frankie shook his head, and Romano released his hold on his arm. "Okay, then, as long as we're both aware of the consequences, you can get back to your celebration." He turned without ever acknowledging

Jordan and walked away with the two big men taking their positions on either side.

When the entourage was far enough away, Jordan stepped in front of Frankie. "Who was that?"

For a second, Frankie looked embarrassed, apparently realizing she'd seen him being bullied. "He's just a business associate. That's all."

"He seemed pretty angry about not getting his shipment." She had no idea what that meant, merely repeating what she'd heard Romano say.

Frankie turned to her, his face now red with anger. "That's none of your business, and you'd be wise to forget what you heard."

"You're right. It is none of my concern. I guess I'll see you then."

He reached for her arm. "I didn't mean to raise my voice to you. It's just that Romano Ortiz did upset me a little, and I could use a stiff drink right about now. I'd love for you to join me."

She wanted to say that since he was well on his way to the proverbial three sheets, the last thing he needed was more alcohol. Instead she pulled her arm away. "Sorry. I'm already getting a headache from just one glass of wine, plus I have a long day tomorrow." Then as if to smooth things over, she added, "I'll be here tomorrow night with my friends, though. We'd love to have that drink with you."

He frowned. "I don't do well with crowds. I was thinking more along the lines of something a little cozier with just you and me."

She fought hard not to wrinkle her nose at the suggestion. "I'm not sure my boyfriend would be too happy about that." Turning, she started toward the exit, wishing she could see his face after dropping that little tidbit.

When she was in the car on her way back to Ranchero, she began to think about what she'd just witnessed between Frankie and Romano. Frankie was definitely afraid of the man—and with good reason. Anybody who looked like Romano and showed up with two goons built like Sumo wrestlers was not to be taken lightly. His thinly veiled threat left Jordan searching her brain, trying to remember an earlier her conversation she'd had with Frankie.

And then it came to her. The first time she'd met him, he'd mentioned that he'd been in some kind of a business deal with Marco Petrone, then covered by saying he meant family business.

Hadn't Romero Ortiz just said he didn't want Frankie to end up like his partner for not delivering the goods? Could he be referring to Marco Petrone?

Holy crap! Had Romano just confessed to killing Marco? And who had Georgette Calabrese been screaming at?

SEVENTEEN

"YOU'VE HIT A home run with this recipe," the tall blonde hollered across Jordan's cubicle, flashing Loretta Moseley a thumbs up.

Jordan's head shot up from the stack of personal ads she'd been working on since she'd walked into the building several hours before. She figured there must have been another sale on them because there was double the usual number waiting for her when she walked in the door. She'd had to put everything else on hold in order to get the ads ready for the weekend edition and hadn't even stopped to heed nature's call. That in itself was a miracle considering the huge amount of caffeine she'd already consumed since she'd arrived.

She'd been so busy she'd totally forgotten about planting the bait recipe in her locked drawer before she'd left the night before. Glancing to her right, she made eye contact with Loretta, who was smiling at her—and not in a friendly way. It was more like an I-bested-you-once-again smirk.

Jordan studied her face for a few moments before grabbing the key from her purse and opening the drawer, fully expecting to find the recipe missing like the last time. But it was there—right where she'd left it. Relief washed over her when she realized Victor's prediction of Loretta breaking into her drawer again had been wrong. She was just beginning to upgrade her faith in the honesty of mankind when she heard Loretta snort.

"You don't think I'd be dumb enough to give you the evidence to run to Egan and report the recipe missing, do you?"

Jordan squinted with a fake-surprised look. "What are you talking about, Loretta?"

"You know good and well what I'm talking about, Red. You just got another step closer out the door." She chuckled. "Go ahead. Check out today's culinary column. Yours is all about how the Italian Festival started back in San Francisco over a decade ago, and mine is a recipe for an awesome braided spaghetti bread." She chuckled again, this time louder. "Which one do you think the readers will like the best?"

Jordan exited the personals page and pulled up the home screen showing today's edition. Even before she clicked over to the culinary column, she already knew what would be there. And she wasn't disappointed. BRAIDED SPAGHETTI BREAD stared out at her in bold letters across the top of the page. Ginny's Braided Spaghetti Bread recipe minus a cup of spaghetti sauce, proving that the woman definitely had lifted it from the drawer.

Ah ha! You've just made your first big mistake, missy.

Biting her lower lip to keep from smiling, she turned to her nemesis. "I hate to tell you this, but the reason I haven't published the recipe myself is because it's missing a key ingredient."

Loretta's face fell. "What key ingredient?"

Jordan shrugged. "I have no idea. All I know is that Ginny left a message on my voicemail that she'd messed up when she wrote it out and that she'd be calling to fix it." She crossed her fingers behind her back as if that would neutralize the lie. "I'm still waiting on that information."

Loretta grabbed the phone and quickly punched in a number. After waiting a few seconds and tapping her nails nervously on the desk, she shouted into the receiver. "Hank, have all the copies of today's edition gone out yet?"

Jordan didn't need to hear the man in the print room on the other end. Everyone knew the day's newspapers had already been delivered in the middle of the night, and she was pretty sure the frown on Loretta's face was caused by hearing Hank confirm that.

She slammed the phone down before turning her fury on Jordan. "You did that on purpose, didn't you?"

Jordan feigned innocence. "I had no idea you would be stupid enough to steal from my drawer a second time, Loretta." She raised one eyebrow. "Maybe you'll get lucky and no one will notice."

"You're a bee-otch."

"Takes one to know one." Jordan turned her attention back to the computer and pulled up the personals again. She had to call on every ounce of willpower she had not to sneak a peek at Loretta's face right then. When she heard her audible sigh of frustration, she couldn't help herself and smiled once again.

Chalk one up for the new girl.

The rest of the day was uneventful, although every time Loretta's phone rang, Jordan's ears would perk up and she'd lean to her right to listen to the conversation. But there were no angry calls from readers or a summons to Egan's office, which made sense since there hadn't been time for anyone to try the recipe yet.

At exactly five o'clock, she gathered up her stuff and headed out, unable to resist a grin as she passed Loretta's empty desk. Shortly after lunch, the woman had pleaded a headache and gone home—probably to work on a damage control strategy.

Driving down Main Street, Jordan glanced up at the overhead banners announcing the festival and felt a surge of excitement. It was a big deal for the area and the vendors who needed a big turnout. She hoped everything went well.

She pulled into a parking space halfway between Lola's Spiritual Readings and Yesterday's Treasures. She, Lola, and Victor planned to meet Ray and Rosie at the festival. Michael and his radio crew had already been there since four that afternoon to broadcast from the fairway.

As if he'd been watching for her, Victor emerged from the antiques shop and locked the door before sliding into the backseat of her Camry. Immediately, he began to babble on about seeing Loretta's recipe in the newspaper.

"You should've seen the look on her face when I told her the key ingredient was missing," Jordan said, waving hello from the front.

"What? Why'd you go and tell her that? Now she can just reprint it tomorrow," he said, looking up when Lola opened the door and slipped into the front seat. "Hey, girlfriend, is that a new mu mu?"

She gave him a disgusted look. "For a fashionista like you claim to be, you should know they don't call them that anymore. I'll have you know I'm wearing a below-the-knee caftan." She smoothed the front of her dress over her generous figure and winked at Jordan.

"Whatever," he said, leaning closer to Jordan. "Back to you. Did you tell Loretta you left out the key ingredient on purpose, or did it just slip out accidently?"

"Are you kidding me? Of course I meant to tell her. She would've run to Uncle Earl so fast, it would've made my head spin. And I suspect after all the complaints they get tomorrow, Egan and his boss won't think our little plan is as funny as we do. I'll be back to writing only the personals before you can say spaghetti bread."

"Who wants to say it? I want to eat it. But you might have a point. I still say you would've gotten more satisfaction out of her not knowing she'd been had until the boss lowered the boom," he said.

"My satisfaction will be keeping my job." Jordan picked up speed and entered the freeway. "Enough about that. How was your day, Lola?"

"Busy. Seems like everyone wanted their tarot cards read today. Even did a reading for the guy we met the other night when the Italian dude took a dive off the balcony."

"What guy?" Both Jordan and Victor asked in unison.

"You know—that well-dressed man who couldn't keep his eyes off Alex's mother. The one whose daughter was supposed to marry the dead guy."

Jordan nearly swerved off the road. "Emilio Calabrese came by your shop today?"

Lola nodded. "Yes. Said he was checking out downtown Ranchero and remembered that I had mentioned owning the psychic shop. And I gotta say, he seemed wound up tighter than…" She paused. "Let's just say he was so wired he couldn't stop his hands from shaking and nearly fell twice getting to the table."

"Do you know why?" Jordan asked.

"He never said, although it was obvious he wanted reassurance that his daughter wouldn't end up in a bad way."

"Those were his words? In a bad way?"

Lola nodded again.

"Wonder what he meant by that?" Victor asked.

"No clue," Jordan said. "Although I do know that Tina was questioned by the Plainville police the other day after Ginny Bruno said she'd seen her go up to the bedroom suite with another man that night, even though Marco was already up there."

"Sheesh!" Lola exclaimed. "Wish I had known that when the guy was in the shop. I could've gotten more specific with my questions to him and maybe discovered if his daughter was the one who offed her fiancé."

"Do you think Calabrese thinks Tina pushed Marco off the balcony?" Victor asked from the back.

"I don't know, but he did say he'd do anything for her. He loves her very much."

"Yeah, so much so that he was forcing her to marry a man she didn't love when she was actually in a relationship with his brother."

"What?" Victor rubbed his hands together. "This is getting good—like our own little soap opera. How'd you find out that little tidbit, anyway? Surely, Tina didn't admit it."

"I talked to Bernardo Petrone a few nights ago when I was at the fairgrounds looking for stories. He didn't actually say he and Tina were having a thing, but I got the distinct impression that number one, he didn't really like his brother, and two, he was in love with Tina Calabrese."

"Jeez. This keeps getting better and better." Victor leaned so far forward Jordan could feel his hot breath on the back of her head.

"Is your seatbelt on, Victor?" she asked, shivering involuntarily as the hair on her neck stood at attention. "Cause you always say I drive like a maniac."

"You do," he replied. "But I'll take my chances. I

don't want to miss any of this. Do you have any other juicy gossip you haven't told us?"

"Yes, but I want to hold off until Alex gets here so I only have to tell it once." She giggled. "Wait till you find out what I heard last night."

He groaned. "You're such a tease, Jordan. At least give me a hint."

"Oh, can it, Victor. You're like a little kid who expects everything the second he wants it. She'll tell us in due time," Lola said, before turning to Jordan. "Okay, now that I've gotten back at him for calling my dress a mu mu, you can give us one little hint, can't you?"

Jordan laughed. "Let's just say someone may have confessed to killing Marco last night." She turned and made a big deal of zipping her lips. "That's all you'll get until I feast my eyes on Alex."

She exited the freeway and drove toward the Plainville Fairgrounds, glad to be so close. Knowing how persistent Victor could be, she knew she wouldn't last much longer before he would somehow wiggle the story out of her, and she wanted Alex to hear it first.

"Just so you know, there probably won't be any spaghetti bread tonight," she said, changing the subject.

"Damn! I was really looking forward to tasting that again. I guess that means Ginny hasn't shown her face at the hotel yet."

Jordan shook her head. "No, and I'm getting really worried, although her sister says it wouldn't be the first time Ginny has disappeared for a few days."

"Let's hope that's all there is to it," Lola said.

After pulling into the parking lot, she spotted Ray's Suburban at the other end. She drove down the row of cars and slid her Camry into the vacant spot beside his vehicle. The minute she was out of the car, Rosie ran up and hugged her.

"Girl, it seems like ages since I last saw you. I've missed you."

"Me too," Jordan said when Rosie finally released her. "But I've been really busy trying to get stories and recipes that will help me keep my job." She failed to mention how much snooping she'd been doing.

"Tell her about the spaghetti bread recipe," Victor said, visibly excited. "It was all my idea."

"I will, but let's get in line first. It's already snaking around the perimeter."

The five of them made their way to the end of the line while Jordan retold the recipe story.

"The old bat finally got a taste of her own medicine," Victor said, obviously proud of himself for thinking of it in the first place.

"It's a good thing Michael's not here," Ray said, thumping the top of his head. "The last time you called her that, he was all over you about it."

Victor ignored him and moved closer to Jordan. "She may know who killed Marco, but she's making us wait until Alex gets here." He stomped his foot. "Come on, kiddo. I'm dying here."

Ray nailed her with a stare. "Tell me you haven't been poking around the murder investigation, little girl. If I'm remembering correctly, every time you start playing detective, you end up in big trouble."

She shook her head. No way she'd fess up to her meddling. "I just overheard something that should help Kate's lawyer get her off. That's all."

"Good." Ray turned to the group. "So, who besides me is going to gorge themselves on homemade Italian food?"

"Me, me," Victor said, raising his hand. "And Jordan may be able to get it for us free."

"Oh no, you don't," she said. "I like free food as much as the next guy, but now that I've met a few of the vendors, I know how much they're counting on making a profit." She punched him playfully. "And weren't you just bragging about how much money you made off that antique bedroom set you sold this week?"

"Shh," he whispered with a laugh. "I don't want to spring for everyone tonight."

"Like that would ever happen," Lola said, unable to keep the mischief out of her eyes. "You, my friend, are the biggest cheapskate I know."

"Have you met Michael? He hoards every penny we make and socks it back into the apartment building. He even has me packing a lunch every day because he said I was spending too much on fast food." Victor frowned. "At least that's what he says, but it doesn't take a brain surgeon to know what he's really up to. He thinks I need to lose a few pounds and makes sure I take the carrot sticks he bags for me every day." He chuckled. "Wouldn't he die if he knew I feed them to the two big rabbits behind Myrtle's Diner in exchange for a greasy cheeseburger?"

"What's up with this line? We've barely moved an inch in ten minutes," Rosie complained.

"It's a different world we live in, my friend," Ray said. "Security is much tighter everywhere you go."

"I know that, but I don't have to like it," she said just as the line finally began to move. "Alright!"

Even so, it took them fifteen minutes to make it inside the gate and another fifteen to purchase food and ride tickets. Then they started down the fairway for a night of fun. Jordan had already decided the next few hours would be strictly all play and no work, and from the looks of it, everyone from Plainville and the neighboring cities had the same idea. There were lines at every food booth, and the Ferris wheel was going nonstop with a full load every time and a line that wrapped around two food booths.

At the end of the fairway, they turned around to walk down the other side to check everything else out. Several booths down, the area had been cleared, and there was a Bocce ball tournament in progress.

When they stopped to watch, Victor asked, "So what's the object of this game, Jordan? Two old guys at one end try to get their big balls close to the smaller one at the other end where another two old guys are waiting their turns?"

She laughed. "It's more complicated than that. The smaller ball is called a pallino, and they score points by—"

"Hey, Jordan, do you want to be my partner and play?"

Everyone turned to the young boy who was now looking up at Jordan with adoring eyes.

"Can't tonight. Sorry."

Victor tsked. "A little young even for you, Jordan. Don't you think?"

"Should I be worried?"

Jordan felt Alex's soft lips on the back of her neck before she even realized he was behind her. She squealed and turned into his body, planting a soft kiss on his lips. "I've missed you so much."

"Ditto," he said. "Now back to your young admirer."

She turned to the boy and gave him a peck on the cheek, which brought out the cutest pink flush across his face. "I call this sweet young man Sure Hands because he's better at catching a touchdown pass than a lot of NFL wide receivers." Playfully, she messed up the kid's hair, causing the blush across his cheeks to deepen. "But his friends know him as Gio. He's Bernardo Petrone's son."

Rosie was the first one to react and extended her hand. "Nice to meet you, Gio. Now tell us why our friend already has a nickname for you."

He smiled up at Jordan. "The other night she threw five touchdown passes to me. We kicked major butt."

"All this time I've been feeling guilty about not being around much. Here I thought my girl was pining away for me, and now I find out she's been carrying on with a bunch of guys."

"Boys," Jordan corrected, before turning back to Gio. "Where's your dad tonight?"

"He's around here somewhere looking for Mrs. Calabrese."

"Georgette Calabrese?"

"Yeah. My dad's been trying to get a hold of her since this afternoon, but no one knows where she is."

"I'm sure he'll find her. After all, she is running the whole show here," she said. "Hey, do you want to have dinner with us?"

He shook his head. "Already ate. I need to find Vince to talk him into getting in on the Bocce ball action with me. They're playing for real money," he announced.

"Then, by all means, go find your friend. I'll catch up with you later." She gave him a gentle shove along with an air kiss.

"That boy's in love," Lola said with a grin.

"Yeah, I seem to attract all the young ones," Jordan said before adding, "Or the screwed-up older ones."

"Hey, wait a minute," Alex protested. "I'm not messed up."

She grinned. "So you're admitting you're attracted to me?"

He did a slow scan of her entire body, making her wish she was wearing something a little sexier than jeans and a T-shirt.

"I think you know the answer to that one, but just in case you've forgotten, I fully intend to show you how much later on."

"Oh no. You're not going to talk about that stuff with me standing right here." Rosie threw her hands in the air. "Single, horny as hell, remember?"

They all laughed and continued down the fairway to the area designated as the food court. Tables covered with red and white checked tablecloths were filling up fast as customers stopped to try the food.

"Grab that big table over there," Victor said, pointing to a vacant one. "That way we can all sit together. We'll take turns getting our food."

Lola and Ray walked over to the table while the rest of them wandered around the food booths trying to decide what to sample. By the time Jordan made her way back there, her plate was piled high with baked ziti, asparagus risotto, sausage and peppers, and three cannolis."

"Don't say a word," she cautioned when Ray glanced down at her plate and frowned.

"How you manage to stay so skinny is beyond me." He shook his head. "And you don't even work out."

"Oh, leave her alone," Lola said. "And go get yourself a plate as big as hers. I'll help you work it off later tonight."

"Criminy!" Rosie said as she joined them. "Did you

not get the memo about keeping your bedroom adventures to yourself?"

"Hey, guys." Michael waved as he walked over with his own plate. "I have thirty minutes to kill before I have to get back to the broadcast. We're having a blast. Come by later, and I might even put you on the radio." He turned to greet Victor when he appeared with a plate piled even higher than Jordan's. "You know pasta has a lot of carbs, right?"

"I do know that," Victor said, before shoving a huge bite of baked ziti into his mouth. "But thanks for reminding me. Now sit down so Jordan can tell us about the guy who killed Marco."

Alex turned to her. "You know who killed Marco?"

Jordan huffed. "That's exactly how rumors get started, Victor. I didn't say I knew who the killer was. I only mentioned that I overheard a conversation where someone may have confessed to it."

Alex put down the fork and wiped his mouth with a napkin. "Okay, let's hear it, because frankly, right now Jeff Hamilton is at a dead-end as far as finding new evidence to clear my sister."

"Oh no. I thought after they talked to Tina and she admitted going up the stairs with another man the night Marco was killed that there would be enough reasonable doubt for them to clear Kate."

"Tina admitted going to the other bedroom up there, but she insists she was alone. She swears the witness—who no one can find—was mistaken. Jeff said we'd have to wait for the actual trial so he could subpoena her and try to get that information when she's under oath."

"I'm pretty sure the other guy was Bernardo Petrone," Jordan said. When all eyes turned her way, she explained. "I met him the other night when I played flag football with Gio. He pretty much told me he hated his brother and that he was in love with Tina Calabrese. I think the feeling is mutual, and that's why she was so mad at her father for making her go through with the marriage to Marco."

"Wow! I need to call Jeff and tell him these new developments. Hopefully, it will give him something to work with," Alex said. "As it stands right now, he's suggesting it might be wise for Kate to cut a deal with the DA. So far they're offering manslaughter with jail time, but he's trying to get that changed to probation only."

"But Kate didn't kill Marco," Lola said. "Why would she agree to something like that?"

"Because there's no proof that anyone else was in the suite except her and Tina. And since Kate's DNA was found under Marco's fingernails and the police have determined that he was definitely pushed, it's a crapshoot about how the jury will go," Alex explained, unable to hide the frustration in his voice.

"How can they be so sure that he was pushed rather than just being so drunk that he accidently fell over the railing?" Victor asked.

"A few things," Alex said. "A jumper lands close to the building, whereas someone who is pushed usually screams all the way down and ends up farther out on the pavement the way Marco did."

"Nowhere in the police report does it mention that anyone heard him screaming," Ray said.

"That's true, but don't forget, the ME determined that the gaping wound on the back of his head couldn't have been caused by the fall since he landed facedown. The theory is that someone cold-cocked him, and he was probably unconscious when he went over the railing." He turned to Jordan just as she shoved the last bite of cannoli into her mouth. "And what's this about someone confessing to the murder?"

For the next fifteen minutes, Jordan relayed the story about Frankie O'Brien and Romano Ortiz from the night before, specifically leaving out the part about Frankie hitting on her.

"This could really be helpful, Jordan," Alex said, visibly excited. "Remind me to give you an extra long kiss tonight." He held up his hand just as Rosie's eyebrows furrowed into a V. "I know. I know. No more talk about that. Let's finish up here so I can take my favorite girl on the Ferris wheel and show her the stars."

By the time they'd finished eating, everyone was fired up about trying the games and the rides. Alex stepped away from the table to make the phone call to Kate's lawyer. Jordan was anxious to see if Gio and his friend Vince had entered the Bocce ball tournament so she could cheer them on.

As they cleared the table, Alex returned to the group with a grin. "Jeff's optimistic about the new developments. Hopefully, he'll be able to use—" He stopped talking when the phone rang in his hand. "It's my mother. If you'll excuse me, I need to make sure everything's okay." He stood and moved away to a quieter spot.

When he returned several minutes later, he shook his head, a grim expression on his face.

"What happened, Alex? Is it something about Kate?" Jordan asked.

"Not Kate. It's Georgette Calabrese. The police just found her body in a car on an abandoned cattle ranch about five miles north of here."

EIGHTEEN

"OH MY GOD!" Victor exclaimed. "Was she murdered?"

Alex shrugged. "They won't know until the ME does an autopsy, but the initial guess is that Georgette Calabrese died of heat stroke. They think she was in the car for several hours, and you know how hot it was today."

Jordan couldn't believe what she was hearing. First Marco Petrone is murdered, then Ginny Bruno goes missing, and now Georgette Calabrese was dead. Could it be that the Italian Festival was somehow cursed? "Are they sure it was Georgette and not Ginny?" she asked as the thought suddenly popped into her head.

"It's Georgette," Alex said. "My mother found out when Emilio called a little while ago."

"Oh boy! I'll bet he's freaking out. First his future son-in-law and now his wife," Lola said. "I wonder if that's why he was so distraught earlier when he came to see me at the psychic shop."

Alex turned to face her. "Emilio Calabrese came to see you today?"

"Right after lunch. He was pretty upset and asked me to read his tarot cards."

Alex tilted his head and raised an eyebrow. "Did you get the impression that he was nervous about something?"

"Oh yeah. He was nervous, alright. I think he wanted me to tell him that everything in his life would be okay."

"Hmm. The cops said Georgette's car was like an

oven with a temperature reading of over 150 degrees when they found her. She had to have been in the hot sun for at least an hour, probably longer. Going on that assumption, it's possible Emilio knew about her when he came to see you."

"Are you saying what I think you're saying?" Victor asked, moving closer to Alex. "You think he might've killed his own wife?"

"Whoa! Don't go jumping to conclusions, my friend. I'm only suggesting that Georgette may have already been dead when Emilio went to Lola's shop. That's all." Alex raised his hand to his mouth to cover a yawn. "Sorry, guys, between the day job and my sister, I've been running on fumes. Would y'all mind if I cut out early to spend some alone time with Jordan? I've got a hot case going on over in Ellis County right now that we're ready to move on, and I have to be in Dallas by nine tomorrow morning."

Jordan smiled up at him, suddenly feeling like a teenager about to get her first kiss. Since his mother and sister had arrived in Ranchero two weeks before, she'd barely seen Alex. She was already anticipating cuddling up to him in her warm bed. "I'm pretty tired, too," she said, turning to her friends. "So I guess we'll see you guys back at the apartment?"

"I'll go home with Michael," Victor said.

Ray waved them on. "Go enjoy each other. I'll take the girls home in a little while. Keep us informed about Emilio, will you, Alex?"

"Will do." Alex reached for Jordan's hand. "Are you disappointed we're not staying around to have that Ferris wheel ride?"

She shook her head. "Let's see. A ride with lots of

people around or just you and me at my apartment? What do you think?"

He grinned, making her wish they were already there. She wasn't sure she could wait much longer to feel his body next to hers.

"That's exactly what I wanted to hear," he murmured under his breath, picking up the pace. When she was slow to follow suit, he nudged her. "Keep up, woman. We've only got about ten hours, and I plan to make the most of every one of them."

WAKING UP IN Alex's arms the next morning felt exactly like she knew it would, and if she were a cat, she would be purring right now. She glanced up and met his gaze, noticing the way his eyes crinkled with mischief when he saw her looking.

Yawning, he slid the covers off. "I would give anything to stay here all day with you, love, but I can't. My guys are closing in on a gang of men selling weapons to all the wrong people, and I need to get to the office to coordinate the takedown." He bent over and gave her a long kiss that made her wish his job didn't require taking on all the evil people in the world.

She pushed out her lower lip in a pout. "I knew you were a love 'em and leave 'em type from the moment I first met you."

He laughed, pointing his finger at her. "After we put the criminals in jail today, and my mom and sister are back in Houston, you just try to get rid of me. And why would I want to leave, anyway? Didn't I use the 'L' word on you not too long ago?"

Her eyes opened wide. "I thought it was something you say casually to everyone."

He pulled her close. "Just for the record, I've only

said it one other time in my life to someone who didn't qualify as close family, so no, there was nothing casual about it." He lifted her chin with his thumb and forefinger. "I don't know if you feel the same way, but I promise that's a conversation we're going to have in the near future." He kissed her lips lightly and then crawled out of bed and padded to the shower.

He loves me! She thought, taking a deep breath and releasing the air slowly. She wasn't sure exactly how she felt about that, though. There was no doubt she had deep feelings for the man, even tingled just being near him, but it had only been a little over a year since her life had been all about the guy she thought she'd grow old with.

And look how that had ended. She had to be sure she was ready to make that kind of commitment, assuming that's what he wanted to talk about. Was it possible he just wanted an exclusive commitment? Weren't they already at that stage?

For the first time since moving to Ranchero, she felt the need to talk to her mother. Sylvia McAllister had been the only one who'd recognized how hurt Jordan had been after Brett broke her heart. Even made a surprise visit to Dallas to make sure her daughter was okay. Jordan's father and brothers, on the other hand, had a much different plan to deal with it. They were ready to hop in the pickup, drive like maniacs, and beat the crap out of her ex.

But her mother had talked them out of that, knowing it was the last thing Jordan needed. Although it might have given her a smidgeon of satisfaction, she'd known even then that the feeling wouldn't have lasted. What she'd needed had been for someone to hold her while she cried and to listen without judging. Sylvia McAllister had come through with flying colors. And although she hadn't bombarded Jordan with advice about what to say or do, she'd helped by letting her talk it out and grieve for a lost love without saying, "I told you so."

Jordan desperately wanted to talk to her now.

"Penny for your thoughts," Alex said, emerging from the bathroom with his hair still dripping and his lower body covered with only a towel.

She smiled up at him. "I was wishing you didn't have to run into Dallas today," she said, before moving her eyebrows up and down. "And how much I'd like to swipe that towel away from you right now."

"You are such a devil. You know I need to be on the road soon and yet you tease." His grin covered his face. "Hold that thought, though. As soon as I put a few criminals behind bars, I'll find a way for us to be together again tonight." He turned and walked back into the bathroom before sticking his head out the door. "Did I mention that I might have a few minutes to run by Myrtle's and pick up a few pieces of her famous Chocolate Chip Coffeecake before I leave?"

That diverted Jordan's attention away from the sexy stuff. "I'll put on the coffee."

Much later, after they'd devoured the coffee cake and Jordan was alone again in her apartment, she pulled out her laptop and began to work on the next day's culinary column. Before long, she was so engrossed in a story about Italian traditions that she'd nearly lost it when her phone suddenly blared out Carrie Underwood's *When He Cheats*.

Grabbing it, she glanced at caller ID. Alex's mother. Why was she calling? She hit *Talk*, more than a little nervous. "Hello."

"Jordan, do you have plans for today?" Natalie asked.

"I was going to work on my story for Sunday's paper. I have to have it in by six tonight. Why?"

There was a pause. "I know you don't like Emilio—"

"I don't dislike him," Jordan interrupted. "There's just something about the man that makes me uncomfortable."

"I know. But I was hoping you'd do something for me that will probably take you out of your comfort zone." There was silence as Alex's mother waited for Jordan to respond. When she didn't, Natalie continued. "Kate took the car and is with Jeff Hamilton at the DA's office, and of course, you know that Alex is in Dallas. I need a ride."

Anticipating something way worse, Jordan was pleasantly surprised at the request, and she chose to ignore the reference about Alex spending the night at her apartment. "Of course, Natalie. Where do you want me to take you?"

"To Emilio's hotel room."

For one of the few times in her life, Jordan was speechless. Out of her comfort zone? What Natalie was asking was more like out of her comfort country. How could she take Alex's mother to her ex-boyfriend's hotel room in all good conscience?

"He called a little while ago and begged me to come over. He sounded really distraught over Georgette's death."

Jordan's first instinct was to say 'Not no, but hell no.' "Are you sure this is something you want to do, Natalie? Because going to his hotel room could be misinterpreted by a lot of people."

"Sounds like you're one of them," Natalie responded a little sharply before her voice softened. "He's an old friend, Jordan, and right now, he has no one else to turn to."

"What about Tina? She must be grieving for her step-mother, too."

"He gave me the impression he's worried about her and doesn't want to add to her emotional state."

"Worried about her? Why?" Jordan asked, getting more confused by the minute. Was Emilio afraid his daughter would do something crazy or harm herself over this?

"I don't know. He only said he'd do anything to pro-tect her, and he wants to talk to me." She paused, as if allowing it all to sink in. "So, will you take me, or do I need to call a cab?"

Jordan mulled this one over for a moment before de-ciding Natalie would be safer if she had someone with her. "Okay, I'll get dressed and be over there in thirty minutes." Even as she said it, she was already praying when Alex found out that she'd helped his mother visit an old boyfriend, he wouldn't hold it against her.

"Terrific. I'll be waiting outside."

Jordan chugged the last of her coffee, shut down her laptop, and took a quick shower. By the time she pulled up in front of Alex's house, Natalie was pacing back and forth on the front porch. When she saw Jordan's car, she raced out to greet her.

"I can't thank you enough," she said after she was settled in the front seat. "I've never seen this side of Emilio before."

"I hope you know what you're doing," Jordan cau-tioned, stopping before she spilled the beans about Emilio's visit with Lola the day before. Better to keep that information to herself, along with the suspicion that it was possible Emilio had already known about his wife's death when Lola read his tarot cards.

"Don't worry," Natalie said, reaching over and patting Jordan shoulder. "This won't turn out badly. I promise."

NINETEEN

THERE WAS VERY little conversation on the drive to the Crown Royale Hotel. Pulling up to the entrance, Jordan couldn't help glancing at the spot where Marco Petrone had landed when he'd fallen from the balcony. She fully expected to see a chalk outline of a dead body and was disappointed there was none. If she hadn't witnessed the horrific event, she wouldn't have guessed that the driveway had once been a crime scene.

"Let the valet park the car," Natalie said. When Jordan shot her a look, she added, "You drove. I'll take care of parking."

"We'll split it," Jordan said, not wanting Alex's mother to think she was cheap. But after spending the extra bucks for the shoes to go with the dress she'd worn to the party, her budget was stretched to the limit.

"Deal." Natalie stepped out of the car when a young man appeared out of nowhere and opened the door.

Jordan was already out of the car when he attempted to do the same for her, and she handed him the keys. After taking the ticket from him, she and Natalie walked through the beveled glass doors onto the marble floor where she was reminded once again how luxurious the lobby was.

Natalie slipped her arm through Jordan's. "Come on. Emilio's room is on the eighth floor, and he said to come right up when we arrived."

On the elevator ride up, Jordan tried to dissuade

Natalie one last time. "You don't have to do this, you know." When Natalie smiled up at her, she finally gave up and added, "Okay, if you suddenly decide you want to leave after we get in there, just ask if I've finished my article for tomorrow's paper. I'll make a big deal out of it and say I have to go home."

"It's going to be okay, Jordan," she said, reassuringly. "Emilio is a powerful man to a lot of people, but to me, he's simply an old friend who needs my support right now. He's just a big old bear sometimes."

Jordan was convinced that nothing she said would change Natalie's opinion of the man. "I get it, but remember our 'get out of there in a hurry' signal just in case."

She still had reservations about coming to Emilio's hotel room in the first place, and even though Natalie viewed him as harmless, Jordan wasn't anywhere near convinced. When Alex had first introduced her to Emilio, he'd mentioned the man was connected, and that didn't happen because he was a 'big ole teddy bear.'

Emilio opened the door on the first knock, dressed in a pair of black slacks and a jacket that reminded Jordan of what the old-time movies used to call smoking jackets.

He hugged Natalie, then acknowledged Jordan with a nod. "I'm so grateful to you for bringing my friend here today."

All she could think to do was shrug as she checked out the room. There was a living area off to one side with a large couch and two chairs. An office of sorts filled the other corner with a desk and a computer. The king-sized bed was in the back along with the bathroom, and she could see what looked like a Jacuzzi out on the balcony. Although it wasn't nearly as big as Marco's suite had been, the whole area was twice the size of her apartment. She wondered if Emilio really wanted Natalie there for support or if he'd planned a nice quiet hot tub party for two.

While he was making small talk with Natalie, Jordan used the time to study the man who had seemed so overbearing and scary when he'd showed up at her apartment a few nights before. His dark eyes, demanding and threatening then, were now reddened and slightly swollen. Realizing he'd been crying softened her opinion of him, and she felt the ball of fire in her stomach beginning to die down. Maybe this wouldn't be as bad as she'd anticipated.

He walked over to a rolling cart beside the couch and took the lids off several trays. "I had room service send these up in case you were hungry," he explained.

"I've already eaten," Jordan said, still not ready to make nice and break bread with him. Then she made the mistake of glancing toward the uncovered dishes and almost slapped herself.

He caught her looking and smiled. "They're éclairs. I was told you have a sweet tooth, and it's my way of thanking you for bringing Natalie here today."

"Maybe later, Emilio," Natalie said. "I don't know how long Jordan can stay because she's got a deadline for tomorrow's newspaper. Why don't we all grab a cup of coffee and sit down?"

Jordan caught the side glance from Natalie and knew she was setting Emilio up in case she decided to bolt.

He walked to the tray and picked up the carafe, but his hands were shaking so badly, he had to set it down again. Natalie was beside him in a flash and motioned for him to move to the couch. Obediently, he did as she'd indicated. Jordan took the cup from Natalie and settled into the chair farthest away from him. Much to her surprise, Natalie sat down beside him and reached for his hand.

"I'm so sorry about Georgette, Emilio. You must be devastated."

Tears rimmed his eyes. "She was a good woman. I met her a year after my Lillian died of breast cancer. I was struggling to run the business with a two-year-old who demanded every second of my attention. Georgette was like a savior to all of us."

"I'm sure you loved her very much," Natalie said, sending another furtive glance Jordan's way.

Jordan wondered if Natalie was thinking the same thing she was about Georgette sleeping with Marco and whether or not Emilio knew.

"I suppose we were in love in the beginning, but at some point, we just became convenient for each other. She needed stability for Frankie, and I needed help with Tina." He stopped to take a sip of coffee and nearly spilled it when his hands began shaking again. "Lately, we'd become more like friends than lovers."

"Sometimes, that can be more important," Natalie said softly. "Either way, her death must have hit you hard, especially coming so soon after Marco was killed."

At the mention of the man who would have been his son-in-law, more tears escaped down Emilio's face. Jordan thought it strange that he showed more emotion for Marco then he had for his own wife.

"I loved that man," he said. "Even though I knew in my heart he was not the perfect match for Tina. It was obvious he could never be satisfied with just one woman, but I kept hoping he'd change."

"Tina didn't love him," Jordan said, before she could stop herself. She pressed her lips together to keep from saying any more and waited for his angry command to mind her own business—which would be totally justified.

Instead of screaming at her, he lowered his head. "I know. But I don't have a lot of time here, and I was praying that eventually, her feelings for him would grow."

"Why was it so important that she marry Marco?" Natalie asked, getting up to refill the coffee cups.

"I'm dying."

Natalie nearly dropped her cup and was by his side in an instant. "What do you mean you're dying?"

He swallowed hard before meeting her intense gaze. "I'm sure you've noticed the way my hands shake and the way I'm sometimes unsteady on my feet." When she nodded, he continued, "Last month I went to see my internist, fully expecting him to tell me that I needed to cut down on the stress in my life."

"And did he?"

Emilio shook his head. "After every test in the book came back negative, he sent me to a specialist at Johns Hopkins." Emilio bent his head all the way back as if to keep more tears from slipping out. "I have ALS."

"What the hell is ALS?" Natalie asked, obviously having a hard time keeping her own tears in check.

"Amyotrophic lateral sclerosis, or Lou Gehrig's disease to the layperson," Jordan answered for him, remembering when she was at the University of Texas covering the athletic events on campus. One very prominent ex-jock had developed this disease and had been the focus of many fund-raising events to pay for his care.

Natalie may not have known what ALS was, but as soon as she heard Jordan refer to it as Lou Gehrig's disease, her mouth formed a perfect circle before clamping shut.

Again, she reached for Emilio's hand. "I'm so sorry. Is there anything I can do to help?"

He shook his head. "ALS is a rapidly progressive disease that attacks the nerve cells responsible for controlling voluntary muscles, like my arms and legs. Eventually, I'll be confined to a wheelchair and will need a ventilator to breathe."

Jordan's mind wandered as Emilio explained the progression of the disease that would eventually kill him. The ex-athlete at UT had died three years after he'd been diagnosed. She'd gone on to research ALS for extra credit in one of her journalism classes and remembered how life-changing it was.

She'd been amazed to discover that ALS affected one to three people out of every one-hundred thousand and usually afflicted more men than women. She'd read that although a small percentage of cases were inherited, the majority of incidences were random without any clear associated risk factors. She wondered which category Emilio fell into, because if it was familial, Tina might want to be tested.

"My doctor has me on a new medicine that's supposed to slow the progression of the degeneration, but the bottom line is, I'll die from this disease, whether it's two or three years down the road…or a little longer."

Natalie sniffed back the last of her tears. "I understand the urgency to see Tina settled before…" She couldn't make herself finish. "But for the life of me, I can't understand why you'd choose someone like Marco for your daughter, knowing what a womanizer he was. You saw how miserable Tina was at the party. It would only have gotten worse."

Emilio lowered his eyes and sighed. "That was my selfish pride coming out," he explained. "Since Tina is an only child, I have no one to take over the reins of my company, which has been in the family for generations. Say what you like about Marco, but the man had an incredible business sense. He took a nickel and dime import/export business and turned it into a multimillion dollar venture."

Jordan stopped herself before she blurted that there might have been another reason for Marco's success. If what she suspected after hearing Romero Ortiz shake down Frankie O'Brien the other night was true, a more criminal element might explain that achievement.

"What about your stepson?" Natalie asked, making Jordan wonder if she'd read her mind.

Emilio threw back his head and laughed. "Have you met Frankie? Besides the fact that his mother coddled him all his life, that boy couldn't run a lemonade stand. I've tried giving him added responsibility on many occasions, and each time, he found a way to screw it up. As if that isn't enough strikes against him, he's an alcoholic who's failed rehab twice now." Emilio shook his head. "I have to answer to my daddy and his father before him when I meet up with them again, and believe me, they would not be happy if I left Frankie O'Brien in charge of the shipping empire they'd worked so hard to build."

"Why not send Tina to business school and let her run the company?" Jordan asked. "I can rattle off the names of many successful women CEOs."

"That may be true, but I know my Tina. She's more interested in shopping than sitting at a desk looking over a spreadsheet. That's why I had Jeff draw up a new will a few weeks ago, naming her husband as my successor."

"And you were willing to bully her into marrying Marco when she clearly wasn't in love with him? All for the love of your company?" Natalie tsked. "Come on, Emilio. Even for you, that's a little heartless."

"Tina's in love with another man," Jordan blurted before clamping her hand over her mouth as if that would stop her from sticking the rest of her foot into it.

Emilio turned toward her, a look of total surprise on his face. "How would you know this?"

Jordan glanced first at Natalie, then back at Emilio. "Remember when I told you about the vendor from the festival seeing her go up the stairs right after Marco and Kate that night?"

"Yes. I still wonder what she was doing up there."

"There was another man with her. I think they were going upstairs for a little alone time."

"Did this vendor say who the other man was?" He leaned forward to give her his total concentration.

"Ginny Bruno's still missing," Jordan said, sadly. "But I believe I know who Tina took upstairs that night."

"Who?" Natalie asked, also leaning closer to Jordan to hear.

She wasn't sure it was the best idea to continue, but she'd already said too much. "Marco's brother, Bernardo Petrone."

"Nardo? He barely makes eye contact with anyone. Marco said he's shy and hasn't ever been involved in the day to day operations of their business. I find it hard to believe he'd be brazen enough to have a fling with Marco's fiancée."

"Marco probably said a lot of things to pump himself up in your eyes," Jordan said. "And if what I suspect is true, Marco was involved with your stepson importing some kind of contraband along with the actual merchandise they sold."

Now she really had Emilio's attention. "What makes you think that?"

Jordan related the conversation she'd overheard between Frankie and Romero Ortiz. When the phone rang in the middle of her explanation, she paused, but Emilio impatiently gestured with his hand for her to continue before picking up the phone and slamming it back down.

When she was finished, the room became quiet, and she watched his face. She got the impression that hearing about Marco's other life didn't come as a total surprise to him. Had he been so desperate for the man to take over his company that he'd been willing to overlook even criminal activity?

"I've suspected something like that for a long time, but I never had proof until—"

"You still don't have proof," Jordan interrupted. "It's only my suspicions after I overheard the conversation."

Emilio leaned back into the couch, deep in thought, before he nailed Jordan with a look. "And you're sure Tina is in love with Marco's brother?"

She sighed. "Again, it's only my suspicion, but if I were you, I'd sit down with my daughter and have a serious talk. This time ask her what she wants. Sounds like you've only been telling her what *you* want." She couldn't believe she was saying these things to a man Alex had said was connected, but it was too late to turn back. "And Emilio, I've met Bernardo, and in my opinion, he's a wonderful man and father."

"A father?"

She smiled, thinking of Gio Petrone. "He's got an absolutely fantastic twelve-year-old son who's a delight to be around. The kid alone could bring a lot of joy to what's left of your life." She leaned closer. "Talk to Tina today before it's too late."

He stared at her before turning his attention back to Natalie. "Thank you, my friend, for coming to me when I needed you and for bringing your cheeky friend who's not afraid to say how she feels." When Jordan started to protest, he held up his hand. "That was a compliment, Jordan. I appreciate your honesty. You've given me a lot to think about."

Just then his cell phone rang, and he glanced at caller ID. "It's Jeff. If you ladies will excuse me for a few minutes, I'd appreciate it. This may be something important."

The two women sat in silence, listening as he spoke to his lawyer. When he gasped, they knew something was up. It took every ounce of patience Jordan had to sit quietly and wait for him to hang up and tell them what was going on. She hoped it wasn't bad news about Kate who was supposed to be with Hamilton right now.

When Emilio finally hung up, he turned to Natalie. "Jeff says the police have dropped all charges against your daughter."

Natalie reached over and hugged him. "Oh my God! You're sure?"

He stared at her, his eyes filled with anguish. "They've arrested someone else in both Marco's and Georgette's death."

"Who?" Both women asked at once.

"My stepson."

TWENTY

"THE POLICE THINK Frankie O'Brien killed Marco and Georgette?" Jordan paused to rub her forehead. "Wait a minute. I thought your wife died of a heat stroke. How can they blame Frankie for that?"

Emilio walked over and sat down next to Natalie on the couch. "Apparently, the tox screen confirmed Georgette actually died of a heroin overdose before the heat of the car could take its toll."

"Heroin?" Natalie had been sitting quietly but now turned to face Emilio and asked the question that was also on Jordan's mind." Did you know she had a drug problem?"

He shook his head adamantly. "That's just it—she didn't. Georgette may have enjoyed an occasional cocktail or two, but that's as far as it went. She wouldn't even take ibuprofen for a headache. Said she didn't need chemicals to make her feel better."

"I'm still confused about why the police think her son killed her. Granted, if what I'm thinking about his import business with Marco is true, he may have had access to some serious drugs, but it makes no sense for him to kill his own mother. You said yourself that she'd coddled him." Jordan thought back to when she'd first met Frankie. Although he came across as a loser, he'd never given her any reason to suspect he might also be a killer.

"Jeff said Frankie had a knock-down, drag-out fight

with Georgette the night before she went missing. He was overheard saying he was tired of her constant nagging—that no matter what he did, it wasn't ever good enough for her." Emilio's voice cracked, and he lowered his head into his hands. "Oh God. She loved that boy so much, and no matter how badly he screwed up, she stuck by him. She was always on my case about giving him more responsibilities in the company."

"I heard her arguing with someone that night," Jordan said, remembering how she'd tried to get closer to hear better when she was at Dezi's food booth. "Although I couldn't see who was on the receiving end of all her anger, I was able to make out the words 'outsider' and 'suck up.' Why would she say that to Frankie if she was trying so hard to move him up the ladder in the family business?"

Emilio shrugged. "The police picked up Frankie about an hour ago, and they're questioning him now. He admitted being in an alcoholic black-out that night and can't remember killing her, but he swears he never left his hotel room." His forehead wrinkled as if he was in deep thought. "I may be able to prove he's telling the truth."

'How?" both women asked.

"Georgette was worried about him—thought he might be in trouble. I decided to check it out myself and had the hotel install a security camera in his room. That should prove his innocence."

Natalie touched his shoulder gently. "What if it doesn't?"

He scrubbed his hand across his face. "Then I'll deal with that, but for now I have to believe he wouldn't hurt his mother.

"Is Jeff at the station with him now?" Natalie asked.

Emilio met her gaze and held it before shaking his head. "Jeff can't represent Frankie because he's already on Kate's legal team. Even though she's been cleared of all charges, we were afraid it might be a conflict of interest, especially because he's the one who overheard the argument between Georgette and Frankie. He pulled some strings, however, and lined up one of the best criminal lawyers in Dallas. The man's on his way to the Plainville Police Station as we speak." He rose and walked over to look at the clock on the nightstand. "I'll need to get down there myself to…" He got choked up and couldn't finish. Swallowing hard, he said, "Georgette would want me to be with him."

"Definitely," Natalie said. "I remember how relieved I was when I heard that you'd sent your own lawyer to make sure Kate didn't say anything that might incriminate her. I also remember how frightened my daughter was, even though she's a lawyer herself and how I wished I could have been with her. No matter what, Frankie needs you right now, so go get dressed. We'll find our own way out." Natalie motioned for Jordan to follow as she started toward the door.

"Oh, I almost forgot to tell you," Emilio said, stopping halfway to the bathroom. "Jeff and Kate had a long morning at the police station, and he brought her back to the hotel for a quick lunch before taking her home. She's down the hall with him in his room."

Natalie's eyes lit up at the thought of seeing her daughter. "I'll keep all of you in my prayers, Emilio. Let us know if there's anything we can do."

"Other than keeping the news of my ALS a secret for now, I can't think of a thing anyone can do. And Natalie, I'm sorry I gave you such a hard time about Kate killing Marco."

She waved him off with a flick of her wrist. "Don't give it another thought. We were both trying to protect our daughters." She whirled around to face Jordan. "Ready?"

Jordan swiveled around and fell into step behind her as she walked out the door and down the hall to room 828.

As soon as Jeff opened the door and Natalie saw Kate by the couch, she rushed over and encircled her in her arms. "Oh my God! Is it really over?"

Kate hugged her mother back and tried to smile but not before Jordan noticed the dark circles under her eyes. "Captain Darnell said we can leave for Houston anytime we want."

"That can't happen soon enough. It's hard to believe that less than two weeks ago I was looking forward to coming to Ranchero to see Alex, meet his new girlfriend, and enjoy the festivities. Now, all I want to do is go back home and try to forget what you've been through—what we've all been through." Natalie was unable to keep her voice from cracking.

"I know, Mom." Kate pulled her closer and rubbed her back as if she were consoling a small child.

"This calls for a drink," Jeff said, motioning for them to sit down on the couch. "What can I get for you ladies?" When they all shook their heads, he walked over to the minibar and bent down. "Normally, I don't like to drink by myself, but it's been one of those weeks." He reached in and pulled out two mini bottles of Scotch and poured them into a glass from the counter. After taking a long sip, he looked up and smiled. "Why is it that liquor always seems to make things better?"

"I don't know, but I agree," Natalie said. "Unfortunately, I didn't have breakfast this morning, and I'm afraid that alcohol on my empty stomach wouldn't sit too well."

"Do you want to have lunch with Kate and me?" he asked, walking over with his now half empty glass and sitting on the chair next to the couch.

"Oh, Jeff, can I take a rain check on that lunch?" Kate asked. "All of a sudden I feel so exhausted and—" When she heard a ring, she leaned over and grabbed her purse. Reaching in, she fished out her phone and put it up to her ear. "Hello." Turning to her mother, she mouthed the word *Alex*. "You won't believe the news. The police have charged Emilio's stepson in both Marco's and Georgette's murders and cleared me of all charges. I'm here in Jeff's hotel room with Mom and Jordan, but we're just about to leave."

She handed the phone to Jordan. "He wants to speak to you."

It would be good to see the sparkle come back in Kate's eyes, Jordan thought as she reached for the phone. "Hey, you," she said, loving the way her entire body tingled when she heard his voice.

"We're getting ready to move in and make the arrests down here. It should be over in a few hours, and then I thought maybe all of us could go out for celebratory dinner before Mom and Kate go home in the morning." He chuckled. "That's when the real fun begins for you and me. Last night wasn't nearly enough for my Jordan fix."

She was glad he couldn't see the way his words had sent a flurry of pink up her cheeks. Glancing around to see if his mother or sister had noticed, she was relieved to see them standing by Jeff's bed looking at a picture he'd taken from his wallet. "I can't wait, either," she whispered into the phone.

"Gotta run. The bad guys are waiting. Love you."

There it was again. The "L" word. Before she could respond, he hung up, leaving her wondering once again what it all meant. After laying the phone on the table near their purses, she went over to the bed to see what they were looking at.

"When in the world do you find time to train for something like that?" Natalie asked. "I know Emilio must keep you busy all the time."

Jeff laughed. "He knows how important it is to me." When he noticed Jordan approaching, he handed her the picture in his hand.

"You ran the Boston Marathon?" she asked incredulously, staring at a picture of Jeff at the finish line in athletic shorts and a tank top. She'd noticed his chiseled body when she'd first met him, but he'd never given any indication that he was a runner.

"The Boston and the New York Marathon," he corrected. "Next on the list is Chicago. I've discovered all that alone time with the wind in my hair is just what I need to bring me down after a long day dealing with the struggles of my job. It's a cheap form of therapy for me."

"I could certainly use an outlet like that for my own stress," Kate said. "Maybe I'll give running a try when I get back to the firm in Houston." She frowned. "That's if I still have a job."

"They wouldn't dare fire you over this, but if they try, let me know. We'll go after them with a vengeance, and if nothing else, you'll walk away with one helluva severance package."

Kate stood on her tiptoes and kissed his cheek. "I don't know if I'll ever be able to thank you enough, Jeff. You gave me my life back."

"Glad I could help," he said. "Are you sure you won't

stick around and have lunch with me? The hotel makes a mean open-faced steak sandwich."

She shook her head. "All I want to do is go home and wrap my head around my newfound freedom." She turned to Jordan. "Would you mind if my mother rides back to Ranchero with me? It seems like forever since I've had a chance to really talk to her."

"Of course not." Jordan waved them on. "I want to run over to the Dream Weaver Motel anyway to see if Carlita Bruno has heard anything from her sister."

"Is Ginny still missing?" Kate asked.

"Yes. I was over there the other day and talked to a hotel maintenance worker. He remembered seeing Ginny walk out of the lower-level into an alley with a man she apparently knew. I'm going to try to locate him again and see if he or one of his coworkers remembered anything else about the mysterious man he saw with Ginny."

"Like what?" Natalie asked.

"For starters, maybe someone noticed what was on back of the man's hoodie."

"You talked to someone at the hotel about the tape?" Jeff's brows were scrunched in question. "That's police business. Why would you do that?"

She sighed. "Because I feel responsible for her disappearance. If I hadn't told the police that she might have information about who was upstairs when Marco was killed that night, she might not be missing. Now that Kate's been cleared of the murder, I'm going to concentrate all my energy on helping Carlita find her sister."

"Hopefully, you'll find something that can help the police locate her." Kate said before turning to her mother. "Ready?" When Natalie nodded, she picked up her purse and then slipped her arm through her mother's.

"Come on. Let's go climb into bed and catch up on our sleep until Alex gets home."

"He wants us all to go to dinner tonight to celebrate," Jordan said. "Let me grab my purse, and I'll walk out with you."

Before Jordan could do that, Jeff said, "Could you stay a few more minutes, Jordan? I'd like to hear about Ginny. Maybe I can help with your search for her."

She swiveled around to face him. "I'm not sure what we can do, but I'd love your help." Turning back to Natalie and Kate, she said, "Go get that much needed nap, and I'll see you two at dinner tonight."

After waving goodbye to them, she sat back down on the couch, once again declining an offer for a drink. "Here's what I know. Ginny disappeared shortly after I told the police about her sitting by the spiral staircase at the party the night Marco was killed. The maintenance man said it looked like she went willingly with the man in the T-shirt hoodie, which tells me she probably knew him."

He eyed her suspiciously. "Good point. What else?"

"The hotel worker also mentioned he saw the word ON written across the man's back. Like I said, I'm hoping one of the laundry workers might be able to shed a little light on the rest of the words on his shirt. If we're lucky, it will be a company logo or something that might narrow down the search considerably."

"Sounds like you've been doing a little undercover work in your spare time."

"I have, but don't tell Alex. I know I'm close. I just can't put my finger on some things that have been bothering me. So, how do you think you can help?"

"I'm not sure. Let me call her sister and find out if she's heard from Ginny." He picked up his phone and punched in a number. "Room 782 please." He tapped his fingers on the side of the phone while he waited. "Miss Bruno? This is Jeff Hamilton. I'm the legal counsel for Emilio Calabrese, and I'm standing here with Jordan McAllister." He paused and winked at Jordan. "Yes, she is a sweetheart and says the same thing about you. Anyway, we're both curious to find out if you've heard from your sister."

Jordan focused on the one-sided conversation, praying that the answer would be yes.

"That's terrific news." He turned to Jordan and gave her a thumbs up. "Of course. Let me write down that address." A search in the desk on the opposite side of the room produced a pen and notepad. "I'm ready when you are." After scribbling an address, he said, "Stay close to the phone, and I'll call the minute I'm there."

Jordan's hopes soared as she waited patiently until he disconnected. "Ginny's okay?"

"Seems she and another vendor went for a drive in the country. Ginny told her sister that the man had been drinking and was looking for more than a nice quiet drive. When she wouldn't comply, he dumped her off in the middle of nowhere and drove off with her purse still on the front seat." He stopped to take a swig of the Scotch. "Probably got home and after sleeping it off, either he didn't realize he hadn't gone back to get her or couldn't remember where he'd left her. If the latter was the case, my guess is that he was too afraid of the consequences if the police knew he'd been with her."

"But I got the impression from your conversation with Carlita that Ginny was okay? Right?" She prayed she'd heard him correctly.

"Apparently only hungry and badly sunburned but

otherwise fine. Ginny's sister got a phone call from some farmer who found her wandering around in his pasture."

"Thank God. That's wonderful news. Are the police on their way out there now to get her?"

He nodded. "Carlita said she was just about to contact me."

Jordan tilted her head, confused. "Why?"

"She's a little worried about the police questioning her sister. Asked if I could go out to make sure Ginny has someone by her side who knows how the police operate when they question someone." He walked to the dresser and grabbed his car keys. "I'll call you the minute I know something."

"I want to go with you," Jordan said, excited that Ginny was okay. When he hesitated, she added, "Ginny doesn't know you. I think she might appreciate a friendly face."

He thought about that for a second before agreeing. "I'm sure Carlita would like that as well."

"Where exactly is she?" Jordan asked.

"About ten miles outside of Plainville. Come on. I'll drive. You can leave your car here, and I'll bring you back afterwards." He reached for his glass and drained the rest of the Scotch. "It looks like we have yet another reason to celebrate today."

When she walked over to get her purse, she noticed Kate's phone lying on the coffee table right where she'd laid it after talking to Alex. In the excitement, Kate must not have seen it there when she'd left. Jordan picked it up and slipped it into the back pocket of her jeans, thinking she'd give it to her at dinner.

She walked out of the room and waited as Jeff followed and made sure the door was closed. Together, they made their way to the elevator, each lost in their own private thoughts. Her mind was on Carlita and how excited she must be that her sister was safe. She hoped Ginny hadn't been too traumatized by it all.

When they reached Jeff's car, he opened the passenger door for her. Smiling up at him, she slid in and waited for him to walk around the car and do the same. She debated whether to call Alex and tell him about Ginny, then remembered that he was in the middle of a drug bust.

For the next fifteen minutes, neither she nor Jeff said anything, both deep into their own thoughts. When he turned onto a dirt road several miles outside the city limits, Jordan was already planning what she'd say to Ginny and hoped the woman wasn't still holding a grudge because of Victor's mustache comment. She turned to him to ask how much longer when she noticed a crumpled shirt sticking out from between the seats.

After reaching down and pulling it out, she realized it was one of his running shirts and held it up to him. "You worked way too hard for this to have it end up in a ball," she said with a grin when she saw BOSTON MARATHON across the back. "Although I doubt you'll get a chance to wear long sleeves in this heat, you might want to make sure this doesn't get left behind in the rental car when you turn it in at the airport."

Her grin faded when she realized the navy blue shirt was a hoodie. As if a light bulb went off in her head, the image of Ginny Bruno walking out a basement door into the alley behind her hotel with the man in a dark hoodie flashed across her brain. Although the back of the shirt had been partially obstructed from view, the janitor clearly remembered seeing the letters ON when the mystery man and Ginny had exited the building. A sudden chill ran up her spine as she realized that the word marathon ended in those letters. Suddenly, other things that had seemed strange earlier now started to make sense. Like how Jeff had known where Carlita Bruno and her sister were staying, and how he just happened to have the hotel's number in his phone.

She stared out the front window as warning bells went crazy in her head. She was trying to make sense of it all when she heard him chuckle to himself.

"I knew you'd figure it out sooner or later."

TWENTY-ONE

SHE DECIDED TO play dumb. "Figure what out?"

She glanced up at the passing landscape, trying to decide if she should jump from the car, but they were already going too fast. The fall would probably kill her, and even if it didn't, there was no guarantee he wouldn't turn the car around and finish her off.

This time he laughed out loud. "You can't tell me in one breath how you're closing in on finding out who left the motel with Ginny Bruno and then pretend you have no clue. I'm a lawyer, remember? I'm trained to read faces."

"Where are you taking me?"

He met her intense stare momentarily, and for the first time, she saw evil radiating from his eyes. An involuntary shudder ran through her body. How could she and the others have been so totally taken in by this man?

"We're going exactly where I said we were."

So far, she'd only seen one other car on the road and figured her chances of catching someone's attention weren't good. She had to think fast and find another way to help herself.

She decided to play the dumb card once more. "Will Ginny be there like you said?"

"Oh yeah," he responded with a snort. "Unfortunately, she won't be much company for you."

"You killed her?"

"Not exactly. Let's just say Mother Nature and the

Texas sun did the job for me, with the help of an old black friend."

Oh God! Even though Jordan hadn't held out much hope of finding Ginny alive, hearing Jeff Hamilton confirm the woman's demise filled her with sadness.

"So it was you in the security footage?" When he nodded, she continued, "Why did you have to kill her?"

"You have only yourself to blame for that woman's death. If it hadn't been for you, I would never have known about her sitting by the spiral staircase with a perfect view of everybody who went upstairs that night."

Jordan shifted uncomfortably in the seat as guilt produced a hard lump in her throat. "Either you went up to Marco's bedroom yourself, or you're protecting someone else who did. You wouldn't be worried about it, otherwise." She turned to face him, thinking if she could keep him talking, it would give her a chance to figure out how to get away from him. "So which was it, Jeff?"

"I knew you were on to me and only pretending not to know." He grinned. "I saw it in your face when you handed me the shirt, which was my mistake leaving it in the car in the first place. I should've tossed it that day, but I just couldn't make myself do that."

"Why were you in Marco's bedroom?"

The question caught him by surprise, and he nodded, before turning his head to glare at her for a few seconds. "I couldn't chance Ginny suddenly remembering and telling the police."

Jordan narrowed her eyes, feeling even more confused. If Marco and Kate were in one bedroom and Tina and Bernardo in the other, where had Jeff been?

"Didn't that make you a fifth wheel? Or did you have something kinky going on with Marco and Kate?" She knew that was reaching, but she was worried they were already too close to wherever Jeff was taking her. He'd mentioned before leaving the hotel that Carlita had said Ginny was ten miles outside of Plainville. Since they'd already driven at least that far, she racked her brain for a way to buy more time.

"Not with Kate. There was something going on between Marco and me, but it's not what you're implying." He slowed down when they came to a pasture enclosed by a four-foot wire fence, and Jordan reached for the door, only to find it locked. "You don't think I'd be that stupid now, do you" He reached under his seat and produced a large automatic weapon. "It's amazing what you can buy on any street corner these days."

Jordan decided if she could keep him talking, maybe somehow, she could escape. "Then why were you upstairs that night?"

He cut the ignition and pointed the gun at her head. "I've been Emilio's trusted friend and counsel ever since I graduated from Harvard, and my daddy held the position before that. Marco only came into Emilio's life last year, and all of a sudden, he's the Golden Boy." Jeff's voice crackled with resentment. "Emilio even changed his will last month to give Marco total control of his company when he dies."

"I know," Jordan said. "That must've made you furious."

"Furious is not the word I'd use. More like thoroughly pissed off. I was the one who gave up a social life to be at Emilio's beck and call for all those years." He eyed her suspiciously. "And how would you know about his will?"

"He told me," she said after Jeff pulled over to the side of the road. "I also know he's dying."

"Yeah, that's a bummer. When I first heard, I thought it was finally my big chance. For the first time in my life, I thought this would be an accomplishment that would make my father proud. Unfortunately, he's wasting away in a nursing home with dementia and will probably never know about my success." He shoved the keys into his pocket, careful to keep the gun pointed at her. "Now get out."

She stole a quick peek at the pasture hoping to see a farmhouse, but there was only flatland for as far back as she could see. After he unlocked the door and got out himself, she relocked her door and grabbed her purse off the floor.

In a flash, he unlocked it with his keys, pulled it open, and wretched the purse from her hands. "Oh no, you don't. I'll need this today when I move your car to a bad part of town to make it look like you were robbed." His eyes hardened. "Now get out before I have to get physical."

With no other option available, she slid her legs out of the car and stood facing him. If she had any aspirations of taking him on, the way his six-two frame loomed over her killed that idea. That and the gun in his hand. She turned her head both ways, searching for an escape route, but all she saw was the gravel road.

Since she wouldn't be able to outrun his car, she tried reasoning with him instead. "You really don't have to do this, Jeff. Right now, you're only looking at Marco's murder." Conveniently, she'd left out the part about him killing Ginny Bruno as well.

This time he threw his head back and laughed out loud. "Apparently, I gave you more credit in the smarts department than you deserve." He pointed to the roof. "Climb up there."

A flash of terror gripped her. "Why? So you can pick me off like I was an animal?"

His grin faded. "I'm trying to help you out. Now get up there before you piss me off."

She had no idea what he intended to do, but right now, keeping him talking might buy some time. "So you went upstairs intending to kill Marco, clearing the way for you to move into the number one spot with Emilio?"

"Hell no. I didn't want him dead. I only wanted to discredit him in Emilio's eyes. I went up there to use his computer to sabotage the liquor shipment for the festival. I knew that would upset Emilio more than anything. I also knew about his affair with Kate—and about a half dozen other women. I thought for sure when things hit the fan at the party with him and Tina, Emilio would think twice about handing over his daughter—and his company—to a man like that.

"I was prepared to marry the woman myself, even though she's not my type. I like my women to turn heads and use her brains for something other than what's on sale at Sak's." He let his eyes roam up and down her body. "Under different circumstances, you and I might have hit it off."

She ignored the comment and plunged right in. "But you were wrong. In a twisted sort of way, Emilio thought Marco would eventually make a good husband for his daughter. In the meantime, not only would his company get a CEO with astute business sense, but Marco's very prosperous holdings in his own family businesses would become part of the Calabrese empire."

She paused to see how Jeff would react to that and was pleased to see she'd hit a nerve. She'd learned a long time ago in her journalism classes that an angry man made mistakes. She might be able to use that to her advantage since time was running out for her.

She decided to try a different technique. "So were you in the room when Kate and Marco had the fight?"

"I'd just finished sending the liquor shipment to the wrong address when I heard Marco come into the room. Quickly, I ran out on the patio with his laptop and hid behind a huge plant. I needn't have bothered because he was so drunk—and high, according to the coroner—that he probably wouldn't have noticed me anyhow. When Kate came in, I had to stand by silently while he assaulted her. Although it only pissed me off more, I still had no intentions of killing him." He shoved her against the car.

Anxiety formed a hard knot in her stomach. She had to find a way to escape. Frantically, she looked around for something—anything to use as a weapon—and screamed when she felt the cold steel of the gun pressing into her back. Using the tire for leverage, she was able to lift herself up until she was standing on the hood of the car.

"Jump," he commanded.

"First tell me why you killed him."

"I don't have to tell you anything, I'm the one calling the shots here."

She decided goading him might buy her more time. "I get it now. You were jealous because Marco was so much more successful than you. The only way to make yourself look good was to get him out of the way."

The hate in his eyes was not lost on Jordan and for a minute she thought she had gone too far. Then he sighed. "I never meant to hurt the man physically, but when Kate went into the bathroom, Marco came out on the patio and spotted me behind the planter. He screamed that when he told Emilio, I would be tossed on my ass—or worse. I guess I lost it and slammed the back of his head with the laptop." He snorted. "Don't you think it's kind of ironic that he bit the dust with his own computer, which, by the way, contained all sorts of kiddie porn." His face grew angry again. "Now jump, Jordan. We've wasted enough time."

"Carlita Bruno will tell the cops you and I came out to get Ginny?"

"Maybe I really was wrong about you. Maybe you *are* just a pretty face." He smirked. "Do you seriously think I was talking to someone back at the hotel?"

"What makes you think our bodies won't be discovered out here? Sooner or later, the farmer who owns this land will venture out this way. Then your little plan will be shot to hell."

She stared out into the pasture, thinking if he left her here in this hot desolate field to die, just like he'd done to Ginny, she might be able to climb back over the fence and walk back down the gravel road for help.

As if he'd read her mind, he grinned. "That wire fence may look harmless, but trust me when I tell you that it carries a five thousand volt charge. You might want to stay clear of it unless you want the jolt of your life."

"I'm still confused about why Ginny would go willingly with you that day, especially if she remembered seeing you go up the stairs that night."

An evil grin crossed his face. "I told her that Emilio wanted to sit down with her to talk about operating a side business selling her Italian food and shipping it all over the country." He tsked. "The stupid woman would have gone with the Boston Strangler if she thought she'd make money doing it."

Poor Ginny! Her taste in men as well as her judgment in character left a lot to be desired. But she hadn't deserved the fate she'd received.

Jeff waved the gun in front of her again. "You have three seconds to jump before I use this." He chuckled once again before firing the gun, narrowly missing her.

Quickly, she jumped, landing on the hard ground and rolling several times before coming to a stop.

"Sorry, I don't have any sunscreen. Have fun out here, though, and say hello to my black friend," he said, before getting into his car, making a U-turn, and then speeding back down the road.

She watched until he was out of sight, staring until the dust clouds left by his car had disappeared. Then she tried to stand up, hoping she hadn't broken an ankle—or worse. Satisfied that she was only sore, she reached into her back pocket for Kate's phone, saying a silent prayer of thanks that Jeff hadn't noticed it back there.

She turned it on, but there were no bars, and she walked farther out into the pasture, hoping to pick up a signal, even a weak one. There was none. Desperate, she ran about three hundred more yards and stopped close to a tree near the outer perimeter, but again, no signal.

Feeling totally defeated, she said a quick prayer to St. Jude, who had always helped her before when things looked hopeless. Swiping at the perspiration that now covered her forehead, she wished she hadn't worn jeans. And as long as she was wishing, a bottle of icy cold water was right up there at the top of the list.

She walked toward the tree, thinking at least she'd be out of the grueling Texas sun. With no clouds in the sky and an open field, the temperature had to be in the high nineties.

As she approached the tree, she noticed something leaning against it. For a minute, she thought it was an animal until she saw what looked like a hand waving to her. When she was closer, she was able to make out the figure of a small woman and squealed with relief as she realized it was Ginny Bruno. Picking up her pace until she was in a dead run, she raced toward her.

Tears filled her eyes when Ginny looked up and tried to smile. Her face was bright red and blistered in spots, and her lips were so chapped, she could barely open them. But somehow, she was able to speak. "I prayed that someone would find me."

"Ginny, it's Jordan. I'm the culinary reporter from the local newspaper who was doing a story on you and your sister. Do you remember?"

Ginny tried to answer, but she was too weak.

"Save your energy. We've got to find a way to get out of here," Jordan said, glancing in the direction of the gate.

"Don't go near the fence," Ginny said. "It's—"

"I know," Jordan replied "I'm going to see if I can climb over the gate down there. Although it's pretty high, I'm hoping it isn't charged like the rest of the fence."

"Okay, but hurry. I haven't had food for three days, and as disgusting as it sounds, I've survived by drinking the water from the stock pond." She pointed to the body of water halfway between the tree and the herd of cattle grazing down the pasture.

Jordan couldn't help it and wrinkled her nose at the thought of drinking that water. But Ginny wouldn't have made it two days in the Texas heat without it. "Stay put. I have a phone, but I'm not getting a signal. Maybe once I get on the other side of the fence, I'll be able to make the call that will bring help to us."

Just then Jordan was distracted by what sounded like a herd of cattle running. She looked up to see a large animal coming toward them at a fast clip from the area where she'd noticed the cows earlier. It approached slowly and stopped about a hundred yards away, snorting and pawing at the ground. A surge of panic hit her as she realized it was the black friend Jeff had mentioned.

When it inched closer, she found herself staring straight into the ominous black eyes of the biggest bull she'd ever seen.

TWENTY-TWO

"DON'T MOVE." JORDAN looked both ways for something she could use as a weapon. There were only a few branches, none big enough to provide protection.

"I've been hiding from him since the first day, climbing up the tree when I was still able to." Her lips quivered. "He's going to kill us, isn't he?"

When she attempted to get up, Jordan reached out and stopped her. "If he thinks we're a threat to him or his herd of cows, he'll charge."

Even as she said it, the memory of one unfortunate cowboy from the Amarillo Rodeo came to mind. He'd been gored so badly that he had to have multiple surgeries to repair the damage. The only reason the man was still alive was because the clowns had distracted the bull long enough for the paramedics to load him on a stretcher and get him out of the ring.

She and Ginny could use a few clowns right now.

"We shouldn't run?"

"No. Despite their size, bulls are fast, and he'll outrun us." Jordan stopped before adding what would happen when he did. "Be still," she reminded Ginny again, keeping her eyes trained on the large animal, which was now staring intently at her and rubbing his head in the ground he'd turned up with his hoof.

She knew from growing up in West Texas, known for its prosperous cattle industry, that this was a danger sign, that the bull was getting ready to charge.

"What are we going to do if he attacks?" Ginny asked, barely able to get the words out. "I don't want to die at the hands of an animal."

"Shh," Jordan whispered. "I'm hoping he'll see that we're not a threat and go back to his herd." She swallowed hard, almost mesmerized by the bull's eyes, black with only a touch of white showing.

As if on cue, the animal began to snort, a low terrifying growl sound that meant he had no intentions of going back to the other side of the pasture. At least not until he got rid of the threat—namely them.

Then he lowered his head and stepped closer, snot blowing from his nose, another sign of imminent attack. Jordan drew in a sharp breath to stifle her scream. With her heart hammering in her chest, she prepared for the onslaught, ready to shout, hoping the noise might slow him down, at least momentarily.

Just as the animal took another menacing step toward them, she took another deep breath and opened her mouth to squeal at the top of her lungs. But before she could make a sound, a wolf-like animal appeared out of nowhere on the other side of the fence, attracting the bull's attention with his ferocious barking.

In a flash, the animal slid under the lowest wire, yelping when he received the jolt. Once inside the pasture he raced toward them, and Jordan found herself wondering which was worse—getting eaten by a wolf or gored to death by a bull. When he closed in on them, Jordan saw that it was only a white Pyrenees with one black paw in front as he ran right past them and stopped close to the bull, challenging him.

Distracted by the dog, the bull turned toward him and pawed the ground with his hoof, just like he'd done minutes before at the two women. Jordan closed her eyes, not wanting to see the dog killed by the much bigger bovine. When she opened them, she was surprised to see the smaller animal zigzagging across the pasture in a race for his life.

Both Jordan and Ginny watched in total amazement as the dog led the bull toward the other cows and away from the tree. When the bull came to the area where the herd was grazing, he stopped and positioned himself in front of them, as if he were standing guard.

The dog stopped about two hundred yards away and lay on the ground, almost daring the bull to come and get him. After a few minutes of staring the bull down, the dog turned and made his way back to the tree. When he approached them, Ginny cried out, and Jordan grabbed her hand. Thoughts of the dog now turning on them were quickly dispelled as the animal trotted closer, wagging his tail.

When he was directly in front of them, he tilted his head, looked at her, and sat down. Cautiously, Jordan reached out and touched his head. When he seemed to like it, she began to run her hands down the length of his body. After he plopped down in front of her, she went to a full-out ear scratching, loving the way he continued to glare at the bovine herd as if daring them to come across to his side of the pasture.

Jordan continued to pet him, feeling the matted fur with her fingers. Although he didn't have a collar on, he was too healthy looking, except for the matted coat, to be a stray.

With the bull crisis diverted, at least for the time being, Jordan looked toward the gate. There was no way Ginny could walk, and even less chance of Jordan being able to carry her. She decided their best shot was to wait until dark, make a run for the gate, and hope the bull didn't have night vision.

For an hour, the dog lay beside them, finally closing his eyes for a much-needed rest after the run for his life. By now the sun had gone down, dropping the temperature to a tolerable level.

Jordan looked over at Ginny, who was staring straight ahead. Her eyes seemed almost lifeless now, making Jordan wonder how much longer she could make it out here without food and clean water. "How are you doing?"

"I was just thinking about all the people in my life that I loved but never told," she said sadly.

"You'll get that opportunity. It's getting dark, and I'll be able to run for help."

"I haven't spoken to my best friend in over two years because of a fight over something so minor I can't even remember what it was. And then there's the preacher's wife." She continued talking as if she hadn't heard what Jordan had just said. "I've been mad at her for months, too, over some stupid thing."

Jordan reached over and pulled her closer. "Ginny, listen to me. You can't get morbid now. You're a fighter. I need you to think positive. Someone will come looking for us. I promise."

Even as she said it, she knew she could offer nothing to back it up. There would probably be a manhunt for her, but no one would suspect Jeff Hamilton or search way out in the country. Their only hope was if she could find help or if a rancher wandered out their way to check on things.

"Close your eyes and try to get a little rest," Jordan continued. "If I can't find help, we'll have to improvise and figure out a way to get you out of here."

She laid her head against the tree trunk and looked

up, marveling at the beauty of the country sky. Watching the sun make its way over the horizon, she was amazed to already see the moon, only a sliver, but there nonetheless. It was dusk now, and the fading sunlight cast an eerie glow over the stock pond, giving a shimmering appearance to the water. As she stared at the sky, only the chirping of the crickets and cicadas interrupted the quiet of the night.

Knowing the fence was charged was comforting when she heard the howls of a pack of coyotes from somewhere off in the darkness. It might not keep them out, but it would slow them down, along with any other animal that saw her and Ginny as a gourmet meal.

"I know I'm going to die out here," Ginny said, her voice cracking. "I would give anything to see Carlita one last time."

Jordan decided no amount of reassurance would work with her, and she tried another tactic. "I wish my friend Victor was here now. He'd know how to make us laugh and forget about all the bad stuff."

At the mention of his name, Ginny's body stiffened. "I was so mad at that man. No one has ever had the nerve to mention my mustache to me before." She turned to Jordan. "I don't know if you noticed, but I had it waxed off the very next day."

"Carlita told me," Jordan responded. "But I have to tell you something about Victor."

Ginny sighed. "I really liked him and wanted him to like me back, but I guess he wasn't interested."

Jordan giggled. "He wouldn't have been interested even if you looked like Miss America."

An awkward silence followed before Jordan continued, "Now, if you were *Mister* America…"

It took a few seconds for that to sink in, and when

it did, Ginny smiled for the first time since Jordan had found her. "My luck! I was never very good at—" She stopped when they heard tires moving on gravel.

Jordan rose to her knees and looked toward the road where a pair of headlights was coming toward them at a fast pace. The dog sat up beside her and began to growl softly, and she choked back a cry.

What if it was Jeff Hamilton coming back to make sure they were dead?

She turned to Ginny, whose eyes were now filled with terror. "It's probably just a farmer. I'm going to walk over to the fence. As soon as I'm sure it's not Hamilton, I'll scream to get their attention. Stay here with the dog."

She stood and made her way to the fence, planning to hit the ground if it was Jeff. Looking around for some kind of weapon to defend herself and once again finding nothing, she prayed the bull was either asleep or couldn't see in the dark.

Her heart felt like it was beating out of her chest as the vehicle moved closer. Although she'd made light of Ginny's regrets for not telling the people she loved how she felt, she couldn't help thinking about her own list of things she wished she had done.

Like making an effort to get back home to see her parents and her brothers more often. It had been over three months, and that was way too long, considering it was only a five-hour drive from Ranchero to Amarillo.

And then there was her fear of saying the "L" word to Alex. Of course, she loved him—had from the very first time they'd made love. So why was she so afraid to tell him? He wasn't Brett and wouldn't break her heart the way he had. And even if he did, she wasn't the same girl who had put her own dreams on hold to follow her ex around Texas while he chased his. She was stronger now.

But she might never have the opportunity to tell Alex how she felt now.

She jumped when the white dog suddenly appeared beside her and ran the length of the fence, barking at the oncoming vehicle.

So much for hiding from Hamilton, she thought.

She stood silently by the fence until the vehicle was close enough to see it was a Suburban and not Jeff's gray rental car. Jumping up and down, she hollered as loud as she could to get their attention.

On the other side of the fence the SUV passed by her, and she recognized Alex in the passenger seat of Ray's car. The dog was beside her now and began to howl to match her screams.

The Suburban skidded to a halt about fifty yards ahead, and Alex jumped out as Ray backed up. When he raced toward her and reached for the fence, she shouted, "Don't touch it. It's charged."

He pulled his hand back and stared at her. "Oh my God! I can't believe we've found you."

"There's a gate about five hundred yards that way," she said, pointing. "Hurry. Ginny Bruno is alive and over by the tree, but there's no way she can walk that far." She turned toward the stock pond. "And there's a bull loose over there. He's already tried to kill us once."

Alex's eyes widened, and he shouted to Ray, "Back the SUV up to the gate. I'm going in." When Ray had the truck positioned, Alex climbed onto the roof and without hesitating, leaped into the field.

"I'll check out the gate," Ray said before he peeled out in that direction.

"Between the two of us, we should be able to carry Ginny," Jordan said. "She can help a little and—" She stopped when she heard a sound that she recognized from when she was up against the tree. "Oh my God, Alex, the bull."

He turned and hollered. "Get Ginny and head for the gate. Hopefully, by then Ray will have found a way to get in and can help you." He turned his attention to the bull that had left the herd and was now charging toward them. "Hurry," he screamed.

Jordan took off running toward the tree and helped Ginny to her feet. "Our only chance of getting out of her alive is if you're able to help me. We need to go as quickly as we can."

Ginny nodded. "I think I can do it."

With Jordan supporting the small woman, they made their way across the pasture as Alex faced off the bull with the white dog at his side. As strong as Alex was, he was no match for the large bull and wouldn't stand a chance one on one with the animal if it came down to that. She tried not to think about that happening and kept walking toward the gate, having to take on more of Ginny's weight with each step. She worried the woman would give out before they got there.

As they approached the iron gate, the SUV burst through, sending parts of the metal everywhere. Jordan turned to check on Alex and the dog, who were still managing to keep the bull at bay. But even at this distance, she could hear the ominous growls of the now incensed animal. Without warning, the bovine turned his attention to the dog and leaped to attack. She watched in horror as Alex jumped in front to the massive animal and grabbed him by the horns while the dog stood his ground and barked ferociously. But Alex was thrown over the animal's massive head and into the air, landing hard on the drought-hardened ground. The bull slowly turned 180 degrees to face Alex and pawed at the ground before going in for the kill.

"Alex!" Jordan screamed, right before she heard a gunshot. She looked up to see Ray outside the vehicle with a hunting rifle.

The bull stood still for a second before racing away from them, back toward the cattle. Jordan handed Ginny to Ray and ran to where Alex lay on the ground, praying he was still alive.

"I'm okay," he said, even though she could see that he was holding onto his chest and his face was twisted in pain. "I may have cracked a few ribs." He attempted to stand, and she gave him her arm to assist. When he was upright, he gave her a quick kiss on the lips and asked, "Where's Ginny?"

"In the car. Can you walk that far?"

He tried to grin. "My legs are fine." He grabbed her arm, wincing when he made contact. "Let's get the hell out of here."

TWENTY-THREE

WHEN THEY GOT to Ray's car, Ginny was already in the front seat, guzzling a bottle of water. Ray handed Jordan one as she climbed into the back seat with Alex.

Ginny turned her head around and stared at Alex. "Please don't tell me this guy is looking for Mister Right."

Jordan laughed out loud. "Absolutely not. But unfortunately, he's already taken." She winked at Alex.

"My luck." Ginny said.

"Hurry up. I need to get the three of you to the emergency room," Ray said. "And you have some very anxious friends waiting to hear from you, Jordan."

She climbed into the back of the SUV with Ginny. "I have Kate's phone," she said pulling it from her back pocket. "But there were no bars, and I couldn't call out for help."

Alex glanced over his shoulder from the front seat. "Bars or no bars, you can thank your lucky stars you had her phone. It led us to you."

Jordan tilted her head, confused. "How did a phone with no service lead you to us?"

"When Kate told me she'd left it at Jeff's hotel and that Jeff hadn't seen it, I played a hunch and had my friends at the FBI ping it."

"Ping it?"

He laughed. "Pinging can determine the location of a cell phone at any given point by using the phone's

GPS location aware capabilities. A lot of people would be upset to know that Uncle Sam can find out where they are with a reasonable degree of accuracy that way."

"It acts like a GPS tracking system as long as the battery is still in the phone, bars or no bars," Ray explained. "When no one could locate you, Alex pinged *your* phone. It took us to a location well known to law enforcement agencies because of the gang activity. They found it and your purse in the abandoned car. Your wallet was missing, though, and the police assumed you had been robbed and kidnapped."

"He said he was going to do that to make it look like a robbery gone bad."

Alex did a one-eighty and looked her in the eye. "Who said he would do that?"

"That bastard Hamilton," Ginny said. "If I ever get my hands on him, I'm gonna kill him."

"Are you talking about Jeff Hamilton, Emilio's lawyer?" Alex asked.

"Yes," Jordan responded. "He's the one who left us both out here to die."

This time Alex twisted all the way around to make eye contact with her. "Why would he do that?"

"Because he's the one who killed Marco," Jordan answered as Ray turned off the gravel road onto the road that led to Plainville.

Alex turned back around and punched in a number in his cell phone. For the next five minutes, he relayed the information about Jeff Hamilton to Captain Darnell.

When he hung up, he turned to her again, "Darnell's going to pick him up and have him brought to the station. He's also sending one of his officers over to the ER to take your statements." A puzzled look crossed his face. "I still find it hard to believe he killed Marco. Did he ever say why?"

"He was furious that after all the years he'd given to the Calabrese Empire, Emilio disregarded his loyalty and allowed Marco Petrone, a man he'd known for only a year, to stroll right in and become the heir apparent." Jordan paused before she said anything more about Emilio. "Did your mother mention our visit to Emilio's hotel room?"

"Only that you and she went to console him as a friend. Why?"

Apparently, Natalie was honoring Emilio's request to keep his ALS a secret. "No reason. I just thought she might've told you that Emilio had recently changed his will and was leaving his entire business operation to the man who married his daughter."

"This is getting good," Ray said, shaking his head in disgust. "So, Jeff killed Marco and then what? Was he going to try to hook up with Tina?"

"Jeff didn't intend to kill anyone that night. He was only upstairs to use Marco's laptop to sabotage the liquor shipment for the festival. He'd already messed up the initial shipment and saw how upset Emilio had been. He was trying to put the finishing touches on a plan to totally discredit Marco in Emilio's eyes. When he heard Marco come into his room unexpectedly, he hid on the patio."

"He was out there the entire time Kate and Marco had their fight?" Ray asked.

"Yes. After Kate ran into the bathroom, Marco poured a drink and walked out there. When he spotted him, Jeff knew he'd run right to Emilio. He also knew if Emilio found out he was the one who had deliberately screwed up the liquor shipment, he would've tossed him

out on his butt. So he saw it as the perfect opportunity
to solve both his problems."

"So Frankie O'Brien had nothing to do with it?" Ray
asked.

"No," Jordan said. "Jeff stayed hidden until everyone
came up the stairs, then just slipped out of the bedroom
and blended in with the crowd hovering around Kate.
Emilio doesn't believe his stepson had anything to do
with Georgette's death. He was on his way to the police
station with security taken from Frankie's room before
Jeff abducted me."

"Why would Jeff feel the need to get you out of the
picture?" Alex asked.

"Because I figured out that he was the one responsible for Ginny's disappearance, but I had no idea he
was the one who pushed Marco over the balcony wall."

Alex narrowed his eyes. "I don't even want to know
how you were able to come to that conclusion. I have a
feeling I would have to give you that snooping-is-dan-
gerous-to-your-health lecture, and right now, all I want
to do is hold you." He grimaced when he tried. "Unfortunately, that will have to wait until I get some pain
medicine on board."

A few minutes later, Ray pulled up to the ER and
jumped out as soon as the vehicle was completely
stopped. He raced around and opened Ginny's door before lifting her out and carrying her to the door, turning to make sure that Jordan and Alex were right behind
him.

"I'm not hurt, Ray. Honestly," she reassured him.
"Take care of Ginny, and I'll help Alex. We'll see you
inside."

He held her stare for a moment before he nodded and
turned around to take Ginny inside. The ER nurse met

them at the door with a wheelchair and led Ginny back to an examining room. Jordan got Alex settled in a chair and approached the desk where she informed the receptionist that he needed to be seen as well.

While they waited for the doctor to examine Ginny, Jordan remembered that no one had called Carlita.

After getting the number from the ER unit secretary, she called the hotel. When the operator put the call through, she tapped her fingers nervously on the side of the chair, waiting for Carlita to pick up, anxious to tell her the good news.

"Carlita," she said when she heard her voice. "This is Jordan. I'm in the emergency room with Ginny. She's badly dehydrated, but she's going to be fine."

"Oh my God!"

"I'm going to call the Plainville Police Station and have them send an officer over to your hotel to bring you here right now. Be waiting in the lobby."

When Carlita began to cry, Jordan tried to comfort her. "You'll see her soon, Carlita. I promise."

She hung up and was about to ask Alex to make the call, but he was way ahead of her and already had his phone up to his ear.

"Darnell, I need you to send a black-and-white over to Dream Weaver Hotel to bring Carlita Bruno to the Plainville Hospital ER to be with her sister. I appreciate it." After hanging up, he gave Jordan a thumbs up.

Grabbing her hand, he squeezed. "I would ask how you always manage to get yourself into hot water like this, but I already know the answer. I can't seem to stop you from nosing around dangerous people." His voice softened. "I'm not sure I'd want you any other way, though, and I hate to admit it, but this time, your incredible knack for sniffing out the bad guys probably saved Ginny Bruno's life."

"And as much as I'd love to bask in the glow of that compliment, I have to confess that I had no idea Jeff was a bad guy. He fooled me just like he did the rest of you. I'm only glad we found Ginny and that she's okay, because I was right all along about why she went missing. Jeff heard me say she'd seen everyone who had gone up the steps that night, and he wanted to make sure that she didn't mention his name." She lowered her head. "I'm not sure I'd have been able to live with myself if she'd been killed because of me."

"She wasn't, so quit beating yourself up." He leaned over and pressed his lips lightly against hers. "Now tell me how you managed to keep the bull at bay until we got there."

For the next fifteen minutes, she told him and Ray about their adventures with the humongous black bull and the white dog who'd saved their lives.

"What happened to the dog?" She asked when she finished. "I feel like I should take him a T-bone or something."

"I don't know. I can't remember seeing him again after the bull threw me."

"He was like a pit bull guarding a junk yard, challenging that bull like he thought he had superpowers or something," Jordan said, remembering how brave the dog had been.

Just then, a nurse came in and asked Jordan to wait out in the waiting room while they took Alex to get x-rays.

Jordan walked back to the waiting room and started to sit down beside Ray when the door swung open and Carlita was escorted in by a Plainville policemen. As soon as she spotted Jordan, she rushed over. "Have you heard anything yet?"

Jordan shook her head and patted the seat next to her. "She's been back there about a half hour already. I have no idea how much longer it will take. In the meantime, I'll tell you the whole story about how I found her."

Carlita sat down and listened intently while Jordan related the story once again. Tears glistened in her eyes when she heard the part about the rescue.

Carlita sat down and listened intently while Jordan related the story once again. Tears glistened in her eyes when she heard the part about the rescue.

Well over an hour later, the ER doctor emerged from the back room and walked over. "I was told Ms. Bruno's sister is here." When Jordan pointed to Carlita, he stepped to his left and stood directly in front of her. "Your sister spent three of the hottest days this month outside in the heat. It should've killed her, but she's a strong woman. Other than being badly sunburned and severely dehydrated, she's fine. We've given her two liters of fluid, and she's perked up nicely. But we'll need to keep her overnight as a precautionary measure to make sure she can keep food and liquids down. Sometimes when a person has been without food and water for this long, they have a problem with that."

Carlita covered her mouth with her hand, unable to hold back the tears. "Thank you. I don't know what I would've done if the news was bad. Ginny can be a pain in the neck sometimes, but she's my only sister."

It seemed like they waited for another hour or more before being allowed to visit with Ginny and to make sure she looked better than when she'd arrived. Her blistered cheeks were slathered in a cream of some kind, and her eyes lit up when she saw Carlita. After hugging her sister, she embraced Jordan. "You and I will be telling the bull story for a long time to come. Thank you for everything."

Jordan smiled at her. "You can count on that."

A nurse came into the room and informed the group that Ginny would soon be moved up to a med-surg floor where she would be more comfortable. Jordan and Ray said their goodbyes and went back out to the waiting room.

Not able to sit still any longer, Jordan paced the floor after checking with the charge nurse multiple times. It seemed like an eternity by the time a nurse brought Alex out into the waiting room in a wheelchair. With his arm now in a sling, he didn't act like he was feeling much pain.

"Apparently, that old bull isn't nearly the bad ass that he thinks he is," Alex said with a grin. "One broken rib and a dislocated shoulder was all the damage he could do." He showed them a prescription bottle. "These will be my friends for a few days."

Jordan leaned down and kissed him. In that moment there wasn't a doubt in her mind that she loved this man.

After being officially discharged, Alex led the way outside where they all piled into Ray's SUV. There was little conversation between them on the thirty-minute drive back to Ranchero, and Jordan used that time to say a prayer of thanks.

When Ray pulled into the parking lot at Empire Apartments, she glanced up at Alex, her eyes questioning. "Don't you want to spend tonight with your family, since they're leaving in the morning for Houston?"

He looked at her and smiled. "You are my family, Jordan, and right now there's nowhere else I'd rather be."

She felt all her fears slowly slipping away. This man loved her. "That's just what I wanted to hear."

THE NEXT MORNING, she and Alex awoke before seven, and she went with him to say goodbye to his mother and sister. Afterwards, he called Captain Darnell to find out about Jeff Hamilton.

When he hung up, he shook his head. "Turns out the police think he's responsible for Georgette's death as well as Marco's."

"What? Why would they think that?"

He sat down at the kitchen table and motioned for her to do the same. "After talking with Ginny, they found out that Georgette had called under some false pretense about the festival, but what she really wanted to know was if Ginny had seen Frankie go up the steps to Marco's room that night."

"Frankie? Why would he go up there?"

"She knew her son hated Marco because of the way he'd treated him. When Frankie's first business partner died in a carjacking, he was the one who'd introduced Marco to Emilio in the first place. When Marco started undercutting Frankie, especially after Frankie had helped him, Frankie was livid. And more recently, Marco had been seriously screwing him in their joint drug smuggling venture. Georgette may have known about Frankie's extracurricular activities."

"Probably not or she would have intervened," Jordan said, remembering her conversation with Emilio about his stepson. "She'd already forced him to go to two different rehab facilities, but he always went right back to drinking and drugging as soon as he was released. He was a thorn in Emilio's side, but because he loved Georgette, he tolerated her son."

"Anyway, according to Ginny, Georgette was so relieved to hear that although Frankie had indeed gone up there earlier, he'd come back down long before Marco went up, that she'd almost kissed her."

"I still don't get why they think all that would make them think Jeff would kill her, too. He must have known the police would find out all this when they questioned her after seeing her on the hotel security tapes the day Ginny went missing."

"The police found a text message from her when they seized Frankie's cell phone. She said she was at the hotel and ended the message by saying she'd just found a way for him to take over Emilio's company."

"Holy cow! Do you think she saw Jeff walk out with Ginny and was planning to use it somehow to force him out of Emilio's life?"

"We'll never know because Jeff certainly isn't talking."

She wrinkled her brow in deep concentration. "Even if that were true, how would they make the connection between Jeff and the heroin overdose?"

His eyes lit up. "Forgot to tell you. Those surveillance tapes Emilio took to the station after Frankie was arrested showed that he'd been so high the night of his mother's murder that he'd collapsed at the hotel and stayed in bed the entire night. There's no way he could have killed her." He arched his eyebrows. "But that isn't all. The tapes also showed Jeff rummaging through the drawers and leaving with some of Frankie's personal stash and a couple of syringes, apparently unaware the room was being monitored. Even though the DA will never be able to convict with only that, they're satisfied with putting Emilio's lawyer away for a very long time for Marco's murder, not to mention Ginny's and your kidnappings and attempted murder charges."

"I'm glad for Frankie. Maybe this will be enough to qualify as his rock bottom and he'll get sober this time. It would be nice if he and his stepfather ended up with a better relationship over this."

"Hope so." Alex stood up. "I need to get going. I have a lot of errands to run, but I'll see you back at your apartment later with dinner."

"How's your arm holding up?" she asked.

"I'm off the hard stuff and only using ibuprofen now." He followed her out the door.

JORDAN COULD HAVE used at least a few more hours of sleep, she thought as she walked into the office. The moment she arrived at her desk, her phone rang, pushing all thoughts of actually catching a break today further out of reach. Jackie Frazier, her boss's secretary, called to tell her that Egan wanted to see her in the office as soon as possible, and promised it wouldn't take long.

She put her purse in her desk before making the dreaded trip up to Egan's office, noticing that Loretta wasn't at her cubicle. Assuming she was already up in Egan's office, Jordan decided it was now or never and headed that way.

She tried to mentally prepare herself for whatever her editor was about to say to her. But she wasn't the same girl today as she was just two days ago. Getting dumped as the culinary reporter seemed miniscule when compared to almost dying by being attacked by the bull in the pasture.

When she got off the elevator, Jackie looked up and smiled.

That was a first! Egan's secretary had never tried to make nice before.

"He's waiting." She waved her in with a hand.

Jordan was surprised to see that Loretta wasn't there, waiting to gloat. She sat down in a chair across from her editor and waited for him to get off the phone.

"I'm glad you're okay," he said after he disconnected. "The story about you and that Italian woman is all over the front page today. I'll need you to give a full interview to one of our reporters."

She nodded, waiting for the hammer to drop. "Where's Loretta?" she asked, too impatient for small talk.

"Downstairs in her uncle's office." He reached for his coffee mug and took a sip. "Want Jackie to bring you a cup?"

She shook her head. "Get on with it, please. Am I back to writing only the personals again?"

He took the last swallow of coffee before he leaned back in the chair and put his hands behind his head, making his oversized ears protrude even further from his face. "Why would you think that?"

She lifted her chin and met his unreadable stare with an icy one of her own. She wasn't in the mood to play games. "Just tell me, and I'll be out of your hair."

"For your information, you are no longer writing the personals," he answered.

There it was—worse than she'd imagined. Not only was he taking the culinary column away from her, but he was also giving her the boot.

"You're now my full-time culinary reporter, and I've bumped up your columns to four a week."

Her head snapped up, positive she hadn't heard him right. "What about Loretta?"

"Seems she posted a recipe in Friday's paper that has a lot of angry people bombarding Uncle Earl with phone calls and emails." He chuckled. "She claims you deliberately sabotaged the recipe so that would happen. That so?" His eyes told her he already knew the answer to the question.

"I did no such thing. I told her the recipe was missing one of the main ingredients, but unfortunately, she'd already stolen it from my desk drawer and posted it."

He leaned forward on his elbows and supported his chin with both hands. "That's what I figured. Well played, if I do say so myself."

"So what's she going to be doing?"

"Uncle Earl reassigned her to the Classifieds, and I can tell you, she's not a happy camper right now."

"And the column is really mine now?"

"As long as you keep the people of Ranchero happy, it is." He shuffled a few papers on his desk. "Now get out of here and get some rest. I'll see you in the morning." He tilted his head and stared at her as if trying to figure her out. "Oh, and McAllister, I'd appreciate it if you'd reprint the correct recipe and get all those people off my back."

She bit her lip to hide the smile. "I'll see what I can do." She stood and walked out when he dismissed her with a nod.

AFTER GATHERING HER PURSE, she went home, and although she didn't think she could, she slept for three hours. Awakened by a knock at the door, she was surprised to see that it was already after five.

When she opened it, her friends poured into the apartment, all talking at once.

"Tell us everything," Rosie said. "And don't you dare leave anything out."

"Then y'all had better sit down, because it's a doozy."

When they were all seated, she started at the beginning of how her snooping had landed her in Jeff's car on the way to the pasture with the bull.

When she was finished, Victor's eyes were wide with excitement. "Damn, girl! I'll bet you needed new underwear after seeing that bull coming at you." He gritted his teeth. "I always miss out on the good stuff."

"Be careful what you wish for, my friend," Jordan said. "This was way too close for comfort, even for me." She waved to Ray who had just walked in with a bag from Myrtle's. "Please tell me that's her Chocolate Bread Pudding."

"Nope. It's her Better Than Sex Cake. I know how much you love it. I had to promise to fix all her smoke alarms in the morning to get her to break it out. She was saving it for a book club luncheon tomorrow."

"I love you, Ray Varga," Jordan said, hugging his neck. "If I didn't know what a great lady you already have by your side, I might consider making a play for you."

"Oh, hogwash!" Lola said, throwing her arms in the air. "On second thought, a shot at that handsome officer of yours might be worth trading for." When Ray nailed her with a glare and was about to protest, she held up her hand. "Oh chill, honey. You'll always be my little teddy bear."

The playful moment was cut short when the doorbell rang, and Jordan jumped up to answer it, expecting to see Alex with a couple boxes of pizza. She flung the door open and couldn't believe what she saw. Looking up at her with big doe eyes was the white dog with one black paw. She bent down to pet him, and he jumped into her arms, almost knocking her over before covering her face with set kisses.

Then Alex stepped out from behind the door. "Jordan, meet Max."

"How did you find him?" she asked, laughing as she returned the affection to her little friend.

"I talked to a farmer who knew immediately what dog I was talking about when I described him. He sent me to another farmhouse farther down the gravel road where I was prepared to pay big bucks to bring him home to you." He laughed out loud. "This dog was made for you, Jordan. As it turns out, the farmer was so glad to get rid of Max, he probably would have paid me to take him off his hands. Seems your little friend has every cattle rancher in the area furious because he chases their cows and teases the bulls." He handed her the leash. "So you're stuck with him."

She looked up at Victor and Michael. "I know there's a no pet policy here but—"

"This dog saved your life, Jordan. How can we say no? Just try not to let the other tenants see him," Michael said bending down to pet the dog.

"Yeah, right. If Max is as frisky as Alex says, that's not going to happen," Rosie said, stooping down to receive her own big wet kiss. "We'll all help you take care of him. He can be the new Empire Apartment mascot."

Jordan looked up at Alex. "Max, huh?" When he nodded, she smiled and mouthed, "*I love you.*"

His eyes sent a slow and sensual message in reply.

"Save that thought for tonight, love." Then he looked at the others. "Okay, who's gonna help me bring in the pizza and beer from the car?

* * * * *

LILL'S SPAGHETTI SAUCE AND MEATBALLS
(From the files of Rose Magistro)

For the Meatballs
3 lbs. ground chuck
3 large eggs
1 ½ cups Italian flavored bread crumbs
1 ½ cups Parmesan cheese
6 tablespoons parsley
3 teaspoons salt
¼ cup virgin olive oil
2 country style pork ribs
1 tablespoon garlic powder *(optional)*

For the Sauce
6 cans (12 ounces each) tomato paste
18 cans *(using empty tomato paste cans)* of water
If making less, use 3 cans water to each can
Salt and pepper to taste
2 bay leaves

Heat olive oil in a large heavy skillet. Mix together ground chuck, eggs, bread crumbs, Parmesan cheese, parsley, and salt and fry in olive oil, along with the ribs until completely browned. Shake some garlic powder on the meatballs while they are cooking.

In large stock pot, mix together all the sauce ingredients. Add as many meatballs as you want along with the two ribs. Bring sauce to a low boil and let it cook for 3–4 hours until it thickens, stirring frequently to keep it from sticking to the bottom. Be sure not to stir too hard as this may cause the meatballs to break up. Remove bay leaves and enjoy!! This sauce, without the meatballs, can be used with baked ziti, ravioli, and lasagna. It makes a large amount, but it freezes well. Any leftover meatballs can also be frozen for a later meal.

DEZI'S BAKED ZITI
Yields 6–8 servings

1 package *(1 pound)* Mostacioli, Ziti,
 or Rotini pasta
1 tube *(16 ounces)* Italian sausage
7 cups Lill's Spaghetti Sauce *(Or you can use 2
 jars (24 ounces) prepared sauce. I use one jar of
 the hot and spicy and one regular.)*
4 cups shredded Mozzarella cheese

Preheat oven to 350°F. Prepare pasta as package directs. Crumble sausage and brown in a separate skillet and drain. In a large bowl, combine pasta, sausage, spaghetti sauce, and 2 cups of cheese. Mix well. Turn into greased 9x13 baking dish. Cover with foil and bake 45 minutes or until hot and bubbly. Uncover and top with remaining 2 cups cheese. Bake 10 minutes longer or until cheese is melted.

ITALIAN MARGARITAS
Yields 4 servings

4 cups crushed ice mix
2 tablespoons confectioner's sugar
5 ounces tequila
2 cups sweet and sour mix
2 ounces orange liqueur
2 ounces amaretto
4 orange slices for garnish

Slightly moisten rims of four 12-ounce glasses and dip in confectioners' sugar to rim the glasses; fill each with crushed ice.

Combine the sweet and sour mix, tequila, amaretto, and orange liqueur in a pitcher; stir. Pour mixture into the prepared glasses. Garnish each drink with an orange slice.

ASPARAGUS RISOTTO
Yields 3–4 servings

1 pound asparagus, washed
4-6 cups chicken or vegetable stock
3 tablespoons butter, divided
2 tablespoons extra virgin olive oil
1/3 medium onion, finely diced
½ teaspoon salt
1½ cups Arborio rice
½ cup dry white wine, warmed
½ cup freshly grated Parmesan cheese

Add the asparagus to a pot of boiling water and cook until a fork can penetrate the tip of the spear *(five minutes or more.)* Drain water and rinse asparagus under cold water. Cut off the spears and aside. Cut the green part of the remaining stalks into one inch pieces and also set these aside. Discard the white part of the stalks.

Using a medium saucepan and low heat, warm stock. While you're doing that, melt 1 tablespoon of butter with olive oil in a deep skillet over medium heat. Add the onions, stirring frequently until they soften, 3–5 minutes.

Add rice a little at a time and cook, stirring occasionally, until it is glossy, about 2–3 minutes. Add white wine and stir frequently until the liquid has evaporated.

Add salt and warm stock, ½ cup at a time, stirring occasionally. When stock is almost evaporated, add another ½ cup until broth is almost entirely gone. When you add the last bit of broth, add the asparagus pieces and the asparagus tips and continue cooking until rice is al dente *(about 20 minutes total time from the time you start with the broth.)* You can add hot water if you need more liquid. Rice should be tender but still crunchy and may take as long as 30 minutes to get to this stage.

When rice is done, remove skillet from heat, add remaining butter and stir briskly. Add Parmesan and stir briskly, then taste and adjust seasoning. Risotto should be slightly soupy. Serve immediately.

MYRTLE'S CHOCOLATE BREAD PUDDING
From the personal recipe file of Jennifer Batchelder,
Jenn's Sweet 'n Sassy Bakery
Yields 10-12 servings

For The Bread Pudding
Nonfat cooking spray
1 *(2-3)* day old whole 3 layer Chocolate Cake with
Vanilla Buttercream icing cubed into ½ inch pieces
3 large eggs
2 teaspoons chocolate extract
¼ cup Crème de Cacao *(chocolate liqueur)*
1 ½ cups half and half
1 ½ cups whole milk

For the Whipped Topping
1 cup heavy whipping cream
½ cups powdered sugar
½ teaspoon pure vanilla extract

I *(the author and not Jennifer. I'm sure she used homemade everything!)* didn't include a recipe for the cake or the buttercream icing. When I made this I used a boxed cake mix and a can of prepared icing. There are many "from scratch" recipes available on the Internet if you are so inclined.

Place pieces of cubed cake into a very large mixing bowl and set aside. In a large measuring cup or bowl, whisk together the eggs, extract, liqueur, half and half and milk. Pour mixture over cake pieces and toss to make sure all the pieces of cake come in contact with the liquid. Cover with plastic wrap and place into the refrigerator for about 15 minutes. Remove and toss gently again. Place into the refrigerator again while your oven preheats to 350°F. Remove from refrigerator and pour into a 9 x 13 inch pan, sprayed with the nonfat cooking spray. Bake for approximately 45–60 minutes. Check after 45 minutes. It will not have the same texture as a cake, but should not be soupy, either. No sauce is required for this since the sauce is already 'in it' from the cake icing. Should you wish to top it, proceed with the instructions below or use a dollup of Cool Whip on each serving.

In a very cold bowl, with very cold beaters, beat the whipping cream until they begin to get frothy. Add the vanilla. Beat for about 30 seconds, and then slowly add the powdered sugar. Once all the powdered sugar has been added, beat the mixture until it will hold a peak. Some prefer the whipping cream to be stiffer than others. Should you prefer it this way, beat it a little while longer, but not too long.

GINNY'S PIZZA BREAD
AKA Lill's and Cathy Magistro's Pizza Bread
Yields 2 loaves

2 loaves of frozen bread
3 large eggs
1/8 cup Parmesan cheese
1 tablespoon Italian seasoning
1 pound Mozzarella cheese, grated
¾ of a 7 ounce bag of thinly sliced pepperoni
Nonfat cooking spray

Preheat oven to 350°F. Grease counter top and place frozen dough to thaw. Do not let it rise.

When bread is thawed, mix eggs, parmesan cheese, Italian seasoning and set aside.

Roll out dough on the greased counter top to a large thin circle. Spread the egg mixture over the entire circle, using half of it. Preserve the other half for second loaf.

Put three rows of pepperoni down the center of the dough, then sprinkle with ½ the Mozzarella cheese. Turn both sides into the center and seal ends securely. Put on cookie sheet that's been covered with a sheet of aluminum foil and sprayed with a nonfat cooking spray. Brush the top with small amount of egg mixture.

Bake for 20–25 minutes or until lightly browned. Repeat for second loaf. Best when hot, May be frozen.

ITALIAN NACHOS
Yields 8–10 servings

For The Alfredo Sauce

¼ cup butter
1 cup heavy whipping cream

1 clove garlic, crushed
½ teaspoon salt
¼ teaspoon freshly ground black pepper
3 cups freshly grated Parmesan cheese
(divided use)

For the Nachos

2 tablespoons virgin olive oil
1 package Wonton wrappers, cut on the diagonal to form triangles
1 pound ground pork, browned, drained, and crumbled
1 package *(6 ounces)* grilled chicken pieces *(or make your own)*
½ jar (16 ounces) mild pepperoncinis, chopped *(heat level to your preference)*
2 Roma tomatoes, diced
1 can diced jalapenos *(optional)*
Black olives, diced *(optional)*

In a heavy, medium saucepan melt the butter over low heat. Add the garlic and stir. Then increase the temperature to medium and add the heavy cream, a little at a time, stirring to blend. Cook until mixture thickens. Remove from heat and add 2 cups of the grated Parmesan *(Preserve the rest for toppers.)* Season with the salt and pepper and stir until cheese is melted and sauce is smooth. Cover and set aside. Place the olive oil in another heavy saucepan and cook on medium heat until the wontons are light brown. *(This doesn't take long, so stay at your stove until this stage is completed.)* Drain on a paper towel and use immediately.

Place the wontons, each separately, on a large serving platter. Drizzle each one with 2 tablespoons Alfredo sauce. Add the ground pork, chicken, tomatoes, and pepperoncinis. If preferred, add the black olives and jalapenos. Sprinkle each one with the leftover Parmesan cheese and serve warm.

GINNY'S CHICKEN CACCIATORE
pollo alla cacciatore
Yields 6 servings

6 boneless, skinless chicken breasts cut into ¾ inch strips
1-2 tablespoons seasoning salt
1-2 teaspoons pepper
1 cup all purpose flour
3 tablespoons virgin olive oil
1 red bell pepper sliced lengthwise in small strips
1 orange bell pepper sliced lengthwise in small strips
1 yellow bell pepper sliced lengthwise in small strips
1 onion sliced lengthwise in small strips
2 tablespoons dried thyme
2 tablespoons dried basil
2 tablespoons dried oregano
2 tablespoons dried parsley
1 bay leaf
Salt and Pepper to taste
½ teaspoon red pepper flakes *(optional)*
1 can *(15 ounces)* tomato sauce
½ cup red wine
½ cup low sodium chicken broth
1 pound bag of linguine noodles
1 bag *(12 ounces)* Mozzarella cheese, shredded

Sprinkle first the seasoning salt and then the pepper on the chicken strips, then dredge in the flour to coat. In a large skillet, heat the olive oil and add the chicken. Cook 3–5 minutes on each side or until both sides are browned and then remove from skillet. In the same skillet, add the peppers and the onion to caramelize. Salt and pepper to taste. After several minutes, add the thyme, basil, oregano and the parsley. Then add the broth, tomato sauce and the wine. When it comes to a slow boil, cover and simmer for thirty minutes.

While sauce is thickening, cook linguine according to package directions. When it is ready, drain the water and place desired portion on a microwaveable plate. Next add about ¾ cup of the sauce *(more if you like)* followed by approximately ¾ cup vegetables *(again, more if you like)* and top each plate with ¾ cup Mozzarella cheese. Put in microwave for 30 seconds to melt the cheese.

Hint: Adjust this to your personal serving size preferences. When I am being lazy, I use my favorite bottled spaghetti sauce instead of the homemade one. It works well, too.

GINNY'S BRAIDED SPAGHETTI BREAD
Copied with permission from Rhodes Bake N Serve's Home Baked Family Favorites Cookbook

1 Loaf Rhodes Bread Dough or 12 Rhodes Dinner Rolls, thawed to room temperature
6 ounces spaghetti, cooked
1 cup thick spaghetti sauce
8 ounces mozzarella cheese, cut into ½ inch cubes
1 egg white, beaten
Parmesan cheese
Parsley flakes

Spray counter lightly with non-stick cooking spray. Roll loaf or combined dinner rolls into a 12x16 inch rectangle. Cover with plastic wrap and let rest for 10–15 minutes.

Cook spaghetti according to package instructions. Drain and let cool slightly. Remove wrap from dough. Place spaghetti lengthwise in a 4-inch strip down the center of dough. Top with sauce and cheese cubes.

Make cuts 1½ inches apart on long sides of dough to within ½ inch of filing. Begin braid by folding top and bottom strips toward filling. Then braid strips left over right, right over left. Finish by pulling last strip over and tucking under braid.

Lift braid with both hands and place on a large sprayed baking sheet. Brush with egg white and sprinkle with Parmesan cheese and parsley. Bake at 350°F. for 30–35 minutes or until golden brown. Cool slightly and slice to serve.

CARLITA'S ITALIAN CREAM CAKE BALLS
Yields 48 balls

For The Cake
1 stick butter, softened
2 cups sugar
½ cup Crisco
5 egg yolks
1 teaspoon baking soda
2 cups flour
1 cup chopped pecans
1 1/3 cups shredded coconut
1 teaspoon vanilla
1 cup buttermilk
5 egg whites

For The Frosting

1 bar *(8 ounce)* cream cheese, softened
3½ cups confectionary sugar, sifted
1 stick butter softened
1 teaspoon vanilla

OR

Use ¾ can *(16 ounces)* prepared Cream Cheese Frosting

For The Candy Coating

2 pounds dark chocolate candy coating chips
Sprinkles, squiggles made with icing *(optional)*

Use wooden sticks or toothpicks for dipping.

Preheat oven to 350°F. Cream the first 4 ingredients. Add the middle list of ingredients *(except the egg whites)* slowly. In a separate small bowl, beat the egg whites until stiff. Fold into mixture. Pour into 3 greased layer pans or a 9x13 baking pan. Bake for 37 minutes or until a toothpick inserted into the center comes out clean. Let cool completely.

When cake is cooled, crumble into a large mixing bowl, making sure there are no big pieces as this may cause the cake balls to be lumpy.

Add ¾ of the frosting mix *(or ¾ of the can of prepared frosting.)* Mix it into the crumbled cake until thoroughly combined. You need this to be moist but not so wet that you can't roll it into balls.

Use a melon baller or small ice cream scoop to form balls of the cake mixture. Place the balls on waxed paper and chill for several hours in the refrigerator. When they are firm, prepare the chocolate candy coating.

Place half the chocolate candy coating in a deep

microwave safe bowl and follow directions on package. *(When melting chocolate, I usually microwave fifteen minutes on medium power. Then check and stir and repeat until chocolate is completely melted but not burned.)*

Take only a few cake balls out of the refrigerator at a time and dip them one at a time into the chocolate using a toothpick or wooden stick to hold them. Decorate with sprinkles or icing squiggles if desired and place on waxed paper to set.